[Bad Boy's Guide to...] Book 1

Being Not Good

D1293146

ALSO BY ELIZABETH STEVENS

unvamped
Netherfield Prep
the Trouble with Hate is…
Accidentally Perfect
Keeping Up Appearances
Love, Lust & Friendship
Valiant Valerie

No More Maybes Books
No More Maybes
Gray's Blade

I'm No Princess Novellas
Now Presenting
Lady in Training
Three of a Kind
Some Proposal
The Collection (Parts 1-4)

[Bad Boy's Guide to...] Book 1

Being Not Good

Elizabeth Stevens

SLEEPING DRAGON BOOKS
ADELAIDE

Sleeping Dragon Books

Being Not Good
by Elizabeth Stevens

Digital ISBN: 978-0648438182
Print ISBN: 978-0648438199

Cover art by: Izzie Duffield

Copyright 2018 Elizabeth Stevens

Worldwide Electronic & Digital Rights
Worldwide English Language Print Rights

*To all the YA romance that came before,
without you, I'd have a realistic view of teen
relationships.*

Contents

Prologue

Avery

I am a morning-person – always had been. As soon as the first rays of sun were peeking through the gauzy curtains on my window, my music started and I woke up among my pillows and throws, excited to start the day.

I just couldn't help it, there was so much to look forward to: friends, family, rainbows, baby animals. Life was worth living and it was worth living loud and proud.

I sang along as I showered, got my makeup exactly right so the teachers couldn't definitively say it was there but no spots were showing, and made sure every curl sat in perfect formation. I sang as I got ready for school, adding the absolute maximum pops of colour to my uniform I knew I could get away with. I sang on my way past Ebony's room as my little sister burrowed into her pillows for 'five more minutes', and was still there twenty minutes later. And I was still singing as I danced down the stairs to start on breakfast for my family, to be joined by my parents a few minutes later.

Dad let me pretend I was helping with his crossword as I

went over colour swatches with Mum for her interior design customers and I tried to get my previous nights' homework finished. I kissed my sister's head as she finally blinked her way into the kitchen and sat her down with her breakfast with mere minutes before we had to leave.

Dad and I bundled Ebony into the car and I talked to him about my upcoming day as he drove us to school and Ebs denied falling asleep in the back seat. I was the first one out of the car with a wave to Dad before I hurried into the building at quarter past eight, with plenty of time to catch up with my friends before first lesson.

And, even though I'd been up for hours and I got to school plenty early, I was somehow still only getting to class as the last bell rang every morning.

Davin

I'm not even a person-person. There was no sort of person that accurately described me. I couldn't remember if I'd always been like that or if I'd once been different.

And I didn't much care what people thought about that. I had two people I considered irreplaceable, and I lived without one fifty percent of the time anyway.

Even the sun knew better than to fuck with me at any time of the day, let alone when my alarm was going off yet again at eight-fifteen in the goddamned morning. I groaned and pressed snooze 'just one more time'. The days my dad was home, he gave a cursory knock on my door. The days he wasn't, 'just one more time' became at least five and I was falling out of bed at twenty to nine.

In the blessed dark – thank you, blackout curtains – I pulled on the first pieces of uniform I could find and was only awake enough to hope I'd put my shirt on the right way round but never decided it was worth actually checking. Two minutes later, I had my bag and I was stumbling out to the car with my clothes still mostly undone and my usual hatred for the world.

I finished doing up my buttons and my tie as I drove to school and promised myself that would be the last morning I didn't get up in time to at least make coffee. Coffee at least made humanity bearable. But then people seemed to go out of their way to avoid me, so that made them slightly more bearable to begin with.

Finding a park wasn't difficult. There was always one park free, the one I'd parked in since I'd got my license. I didn't know if everyone else left it free because they thought I'd retaliate somehow – if I could be bothered – or if it was because it was the furthest from the school building and no one else wanted it.

And I managed to skid into my classroom just before the last bell rang most mornings.

One: Avery

"Rundown!" I giggled as my best friend and I walked to first lesson, our arms linked as usual.

"Aye aye, captain!" Blair answered as people in the hallway called hello to us as we passed. "So we meet at ten on Saturday which will give us plenty of time for–"

"Best friends' day shenanigans!" I chorused with her excitedly.

She grinned as she finished, "–before we have to get you ready for *the big one*!"

I squeezed her arm and gave her a smile.

Blair and I had been BFFs since forever and we'd risen to the top of the Mitchell College hierarchy side-by-side. Unlike me, she was tall, leggy, and slim. Her hair was black and she had these gorgeous big brown eyes like melted dark chocolate. Like me, she was always smiling and loved life.

We'd made up Best Friends' Day when we were twelve and it always fell on the first Saturday after Valentine's Day. Unless Valentine's Day was on the weekend, then it was the day Valentine's Day wasn't. Each year we spent the whole day together and no one else was allowed.

But this year presented a slight problem in that Miles, the best boyfriend in the whole world, had planned months ago for our first anniversary celebration to be that night. Our anniversary was actually the week after but, after discussing it with Blair, we decided that I could totally do Best Friends' Day *and* an anniversary celebration on the same day.

I sighed happily. "I can't believe it's been a year already!"

Blair nodded enthusiastically as the door to our classroom came in sight, which was good because the last bell had just rung. "I know, right. A whole year! It feels like forever. But at the same time, how has a whole year already gone past?"

I nodded back. "I know."

An unrealistically tall body crashed into us with an annoyed grunt, his hair hanging over his face as always. Blair and I stifled giggles to each other as we paused to watch him slouch to his chair at the back of the room and drop into it unenthusiastically.

"Quickly class," the teacher called as we traipsed in.

"God. You are so lucky to have Miles," Blair said wistfully.

I smiled as I looked at Miles talking to his best mate Becker.

Miles with his light brown hair swept off his face, those flashing hazel eyes, that hunky grin. The perfect boyfriend. He was sweet and kind and funny and totally popular. Everyone said we were the perfect couple. Fairy-tale perfect.

We'd won Mitchell College's Perfect Couple award the year before and it was *never* awarded to a Year 11 couple, it was *always* awarded to a Year 12 couple. I *was* totally lucky to have Miles.

Sure he'd cheated on me about a month back, but it had just been a drunken kiss. I figured everyone was allowed one mistake and what we had was worth more than one stupid mistake.

I didn't think I was supposed to know about Cindy Porter – no one talked about it and nothing about either of them suggested that there was anything more going on between them than that one mistake. So when I'd overheard Becker and another of their friends talking about it once, I'd put the hurt aside and told myself that that was Miles' chance. I'd forgive him – he'd get that ONE mistake – and we'd move on.

Blair and I sat down and, as the teacher finished getting himself ready for the lesson, I watched as Miles talked with Becker. I never really paid much attention to them when they were talking because it was usually about sports and teams I knew nothing about. But I liked to watch the way Miles laughed and how excited he got about things that mattered to him while I waited to say hi to him.

Usually now was the time he turned to kiss me between his conversations with Becker. But that morning he didn't. He didn't even seem to notice I was there until Mr Richards called for our attention again and Miles gave me a weird nod

6

and not even a half-smile before opening his books. I was left confused, but assumed he wasn't snubbing me on purpose. Because Miles didn't do that.

I shared a look with Blair, whose eyebrows crinkled in confusion. But we didn't have a chance to talk about it until we were on our way to our next lesson.

"He did it again!" Blair whispered to me harshly.

I watched as Miles walked away with Becker without even looking at me.

Becker threw me a look over his shoulder, but I couldn't really tell what it meant. I wasn't sure if it was sympathy, confusion of his own, or if he knew something I didn't and couldn't wait for me to find out.

"Did I do something wrong?" I asked, completely baffled.

"You never do anything wrong," Blair reminded me and I nodded vaguely.

"No. No, of course not."

"They're playing their biggest rivals for their first game of the season on Saturday," Blair said thoughtfully. "I'm sure they're just wrapped up in that.

I nodded. Of course they were. Miles took his sport very seriously and I was very proud of him for that. So the matter was off my mind for the rest of the lesson as I got totally engrossed in Miss Nithin enthusiastically going over the diagram she'd put up on the board.

Except, when I went to find Miles at his locker as usual at the start of Recess, I started to suspect the cold shoulder he'd shown me didn't have anything to do with that weekend's sport match at all.

"Hi," I said as I leant up to kiss him. But he pulled away quickly.

"Hi Avery…" he said slowly, looking around the crowded hallway carefully.

He seemed tense, so the only solution was for me to be my usual upbeat self to cheer him up.

"How are things? I was thinking… If you're – I dunno – worried about Saturday, Blair and I could come past for a bit and cheer you on? I've got my big 'Go Miles' sign from last year. I saved it especially for this year. I *was* going to keep it for–"

Miles cleared his throat and I hurtled to a stop. "Look. Avery, I don't need you to come to my games anymore. Okay?"

I blinked at him, my smile firmly in place despite not really understanding him. "This weekend's just an outlier. I'm sure Blair won't mind if–"

"That's not what I meant…" he said slowly, waiting for me to catch up.

And catch up I did as my heart thudded heavily in my chest and my stomach churned. I suddenly felt like up was down and down was up and I was sitting sideways.

"You're…breaking up with me?" I asked slowly, trying to put it together in my head.

Miles had the decency to look like it was a hardship.

8

"Yeah."

"Um… Okay." I looked around and saw that the kids, who had previously been going about the usual business of swapping books in lockers and heading out from lessons, slowed and stopped around us. I was suddenly feeling an odd sense of…detachment. No thoughts. No feelings. Even my heartbeat felt like it had paused. "Can I ask why?"

He shrugged, those big hazel eyes looking anywhere but my face as he ran his hand through his hair. "We're going in different directions. We had our fun, you know? But now it's time to move on."

"Right." I took a deep breath as some emotion returned, but I wasn't sure yet what it was. Nothing was really registering past shock and a sudden thudding of my heart. "And does this have anything to do with Cindy?" I asked, my voice even. There was no anger, no accusation. It was just a question. Something I needed to know.

The now-formed crowd muttered among themselves. Although I wasn't sure if everyone else knew about Cindy and had thought I was oblivious, or if they were surprised at my question.

"It's not what you think, Avery."

It never was. "Isn't it?"

Miles looked at me then and I saw the briefest flicker of guilt. I suddenly got the impression that he hadn't been wrong. It wasn't what I thought. Was it worse?

"It… It wasn't just a kiss. Was it?" I stuttered, my throat

9

feeling very tight, and his expression pinched. I nodded slowly. "Ah. It wasn't…" I nodded again. "When Becker said you 'hooked up', he didn't mean…" I waggled my head. "He meant…" I took a deep breath. "I see."

He shook his head like his explanation was going to make it all make sense, like I'd forgive him once I knew why he'd done it, like it was all in aid of world peace or something, the greater good, even. "You're just so… You're too good."

"Too good? How is that even a thing?" Even the kids in the crowd didn't seem to think that was a decent excuse based on their facial expressions – although I didn't hear them disagreeing out loud. "What?"

Miles shrugged almost apologetically. "Good. You're so sweet and pure and innocent and…such a *good girl*, you know?"

"We've had sex." And now the *whole* school knew. Brilliant. Although we'd been sleeping together for almost six months, so the bets were it wasn't all that much of a secret anyway. Even still, my cheeks heated a little as I fought to remain on the positive side of neutral.

He shrugged again and I could see me giving up my virginity to him had made a lasting impression. Not. "I just…" He shrugged again.

I think I got where this was going. "Ah. You want the girl who wears the pretty swing dress to meet your grandma and then lets you do her dirty in your car after, huh?"

There was a small gasp of shock from the gathered

10

watchers at my unusual display.

No. That wasn't something Miles and I had talked about doing, but I could guess what he wanted if I was *too* good. Blair called it Gryffindor in the streets and Slytherin in the sheets. Miles liked the fact that I presented well, that his family liked me – he'd essentially told me on numerous occasions – but pretending our sex life wasn't as vanilla as it came would be overly optimistic. Even for me.

A strange series of looks crossed Miles' face. He looked sorry that what I'd said was true. Then he looked surprised I'd said something like that out loud. Then he looked like he was beginning to wonder if he was making a terrible mistake all of a sudden by dumping me. But he could second-guess himself all he liked. I wasn't wasting another minute on a guy who'd dump me the day before Valentine's Day, a week shy of our first anniversary for a girl like Cindy Porter just because she was (I assumed) better in bed than me. Not even if he regretted it, or changed his mind, or whatever he was likely to do.

I nodded.

"I mean…" He winced. "It's everything. It's not *just* the sex, Avery–"

I didn't need nor want to hear more. "No. I get it, Miles. I wish you and Cindy all the best." Before I turned to walk away, I decided to go right out on that limb and say one more thing totally out of character for me. "By the way…" If he was going for the girl who'd let him do her dirty in his car,

11

he might need one more thing. "I have the number of an excellent cleaner. Specialises in stains. You know… If you ever wanted to sell your car…"

The crowd around us all burst into laughter as Miles looked around self-consciously. I smiled at them all sweetly as I pushed my way through and started heading for my locker down the hall. And, as I did, I started recognising what I was feeling. It was anger. It was foreign, but I knew it was anger.

"Avery!" I heard a recognisable voice call and I slowed a little to let Blair catch up to me. "Oh my God. Are you okay?"

I actually smiled at her. "Weirdly, yes."

Blair looked me over suspiciously for a moment, but she knew the way my head worked almost as well as I did. She knew when I was okay, when I wasn't, and when I needed a distraction to give me time to properly process. She smiled.

"Then… That was epic!" she laughed.

I nodded. "Teach him to break up with me."

My best friend looped her arm through mine. "Okay. Best thing for heartbreak is getting right back on the horse. Any preferences?"

I shook my head then she started listing guys I should go out with as payback. We both knew I wasn't the sort of girl who dated for payback – that was probably one reason I was too good – but Blair liked to plan. She wasn't particularly fussed what she was planning, as long as she got to plan it. She'd plan the apocalypse if it meant she got to plan

12

something.

"I think Josh is single," Blair was saying. "Although there's that unfortunate situation with the broken leg. But!" she said brightly. "That's totally coming off in like…" She muttered as she was counting, "I dunno, actually. But, like, before the formal at least!"

"I dunno…"

Blair paused for a moment as we stopped at my locker and the force I used to wrench it open was the only outward sign about how miffed I was. My locker door crashed into the one next to mine, leaving a little dent in it.

"Woah. All right, iron woman. Am I going too fast? Is it too early? Do we need to wait until you're not in love with Miles anymore?" she asked gently as I put my books away and got my recess out.

Miles had been my first real boyfriend. I *thought* I'd been in love with him. But the simmering anger – rather than actual heartache or sadness – in me suggested I hadn't been quite as in love with him as I'd thought. Maybe I'd been a little bit in love with him. But I sure as heck wasn't anymore and I sure wasn't going to let another guy treat me that way again.

Too good? I'd show him and everyone else that Avery St John wasn't *too good*. I could let loose like everyone else. I wasn't some stupid little girl. I wasn't innocent and sweet. I was normal. I was just a normal teenage girl.

I just had to work out how to prove it.

"No. I'm not sure I was in love with him to begin with," I told her as Miles walked past with a few girls who fluttered around him like it was him who'd just had his heart broken.

Not that I was the one who'd had their heart broken. Because I wasn't going to let a guy who cheated on me – properly, full blown, no concessions cheated on me – to break my heart as well.

Too good? How could you be too good?

"Hey Avery!" Trina interrupted my thoughts as she passed.

"Hi, Trina," I replied, forcing a smile.

"I'm going to need you to make some photocopies for the Formal Committee meeting on Thursday. I've emailed them to you." Trina was head of the Formal Committee, so it made sense she had other things to do.

I nodded. "Sure. Can do."

"Thanks!" Trina said as she swanned off with Louise and Nina.

Too Good? I couldn't believe this.

I'd thought Cindy was Miles' mistake. I'd thought it had only been a kiss. Now I was starting to think that I was Miles' mistake, that he saw me as nothing but weak and stupid and that made it okay to cheat. And I wasn't going to stand for that. I wasn't going to be anyone's mistake!

Wait… Mistakes? I thought to myself, that simmering anger intensifying as I slammed my locker closed.

Oh, I had a brilliant idea. That brilliant idea bumped up

14

against my brain the same way the subject of the idea had bumped into me that morning on the way into first lesson.

"Blair, hear me out," I said, whacking her in my excitement.

"Oh, what?" The planner was definitely willing to take my input.

"Am I really as good as everyone thinks?" I asked her.

"Uh… Yes." She nodded.

"And I'm innocent and sweet and nice?"

"Yep."

I thought about that. "And that makes people assume I'm an idiot…"

"Yep." She paused. "No, wait… Well…sort of," she said apologetically.

I shook my head, holding up a hand to her. "No. That's good."

"What?" Her confusion was understandable.

"Well, if not, my plan wasn't going to work was it?"

"I don't know. What's your plan?"

"Okay. So everyone thinks I'm this goody-two-shoes and I'm too good? Well, would a goody-two-shoes go out with the worst boy in school?"

Everyone knew who the worst boy in school was.

Blair scoffed, "No, she wouldn't. She'd steer clear of him!"

"She would."

"She'd be like, 'no thanks, I'm not even going to talk to

you'."

"Exactly. That goody-two-*loser* would be just like that."

Blair's smile dropped. "Oh?" Then brightened again. "Oh! " Now a slight tinge of confusion. "You mean *you're* going to go out with *him*?"

I nodded. "Yep."

Now it was full confusion as her eyebrows knitted together. "Why?"

"Everyone thinks I'm the girl who never makes mistakes, right?"

"Well, duh," she scoffed with a smile. "Because you don't. You're perfect. You're nice and kind to everyone."

"And they treat me like an idiot because of it."

Blair frowned. "Not everyone. I don't think you're an idiot."

"Almost everyone," I amended.

Blair nodded in begrudging agreement. "Okay…? So what's *he* got to do with that?"

I might not have been the kind of girl who'd date for payback. But I could date to show everyone I was normal. Maybe that was kind of like payback. But I'd be doing it for more than getting back at Miles – he was the last one I cared about. I was doing this for me.

"Because *he* can ruin my image. With his influence, there'll be no more Little Miss Goody-Two-Shoes. We can say goodbye to her and I can be normal."

"Normal?"

16

"Yep, normal. Normal girls don't get called sweet and innocent and *too good*. People don't talk down to them, or never yell at them, or expect them to cover on Formal Committee, or try to do everything for them like they're incompetent. Their boyfriends don't cheat on them. They're just…normal. Their defining feature is they're smart, or their piercing's infected, or they're sunburned, or something."

Blair was looking unsure. "So you're going to date the worst boy in school and tank your rep?"

I nodded. "Yep."

She wrinkled her nose like she was thinking it through. "I feel like this is *not* the way to get Miles back…"

I waved a dismissive hand at her. "Cindy Porter can have him. I don't want him back. I just want to prove to him, the school, to me that I'm not too good." I finished with a mutter, "How is that even an insult?"

Blair shrugged. "I don't know." She ran a hand over her chin. "*He* would be perfect for the mission, though," she mused. "But how are you even going to get him to go out with you?"

I sighed. That was going to be the one potential snag in an otherwise perfect plan. "Don't know. I guess I'll just have to figure it out as I go."

"Okay." Now she was getting excited. "When are we starting?"

"Now."

"Now?"

17

"Yep. He's like almost always inside at breaks. I'm going to go find him."

"Do you need a lookout?"

I shook my head. Approaching him was dangerous enough. Approaching with more than one person would be suicide. "Nope. I've got it covered."

Blair nodded encouragement. "Okay. Come find me after?"

"Yep. Will do."

"Good luck!" she called as I hurried off.

I went from room to room. I knew exactly who I needed – exactly who the worst boy in school was – and I had a feeling I knew where he'd be. Finally I found him, tucked away in one of the meeting rooms off the library.

Davin Ambrose.

Mitchell College's very own bad boy was at least six feet of indeterminate frame under his baggy uniform. His almost black hair was far too long all over and he was constantly flicking it away from his black glasses frames. So between those two, I wasn't sure I'd ever even seen his eyes. Although that would require any kind of eye contact from him and that was also something I'd never witnessed him give to anyone but those who ventured too close. He was rude and sarcastic at the best of times, and in detention the rest.

I don't think I'd ever seen enough of him to determine if he was attractive or not. He was always hunched in his blazer, hair hiding his face, buried in a book, or behind his computer screen. And that was when he wasn't programming the fire alarms to go off or distributing the popular kids' embarrassing photos.

Well, all the popular kids but me, since I was apparently too good to have anything worth distributing. Then again I guessed pictures of me doing things like hanging out at the beach with Blair or Miles hadn't been very interesting compared to the pictures of Cindy and Trina drinking at Rich's party, or Nina and Becker making out.

Davin was on his ever-present laptop and wore his headphones. I watched for a moment as his fingers played over the keys way faster than any one person should be able to do that, and tried to work out how to get his attention.

"Hey, Davin?" didn't seem to work, so I was going to have to try another tack.

I walked over to him and bent over to stick my head between his screen and his face. Hypnotic green eyes blinked slowly behind those glasses then stared at me in confusion.

Two: Davin

There was a head hanging over my screen.

There was a head with a mass of blonde curls spilling onto my keyboard, shining bright blue eyes, and a bubble-gum pink smile.

I pulled away slowly and realised the head was in fact attached to a body that was standing in front of my table. And I did recognise the whole package.

Avery St John.

Mitchell College's answer to what would happen if you got a teletubby to fuck that weird elf from *Disenchantment*, or what would you get if a rainbow slinky fucked a bucket of glittery fairy floss. She was nauseatingly peppy, didn't understand that there was such a thing as too much colour, and I didn't think she knew how to frown.

After going to school with her for four years, I had started to wonder if she was a robot. And not even something useful like a sex-bot. Just some annoying throwback from the fifties created to serve as an example of the perfect girlfriend. She was like a fucking Stepford Wife, minus the pearls.

Ugh and she was talking to me.

I debated not taking off my headphones so I wouldn't have to listen to her. But touching might have been involved then if she decided to remove them for me and I didn't want to risk catching whatever the popular kids had that made them so annoyingly happy all the time.

I slid my headphones down around my neck and rose an eyebrow at her. Her lips had stopped moving, propped open in a little 'o' like I'd surprised her.

Well, I wasn't the one interrupting.

"What?" I asked her.

"What, what?" she replied, pulling back and standing up straight.

Was she slow? Maybe that was why she was so happy all the time.

"What do you want?" I enunciated carefully.

She blinked like it was a foreign concept, then was back to smiling. "Oh. So I wanted to know if you wanted to go out with me." She caught her bottom lip in her teeth as she gave me this smile that confused me further.

Now I was blinking. Avery St John was asking me out on a date. Either Satan was skating to work this morning or I was the most recent butt of a rather ambitious joke. Well two could play at that game.

"What?" I scoffed, looking back at my screen. "Did that muppet Miles finally dump your goody-two-shoes frigid arse for the super tramp?"

"Yes."

Ouch.

I slid my eyes up and saw there was no sign in her eyes of the perfectly peppy smile she had plastered to her face. Girl was hurting and I wasn't helping.

Oh, well.

"Well. That is something I can't help you with."

"Can't or won't?"

"Take your pick." I shrugged. It was all the same to me.

"Come on, Davin." Did she just stamp her foot? "Go out with me."

"Why me?"

"Why not you?"

I looked at her, highly suggesting she take a moment to remember who she was talking about here.

"What? You're such a bad boy that you're too good for me?" she asked, crossing her arms.

Ignoring the idiocy of that statement, I slowly stood up from my seat and rested my hands on either side of my computer to lean towards her. Even then, I towered over her.

"I was thinking more along the lines of the fact you're the human equivalent of every overly optimistic Disney character somehow squashed into one unfathomably tiny body and I'd have no interest in dating you even if I suddenly had a lobotomy and forgot my own name."

You had to hand it to her, girl rallied like a fucking pro. I doubted she'd ever had anyone say anything less than positive to her in her entire life, but that enthusiasm was so ingrained in her that she wasn't going to let me come along and rain on her parade.

She drew herself up to the tallest her preposterously short height would allow and somehow managed to look infernally happy and glowering all at once. "Just because you've got the personalities of Marvin, Squidward, Eeyore, Bender, Dr Cox, Stewie, and…and a wet towel controlling every function of your unrealistically tall body does not make you better than me, Davin."

I wasn't sure if I should be more impressed that she knew Hitchhiker's Guide, SpongeBob, (was that Breakfast Club or Futurama, though?), Scrubs and Family Guy, or that she'd actually delivered a clean insult. I think I'd just found a shred of respect for the tiny gnat of positivity.

"She's fierce, this one, eh?"

There was an actual frown on those pristine features as she looked around. "Who are you talking to?"

"No one." You know who. I ignored her look of confusion and picked up my computer. "Look. Great talk. But I don't really do people. So I'll save you the bother of leaving and just do it for both of us."

I gave her my least sincere grin and strode out before she drowned me in any more saccharine annoyance. Just her voice had me left feeling like I needed to check my blood-glucose levels. If a person could give you diabetes, Avery St John was that person.

It wasn't even halfway through the day and I felt like I needed to go home and lie down. It was worse than a heavy night of drinking.

"Only… What? Five more hours? I can make it through that. Can't I?"

But I didn't. I did not make it through that. Not sane or relaxed.

Avery bounced up to me at the beginning of our pre-Lunch Home Group two lessons later – with a cursory smile to her friend Blair over the other side of the room, of course – and just radiated joy at me until I felt like I'd been blinded.

"Can I help you?" I asked her, not missing the fact that people were staring at the Queen of Pep talking to little old me. I didn't really care. It's not like I had a reputation to ruin. But it did serve to be annoying.

Blair was staring the most avidly, presumably being totally clued in to why Avery was bugging me incessantly. The two friends looked totally different. Blair wasn't just tall and willowy, she had black hair and brown eyes and her skin was darker – there are probably a thousand more PC ways to describe her, but that's all I've got. However as soon as Blair opened her mouth, the two of them could have been twins.

"You can."

Why did she smile *all* the time? Was she a walking dental ad? "Oh, good. What with?"

Her eyes lit up with hope. "One date."

Sarcasm obviously wasn't her forte. I rolled my eyes.

24

"Seriously?"

She nodded. "Blair's sister's into the whole Goth thing, so she'll give me tips and everything."

Tips? Tips for what? "Sorry. What?"

Whatever she'd come up with in her mind had obviously made her very proud of herself. "So I don't stand out so much. I do own black, you know."

I was still confused. "Still not following. Are we going to a funeral on this hypothetical date you've created in the fantasy land in your head?"

Her head cocked to the side like she was confused but she still smiled. "No?"

"No?"

"I just thought you'd be more comfortable if I looked more…like you?"

I leant my elbows on the desk towards her. "Firstly, in what universe would we ever date? And secondly, Avery…" I scoffed. Are you listening to this drivel? "*If* Hell ever froze over to the point we did go on a date, I wouldn't want you changing who you were."

She looked at me like I'd just spoken Chinese.

Was this really what she believed? Strike that. I didn't even want to begin to contemplate any of her belief systems. "Just… You be yourself, Avery…"

Nope. Still nothing. I wasn't sure if it was just because I'd dashed her grand plans or if she'd spent however long with Muppet Miles thinking she was supposed to be whatever he wanted.

"So… No?" she asked.

I shook my head, feeling like I should be sorry but not finding it in myself. I sat back in my chair and crossed my arms. "That's a hard pass."

She was still smiling. "That's what you say now."

I was flabbergasted as I leant further forward with every word. "That's what I say… Always… I will never not… Wait, what?"

She'd walked off halfway through my blither, so I was really just left talking to you.

I sat back in my seat and had to at least admire her tenacity.

I was admiring it less at the end of Lunch when she found me again.

She just appeared next to me like some sort of personal demon intent on tormenting me with something hideous like fun for eternity. I jumped when I saw her, my heart racing and my hand steadying myself on my locker.

"Don't do that!" I hissed at her.

"Do what?" she asked, hands clasped behind her back and that perma-smile firmly on her face.

"Fuck. You're just a little ray of sunshine, aren't you?" I commented dryly.

"Thank you."

I barked my equivalent of a laugh. "Oh, that wasn't a compliment." I looked her over quickly when she didn't leave. "Did you want something?"

"One date."

"Oh my God, woman!" I sighed. "How many times do you need to hear 'no'?"

"Until it's 'yes'."

"Fucking Jesus." I took another look at her and I was starting to think she wasn't as saccharine sweet as she acted. That, or… No. The counter option did *not* bear thinking about, but I had to cover it anyway. "You do know that 'no' *never* means 'yes', right?" If this was another Muppet Miles lesson, I was considering risking social interaction to teach that arsehole a lesson.

"It's one date. You can't be too cool for one date."

"Yes. That is the problem. You've got me. I'm too cool to date." I sighed deadpan. *"Get a load of this one,"* I tell you.

"What?"

I waved a hand at her to dismiss her questions. "No date."

She actually batted her eyelashes at me as she bit her lip again. "Please? I'll wear my most colourful outfit if that will make you feel better?"

"Nothing about this could make me feel better. I'm actually nauseated."

"You say that, but you keep talking to me."

I did. I did do that. And I didn't know why I kept prolonging my suffering. "Under extreme protest, yes."

She giggled and I didn't care for it. "Still a no then, Davin?"

"Forever a no then, Avery," I replied just as sweetly though with infinite more sarcasm.

Again with the smiling. "Talk to you later, Davin," she said as she walked away.

"No. I'm actually all good on that. Thanks, though!" I yelled after her, giving zero fucks about what I looked like to the general populace as long as she stopped talking to me.

But no dice.

There was something almost to be admired about those eternal optimists. I mean, it made them stubborn as fuck. And Avery was proving no exception to the rule.

"Davin!" she called at the end of the day and I felt like I'd just eaten a whole block of Cadbury in less than five minutes. I could actually feel the sugar-high buzzing in my veins. "Davin!"

With a sigh, I spun to face her as unenthusiastically as possible. "What now?" I sighed dramatically.

She beamed at me like I'd just greeted her with the most romantic sonnet. "How are you?"

"I'd be better if you stopped dousing me in this annoying buoyancy." A touch of confusion crossed her face and I sighed, "Fine. How are you?"

"Great!" Of course she was. "What are you doing on Friday night?"

"The same thing I do every Friday night."

Her delight burst a little. "Oh. What's that?"

"I'm not getting out of this anytime soon, am I? Engage

28

placate-mode."

"What?"

"Nothing." You know. "I'm going to be at home, I'm going to have dinner with my dad, then I'll probably read or watch a movie not from this century," an important addition so she didn't think there was any chance we'd have anything in common, "or maybe game. If I feel particularly sociable, I'll give a mate a call and we'll probably get drunk and argue about something stupid unless we meet up with some girls."

"Oh," she said brightly, "what will you do then?"

"Really?" *Was* she slow? "Sex, Avery. Sex will usually happen at that point."

"Oh." There went that little 'o' shape her mouth did.

"And Miles let that go..." Maybe he was the slow one – there were a few things I envisioned one could do with that mouth.

Oh! And a second frown. That had to be some kind of record.

It suddenly became my life's purpose to make her frown as often as possible.

"Again, great talk," I told her. "But I think you've just about used up my socialisation credits for the day."

"What happens when you run out?" she asked and I couldn't tell if she was genuinely interested or the previous display of sarcasm hadn't actually been a fluke.

"Well I either explode, or..."

She leant towards me eagerly. "Or what?"

29

"Or I might have to kiss you." Why the fuck did I say that?

She flushed pink and pulled back. "Oh."

I cleared my throat. "So… You were asking about Friday?"

Her smile was one that I wasn't sure if it affected me or not. "You interested?"

No. Pfft. I was not interested at all.

"I'm interested in there being less interaction between us. If that means one date, then I'll do it."

"Really?"

Oh God. It was like being doused in glitter and puppies.

Wait…

Oh!

I saw what was happening here. This was like the start of one of those gag-worthy romance stories wasn't it? Well, no thank you. I would go on one date if it meant she stopped talking to me and that was the end of it. No opposites attract. No good girl for the bad boy. No enemies to lovers. Whatever trope this was, I was having no part of it.

One date. Nothing more.

I nodded. "Really."

"Super. Friday?"

I nodded again, the level of my enthusiasm so low it didn't even make a blip on the scale of hers. "Friday."

She actually touched my arm. Physical interaction occurred. "Great," she trilled and bounced off again.

I was regretting it already.

Three: Avery

It didn't take long for word to spread around the school that I was going on a date with Davin Ambrose. Probably because Blair and I ensured it didn't take long. I just had to get him to agree on what the date was going to involve.

While Miles and Cindy were busy being loved-up on Wednesday, and cards and flowers and chocolates spread like bushfire, Blair and I were in planning-mode as we tried to come up with something Davin might agree to doing.

"It doesn't bother you?" Blair checked again at Recess.

I looked over the Year 12 Common Room to see Miles and Cindy hugging while people watched them like some celebrity couple. I felt a small twinge in my chest. I guess I was a little bit jealous. Not because it was Miles, but because I used to be looked at the way he was looking at her.

"I still don't want him back, if that's what you're really asking," I told her.

"Maybe."

As we walked to class I kept an eye out for Davin, but he managed to avoid me like the plague. Ebony found me though.

"What's this I hear about you going out with someone not Miles on Friday?" she asked me as we passed in the hallway.

Ebony was in Year 9 and, like me, she was the shortest in her year. Unlike me, she was the fiercest in her year. No one was going to be calling her too good. Grandma always called Ebs my mini-me; her eyes were the same as mine – the piercing blue we got from our parents – but her hair was a little darker than mine. We had the same nose, chin, and cheekbones. But appearance was about where the similarities stopped.

"Miles and I broke up," I told her.

"He dumped her for Cindy Porter," Blair added and I rolled my eyes at my BFF.

"He dumped me for Cindy Porter," I repeated, acknowledging the truth of it.

Ebony looked Blair and I over with a calculating gaze far beyond her years. "Uh huh. We'll talk about this later. I'm frankly disgusted I found out from the rumour mill." She pointed at me like a villain in a movie as she started walking away.

"Your sister scares me," Blair whispered and I nodded.

Sometimes she scared me, too.

I got through Valentine's Day with my usual pep and vigour. I had a date to look forward to and my image to ruin, so the fact I'd been dumped only the day before paled in comparison to the excitement I lost myself in.

I finally cornered Davin before school on Thursday by his locker – which I'd managed to find thanks to the lovely Mrs Hines, the principal's PA, who gave me its location.

"Do you bowl?" I asked.

"Do I what?" he replied in a gravelly voice, flicking his hair out of his face as he pulled books out of his locker.

His tie was still undone, the ends hanging loose over his shirt. The top two buttons were undone and his blazer collar was sticking up on one side. I resisted the urge to fix it, helped by the hostility spreading off him in waves.

"Bowl. You know. Funny shoes, heavy balls, slippery… What?" I asked as he looked at me weirdly.

"Did she really just…?" he asked like he was talking to someone who wasn't there. "Let's keep talk about balls to a minimum, yeah?"

"Fine. No bowling." The last bell rang. "We'll continue this conversation later."

"We really don't have to."

"A first date should be something both parties agree on," I told him.

"Exactly. So remind me why we're having one…?"

I smiled at him as I started backing away and he got one of those weird expressions on his face. "Because you agreed."

"Under protest and against my better judgement!" he yelled after me as I turned and met Blair to go to class.

"What's he protesting now?" she asked, throwing him a

look over her shoulder.

I followed her gaze to find him looking utterly fed up and muttering to himself. I smiled and told her, "First dates."

She nodded. "Ah. But he did say yes."

I grinned. "He did."

"Step one accomplished. What's step two?"

"Step two is deciding on a date activity."

Blair nodded in agreement. "Step three?"

"Step three is convince him to be my boyfriend."

Blair squealed in excitement. "Step four?"

"Step four. Shed stupid goody-two-shoes image with Davin's help."

"Yay!" She paused in her excitement for a moment. "Any idea about the date activity?"

I shrugged. "I'll come up with something."

And I would. Not that Davin was very helpful. He was either hesitant or downright opposed to everything I suggested whenever I saw him for the rest of the day.

Movies? Eh.

Tunza Fun? No. Should have guessed that one really.

The Lake. No. Also pretty obvious; people having way too much fun there.

Even my semi-sarcastic suggestion of just taking his car up to Make Out Point was met with a serious lack of anything.

"How about dinner?" I asked, hoping my last idea was going to be met with a little more than nothing.

"Dinner?" He looked me over with his usual level of boredom.

"I assume you eat."

He looked mildly surprised. "I've been known to."

"Do you do restaurants? Or is that level of human interaction going to cause you to explode?"

He stopped avoiding looking at me and I couldn't get a read on his expression. "I'm not dating you in public."

I huffed. "Fine. How do you feel about the beach?"

"Horrified such a thing be allowed to exist." I looked at him expectantly and he sighed. "Still public. But what would the beach involve?" he asked.

"Just hanging out, maybe grabbing some chips. I'll even give your bad mood a pass."

His eyebrow disappeared under his hair as those green eyes looked me over. "The beach?" he asked and I nodded. "Chips and…talking?" I nodded again and he sighed again. "Fine."

"Really?"

He took a deep breath as he went back to shuffling books. "Really."

I tried to contain the feeling of victory that was threatening to make me do a happy dance. I knew how Davin would feel about that, but it apparently wouldn't be contained and I still wriggled a little. And I know he noticed.

"See? Incessantly happy," he said in that same way as though he was talking to someone who wasn't there.

"What?" I looked around in case there *was* someone there.

He shook his head. "Nothing. Okay. The beach it is." He sighed heavily like something truly unpleasant was coming, then asked, "Did you expect me to pick you up?"

I nodded. "Sure. That'd be great. Thanks."

"Of course." He paused and, if I thought he looked horrified before, he looked thoroughly terrified now. He held his hand out. "Give me your phone."

I pulled it out of my skirt pocket, confused. "Why?"

He took it and did something with it. When he passed it back, I saw he'd given me his number, although I was pretty sure he wasn't pleased about it. "Text me your address. I'll pick you up at – what? – six-thirty? Seven? What time do these things usually start?"

I couldn't help but laugh at him.

"What?" he asked, his eyes narrowing.

I shook my head. "You're just not very good at this, are you?"

He frowned. Although for him, that wasn't really a change to his normal expression. "No. Strangely, I'm not trying to be."

I smiled. "All good. I'll text you my address. Six-thirty is good."

He nodded resignedly. "Can't wait," he muttered sarcastically. When I didn't leave straight away, he looked at me out of the corner of his eye. "Can I help you with anything else today, Avery?" I had to admit he was very good at the

36

sarcastically simpering sweet tone.

I clasped my hands behind my back and shook my head. "Nope. All good."

"Excellent." He gave that weird rising of the corner of his lips that was in no way a smile and nodded to me. "I'm sure our date will be more successful the less interaction we have between then and now…"

My mouth dropped open as I realised he wanted me to go away. *Well duh, Avery*. "Oh. Right. Sure. I'll see you at six-thirty tomorrow."

He gave me a single nod and watched me leave like he was worried it wasn't really happening.

As I made my way out to find Blair, I ran into Trina. She ran a hand over her light brown hair as her brown eyes looked me over suspiciously.

"You're going on a date less than a week after Miles dumped you?" she asked me, looking me over in a way that told me exactly what she was thinking.

But I wasn't going to let her get me down. "I am."

"How could you do that?"

I looked at her. "Really? It's okay he was dating Cindy *before* he even broke up with me and I'm not allowed to go on one date after?"

Blair had heard from Krista who'd heard from Molly that she'd overheard Cindy telling Miles that she couldn't believe they didn't have to be a secret anymore. I'd had a moment of sadness where I'd felt the betrayal like a white hot poker in my chest. But then I'd told myself it was just more proof that Miles and I hadn't been right for each other.

"Aren't you like devastated he dumped you or whatever?"

Not in the slightest. I knew I was worth more than the way he'd treated me. And I wasn't just too good. I'd show them and I'd start now.

I shrugged. "Miles was right. We had fun, but it's over." Plus if I was honest, since I'd found out he'd cheated with Cindy it hadn't felt the same and a part of me was relieved it was over. "I really liked him, but I guess it just wasn't love after all."

Did that make me callous? By the look on Trina's face, yes. But come on! I was seventeen. What did I know about love and relationships? Well I wasn't sure either; sometimes I thought it was lots and other times I thought it was nothing. But it was enough to know that Miles was not my happily ever after and what we'd had, in hindsight, wasn't love.

So yeah. I was going on a date with Davin Ambrose and I didn't care what anyone thought about it. Trina, obviously, thought something.

"But…Davin?" she whispered as though saying his name out loud was going to conjure him and he'd smite us or steal our innocence or something.

"Yes, Trina. Davin. Is there something wrong with Davin?" I asked.

She looked around the hallway like she wasn't quite so sure anymore. "He's just… Did you know he got detention

38

for having sex in Mr Feeny's office last year?"

I'd heard the story and made a mental note to ask him if that was true. But to Trina, I decided now was the time to try out that being not good thing.

"Maybe I'll be next," I said to her in a terrible attempt at playful.

She stared at me, mouth opening and closing, obviously at a loss for words. "Oh," was all she finally managed, then her cheeks went a little pink and she laughed. "Yeah, right. Like you'd do that. Don't forget the photocopies for the meeting after school." Then she walked away.

And this was exactly why I wanted to go out with Davin. After hanging out with him for a while, I'd know exactly what to do and to say in this situation to make Trina and everyone else see that I wasn't that goody-two-shoes. Okay, so the likelihood of me having sex at school, let alone in Mr Feeny's office, was next to none. No, it was definitely none. But I didn't want people to laugh at the idea because I was supposedly so sweet.

Looking at Trina, I felt like I knew what to say. I just couldn't remember it properly and I couldn't bring myself to say it out loud. Miles had been right. I was too good. But Davin would fix that.

****

After school on Friday, I was hanging out in the kitchen with

Mum while I waited for Blair to arrive and help me get dressed for my big date.

"Do you think Mrs Lewis would prefer the periwinkle or the forget-me-not?" Mum asked as she held up the swatches.

"Periwinkle," I told her without a doubt.

"Good eye, sweetie." Mum smiled at me before looking back down to her board.

Mum was one of the reasons I was the way I was. Her interior design company prided itself on its bold use of colour and I'd been in love with the swathes of bright, vibrant fabrics that had been littered around our house since before I could walk. It was virtually impossible to be unhappy when you were rolled up in a toga of canary yellow with a hat of magenta flowers and a staff in chartreuse for bopping your little sister on the head.

Colour in my world meant happy.

I remembered when Mum's dad died. I was only about seven and I'd been devastated – he'd always been a bright and bubbly force in my life. Mum had told me not to be sad he was gone, but be happy he'd been in our lives. She said that's what he would have wanted. I hadn't quite known what she'd meant for what felt like the longest time. But for his funeral Mum had insisted I wear the dress he always loved me in. It was a bright pink thing more suited to a Disney dress-up party than a funeral, but Grandpa had always said it was his favourite dress.

So I wore it and I started to see what she meant. I

remembered all the good times I'd had with him and it made me feel better. I'd realised that looking at the good in things, being positive about life, was what made me happy and I liked it. So it had become my life philosophy and I looked forward to every day I had.

"How long until dinner?" Ebony asked Mum as she sidled into the kitchen and pulled me out of my thoughts.

"What time's your date coming, sweetie?" Mum turned to me.

"Davin," I prompted.

Mum's face twitched a little until it landed on a smile. "Yes. Davin. What time is he coming?"

"Six-thirty," I replied.

"And Dad's home about seven... About seven, then," Mum said as she looked up at Ebony.

Ebony moaned. "That's forever away."

I looked at the clock on the microwave. It was four-twenty-three.

Mum chuckled. "Find yourself something, then."

"But won't that ruin my dinner?" Ebony asked sarcastically.

Mum and I shared a look before she told my little sister, "You're fourteen. I think you can decide for yourself if you're going to ruin your dinner."

"Ebs doesn't do ruined dinner. She can eat for days," I said with a laugh.

Ebony frowned at me. "Calling me fat?"

41

I scoffed. "I wish I could eat as much as you. Think of all the chocolate I could fit in!"

Mum laughed and Ebony's frown eased up.

"Just practise some more," Ebs said as she went to the fridge.

"You just want to see her throw up again," Mum chided.

Ebony shrugged wildly. "What? Like watching her throw up after too much birthday cake *wasn't* hilarious."

My phone went off and I looked at it to see a text from Blair saying she forgot to tell me she was on her way and she was nearly here.

"Blair?" both Mum and Ebs asked and I nodded.

"She's coming around to help me chose a date outfit."

"Woo," Mum cooed. "Exciting. Your second first date!"

I stuck my tongue out at her. "Remind me of my recent heartache why not."

"If you're so heartbroken," came Ebony's muffled voice from behind the fridge door. She emerged with her mouth full of what looked like leftover tiramisu, "why are you going out with some guy tonight?"

"Because I'm moving on with my life. If Miles gets to have a new girlfriend, I get to go on one date."

Mum added, "It's not like she's marrying the guy, Ebs."

Ebony leant on the kitchen bench and looked Mum over. "Do we not care that she's going on a date with another guy mere days after her long-term boyfriend dumped her?"

Mum slid her eyes to me for a moment, then smiled at

42

Ebony. "Avery's dating choices are her own," she said carefully. "Besides, she's a good girl. Your dad and I never have to worry about her because the choices she makes are always good choices."

I didn't want to be making good choices. But revealing the fact that going out with Davin was for that express purpose to my mother would hinder my ability to make not good choices. So I kept it to myself. It wasn't like I was lying... Not really.

"Uh huh," Ebony huffed as the doorbell rang. "So we're just going to let her go date some random guy, then."

"He's not random. I've gone to school with him for like four years," I answered.

Mum opened her mouth, closed it, and then nodded to Ebony. "There you go, hun."

Ebony didn't look convinced, but I didn't need my little sister giving me dating advice. The doorbell rang again and I jumped before running to let Blair in.

"What took you so long?" she whined dramatically as she closed the door behind her. "Do you not want to start tank–"

"Shh!" I hissed as we walked passed the kitchen and stuck our heads in.

"Hey, Blair," Mum said, looking up.

"Hey, Heather. How are you?" Blair asked.

"Good, hun. How about you? Year Twelve treating you okay?"

Blair nodded. "Three weeks in, it's okay."

43

"Good to hear. You two have fun."

"We will!" I called as I grabbed Blair by the elbow and dragged her up to my room.

"So I asked Grace if she had any clothes you could borrow…" Blair started. Grace was Blair's older sister. The one who knew all about Goth stuff.

"And?"

"She shut the door in my face."

I nodded. Grace was like that. "Oh well. We'll have to do me!"

"Yay!" Blair squealed. "Plus didn't Davin say he didn't want you changing who you were?"

I nodded at her as I pulled open the wardrobe. "He did."

"You know? That's almost romantic…" Blair said.

"What's almost romantic?" Ebony asked as she wandered in.

"Avery's date," Blair explained.

"And does Ave's date have a name? Or is he just one of your little sycophants?"

Blair went up to Ebony and put an arm around her as I started pulling things out of the wardrobe. "So morbid, little Ebs."

Ebony glared at the world in general as I held up a dress for their opinion. "Are you going for the giant marshmallow look?" she asked me, completely unimpressed.

I looked at the dress in question and decided that the marshmallow look on a first date, particularly with Davin

Ambrose, was not the right look.

"We're going to need some help," Blair said, all business-like, and I nodded in agreement.

Blair put the music on and we went to work while Ebony sat on my bed and disapproved of everything we suggested. Not that I paid all that much attention to her, but I liked that she was hanging out with us even if it was to be purposefully unhelpful.

It was a parade of outfits, hairstyles, shoes and accessories as we went through my entire wardrobe. Choosing an outfit for a date with Miles had never been that difficult. Ebony objected very vocally every time we tried to dress her up in one of my fluoro tops or neon scrunchies. But she was also begrudgingly laughing.

At about six, Ebony moved from the bed and over to window seat while Blair finished my hair and helped me perfect my liquid eyeliner.

"That's your date?" I heard Ebony ask eventually and Blair and I rushed to the window.

"Ohmigod! He's here!" Blair cried, grabbing my arm and infecting me with enthusiasm.

We jumped around for a few moments, excited that we were making good progress towards Step Three in trashing my reputation. Then I stopped to actually take in that Davin Ambrose was actually at my house to take me on a date.

He was staring up at the house like it personally offended him. But I wasn't focussed on that. I was focussed on what he was wearing.

I'd never seen him out of school clothes – it was said he went to school parties, but they obviously weren't ones I went to – and I wasn't disappointed by what I saw. He was wearing dark jeans with a dark button up shirt, with only the top couple of buttons undone. The only bit of non-black he was wearing was the splash of white on his sneakers, and even then it was a dirty white. But even I knew enough about Converses to know they were supposed to be well-loved.

As we watched, he raked his hand through his hair slowly, shook his head, and started towards the house.

And it suddenly occurred to me that I was about to go on a date with Davin Ambrose. Like *a date*. With Davin Ambrose. My heart started beating a little harder as I grabbed my clutch.

"You right?" Ebony asked me. "You just lost a little of your…pep."

Oh, yeah. Fine. I just needed to convince Davin to be my boyfriend and trash my reputation. Simple. But I could do this. I was going to do this. No more Little Miss Goody-Two-Shoes.

I nodded. "Yeah. Yeah. Fine." I grinned widely at her.

"Ye-huh." Ebony was obviously not convinced.

I pulled myself together and Blair and I raced down the stairs, followed at a more sedate pace by Ebony.

"Oh! One more layer of lip gloss," Blair said and I paused at the mirror in the hall to touch up my makeup.

Mum came out of the sitting room and smiled at me.

"Is he–?" She was interrupted by the doorbell. "Yes, he is."

Mum, Blair and Ebony followed me to the front door and I pulled it open.

"Hey, Davin," I said with a big smile. "This is Ebony. You know Blair. And this is my mum, Heather."

He just nodded and stared at me like he had no idea where he was.

Four: Davin

Okay, so she looked great.

But when did she not?

Avery St John must have been born looking great.

'Oh, nurse, we'll just need to clean the baby before passing her to Mrs St John.'

'No need, doctor. She's perfect just the way she is.'

Yeah, of course she was.

There was thankfully no sign of whatever Blair and Avery thought Goths look liked these days. But I was hopeful that this was the most colourful she got because I couldn't handle any more than that.

She wore a cropped singlet thing covered in flowers and colours that assaulted the eyeballs while they were busy trying to cop too long a look at the smooth skin of her stomach. Her skirt was short and floaty and pink with a bow at the front. The monstrous heels on her feet were yellow and made you instantly forget the seemingly miles of leg you'd just got to perve on as you made your way down. Add to that the purple bow in her tumbling blonde curls and the little green bag she held and I felt like I was going to be ill.

But she'd look great while I was doing it.

Still. One date.

I could do this.

I felt totally underdressed, but I could do this.

One date and we never had to talk again.

"Hi," I finally said because it had just occurred to me that she'd said hi when she opened the door and I'd been standing there ogling her like a total twonk in front of her mother, her best friend, and what I assumed was a little sister rather than just some rent-a-kid play-date.

Avery giggled and I still didn't much care for it. "Hey."

"You ready to go, then?" I asked her, keen to get this over with as quickly as possible.

"You two have fun," her mum said, her smile not quite reaching her eyes, and I nodded to her.

Avery stepped outside and I'll admit I didn't hate the fact she wasn't quite so short as usual. As we walked towards my car, I pretended I couldn't feel the searing hot stares of the three we'd left at the door.

"*This* is your car?" she asked and I looked at it like I'd forgotten if it was my car or not.

I tried to regain some control over myself. "Yes. That okay?"

She nodded as I opened the passenger door for her. "Yeah. It's nice."

It wasn't that nice. I mean it was a Jag, yes. But it wasn't all that. And I only had a Jag because my dad hadn't had the heart to get rid of my mum's car after she'd died. Fast forward eleven years and he's driving her old car because I refused to get in it, leaving his car – said Jag – waiting for me to drive.

"Thanks." To cover the sudden weirdness I felt at the thought of my mum, I added, "Backseat's nice and roomy, never been used, stain-free guarantee," gave her a wink and closed the door on her laugh. Hang on. "Do not cover weirdness with jokes. You'll just encourage her."

I paused before I went to the driver's side, totally conning myself that I was able to see through this nightmare.

"Jesus. It's just one date. How bad could it be?" I ask you.

Taking a deep breath, I went around and got in the car.

"You heard about the break up, then?" she asked as I started the car.

Eventually the rumours had got around to even me. "Who didn't? I think it's about the only thing getting through the Great Firewall of China this week."

She snorted as though she'd actually understood me. "Wow. Thanks."

I shrugged and, when she'd been silent for too long, I snuck a look at her as I drove along to find her staring at me. "What?"

She smiled almost wistfully. "Don't know. Just wondering if you're really as prickly as you come off."

I looked back at the road. "Pricklier."

"Is this the best version of you?"

I nodded. "Definitely."

"I'd hate to see the worst, then," she laughed.

"Let me go back to my quiet existence after this and you won't."

"You don't scare me, Davin."

More's the pity. "Good. I was only aiming for unapproachable."

She laughed again. "Oh, well then you've nailed it."

"Yet, here you are."

"Here I am."

I felt the corners of my mouth tugging weirdly as I snuck another look at her. But she just flashed me a smile with an unusual hint of insecurity in it and turned to look out the window.

I took us down to the beach and found a park without any more unnecessary talking.

As I watched her get out of the car, I wondered why on earth she'd worn such ridiculous shoes on a date she knew was happening on the beach.

"Because it means you spend at least some of the night being less stupidly tall," she answered and I was reminded my internal monologue and external dialogue often became confused. "And they have the added benefit of coming off easily."

"Unlike that top, I'll bet," popped out of my mouth.

She gave me a crooked smile. "You can stop thinking about taking my top off."

"I promise I'm not." Because I hadn't been. I was very close to thinking about it now, though.

"Come on. Let's go."

I followed wherever she led. Which for starters was to the sand where she pulled off her shoes and dug her toes in.

"You're not taking yours off?"

"My heels? No. I thought I'd leave them at home."

She laughed yet again. "No. Your shoes."

"Yeah, no."

She shrugged as she pulled the strap of her bag over her head so it sat across her body. "Suit yourself."

"Trust me, I will," I muttered as I followed her overly enthusiastic person down the beach.

It was like she found goodness and excitement in something as boringly mundane as the beach at sunset. Did she not realise this happened here every day? She was either skipping or waving her arms around or – God help me – holding my hand or arm while she pointed at something she wanted me to look at.

There was even a single-handed hand stand at one point which took me completely off-guard when she said, "Oh! Oh! Okay. Watch this."

Shoes in one hand, she'd just thrown herself into it and I'd watched, temporarily spellbound, as gravity took hold. Her bag wasn't the only thing that fell towards her head and I took in a decent view of her black undies. Then she was right way up and smiling at me.

"You, uh…" I coughed. "You do know how gravity works, right?" I asked and she cocked her head at me in confusion. I pointed to her skirt. "Black panties were a nice touch."

Her face flared pink and she turned back and forth from me so many times I wasn't sure if she was going to just walk away and leave me there, or if she was going to come back with some rebuttal.

"I… Uh…" She huffed a self-conscious laugh as she smoothed her skirt like that was going to make it stay in place regardless of the Earth's gravitational force. "So, you know that assignment we had to do for Miss Nithin?" she started more confidently as she kept walking and she didn't stop talking.

I don't even know what we talked about. Avery had this uncanny ability to just talk and talk. Anytime there was a slight pause in the mostly one-sided conversation, she found something with which to fill it. As I watched her, I had to wonder if it was just her inanity showing, or if she was covering nervousness with that motor mouth.

But whatever was behind the never-ending stream of consciousness emanating from her mouth, I found myself with answers for her. Whatever the answers were, they made her laugh too often and I was just working out how to stop doing that when she pointed to the road and I saw a shop.

She skipped up to it and was ready to order by the time I got to her. The man behind the counter frowned as she went up to him, still with that skip in her step. But as soon as she'd said, "Hi, how are you?" and turned that blinding smile on him, he was smiling back like she'd just made his day.

"Remind me again why I'm doing this?" I ask you as she finished ordering, then she came back to stand with me to wait.

I would have thought the wait would be as fantastically awkward as the rest of the date had been so far, but she talked easily enough for the both of us and I managed to find something to interject with now and then when she paused long enough and with the intention of waiting for me to answer.

When we got our packet of chips, she carefully carried it back to the beach and found us a spot to sit, finish watching the sunset, and eat. At least there was a small moment of silence in the otherwise incessant noise.

Just as I was beginning to wonder how long I had to sit on a patch of warm but slightly damp sand for it to count as a complete date, she spoke.

"So, Davin. Do you want to be my mistake?"

I had to have heard wrong. "Sorry. Your what, now?"

"My mistake. Everyone has them. And I want you to be mine."

This night was either going to be the best or the worst of my life. "You're going to need to explain that to me some more…"

She was still smiling. "You know." I didn't. "You're supposed to go through the 'bad boy' phase. I want you to be my bad boy phase. Help me show Miles and everyone else I'm not such a goody-two-shoes."

Ah, this was making more sense and we were veering into worst night ever territory. "So, you want the muppet back, then?"

She shook her head as she popped one of the last remaining chips into her mouth and looked out over the water. "No."

Less sense again. "No?"

"No. I just don't want to be that stupid little girl everyone sees when they look at me. And," she shrugged, "I figured who better to help me trash my reputation than *the* Davin Ambrose?"

"You want me to what?"

She nodded, her smile widening. "I want you to be my boyfriend and I want you to teach me how to not be good."

Well, I was probably capable. But was I willing? "How not good are we talking here?"

"I dunno. Start small, see where it leads us."

I ask you, *"Is that even how this works?"*

"What?"

"Nothing." Cue knowing look. "You know, I do have a life. I'm not just waiting around for some girl to decide she needs a makeover to go like 'oh. Hey, yeah. I can do that'.

I'd have no idea how to…trash your image."

"Well, what did you do to yours?"

I blinked. "I was born."

"Funny," she giggled, turning back to the water.

Oh, cute. She thought I was joking.

Now was supposed to be the time the guy goes all weird over her laugh, isn't it? Like, it sounded like tinkling rain and made my chest flutter at the same time my cock stood to attention or some shit. Well sorry to disappoint you, but there was none of that. Her laugh may as well have been nails down a chalk board for all the lack of activity in my chest cavity and pants. I had never felt less erect since I'd learnt what an erection was or why I got them.

"I'm not joking. It's my life. I can't just up and change who I am because it's…less than ideal."

"You're life's not ideal?" she asked, turning her whole body to face me with way too much interest.

Nothing about this was going the way I wanted. "No. My life is fine." Although, define fine. "I was referring to yours. You can't just change who you are–"

"Why not?"

I breathed, "Why…?" as I raked a hand through my hair. "Jesus. Right. Well, let's boil this down to a cliché, shall we? You want to not be the good girl? How many guys have you fucked?"

"One."

Well, at least she didn't shy away from the question. That

actually surprised me. Although, not as much as I *wasn't* surprised by the number.

"Okay. Kissed?" I asked.

"Two."

I sighed. This part was going as well as expected. "Okay. You want to be bad–?"

"Not good."

There was a difference? "Right. Start with hooking up with some more guys and see where that…leads you."

"All right."

She moved towards me and I pulled away with a speed I didn't know I was capable of. "Whoa! What are you doing?"

"I was going to start with you."

I seriously couldn't tell if this was incredible naiveté she was showing, if she was far too serious about this changing business that she was listening to whatever drivel I spouted off the top of my head, or she was just scarily adept at taking the piss out of both of us.

"Me?"

She nodded. "Why? You don't want to kiss me?"

"Not really."

"Why not? We don't know each other well enough?" She was actually teasing me.

I scoffed, not one to be easily teased. "No. If anything, we know each other too well."

Another frown. "How is that a thing? You don't want to know the people you kiss?"

"Uh, I'll kiss anyone–"

"Except me."

Apparently. "Except you."

"Because you know my name?"

If that would mean I didn't have to kiss her, yes. "If I didn't know your name, might be a different story."

She paused for a second and I wondered what she was going to say until, "Then pretend you don't know my name," came out a little less assertively than I thought was the intention.

"Pretend I don't... What?" I was not going to fall for this... Was I?

"Go on. Pretend you don't know me and kiss me," she said, that confidence returning.

She was serious about this.

Maybe if I kissed her and she realised there was bugger all between us then I could go home. I could be her temporary mistake only and we could put the whole uncomfortable experience behind us.

Right. One kiss.

"Kiss you?"

The tilt to her lips was less unicorn farts and lollipops and more wry and calculating. "I assume you do actually know the concept and all the stories aren't rubbish?"

I frowned. "Of course I know the concept. There just isn't usually this much discussion about one kiss."

"Oh, sorry. How does it usually work?"

I shrugged. "I don't know. We see each other, then we kiss."

"You truly are the Jane Goodall of humanity, aren't you?" I knew that was sarcasm for sure. I wasn't sure if I was more impressed with the obvious intentional use of the sarcasm or that she knew who Jane Goodall was.

So I leant over and kissed her if only to shut her the hell up. Avery St John was not supposed to do sarcasm. She wasn't supposed to do wry. And she certainly wasn't supposed to kiss like she knew what she was doing.

But she did.

For a second, I thought she was going to pull away. But after she got over the momentary surprise of me kissing her, she kissed me back like she meant it. She wasn't shy, she wasn't hesitant, she certainly wasn't a goddamned wallflower.

Somehow she ended up straddling my lap and I wasn't sure how much of that was because I'd dragged her to me or she'd climbed on. I felt like maybe it was half and half, and there was definitely a little more action going on in my chest and my pants than there had been earlier.

I hated everything about Avery – her incessant happiness, her obsession with colour, the way she talked non-stop, the way I felt like I was crashing from a massive sugar high after every encounter. She annoyed me to the point I'd rather be in detention with Mrs Mack than anywhere Avery could find me. But the way she kissed me? Holy Jesus.

She was soft and warm in my hands as her body pressed against mine. She was dominating me more than I was dominating her, and that was a fucking turn on. She kissed me like I wasn't just that guy, whoever that guy was. God, and when she took that playful bite of my lip? I felt like I'd toppled off the edge of a fucking precipice.

Only after my hand slid up under her skirt did she pull away. But she didn't go far, her nose was still close enough to bump mine. And she was smiling as usual, but there was a different look in her eyes. Something I did not associate with Avery St John. Something I didn't think anyone would associate with Avery St John.

"You kiss all the girls you don't know like that?" she asked teasingly.

I had no idea. "You kissed Muppet Miles like that and he still broke up with you?"

She shook her head, her curls bouncing. "Maybe he might not have broken up with me if I had?"

"Yeah. I don't think I'd make that mistake," I breathed.

"So does that mean you'll be *my* mistake?"

God, she just had to wriggle in my lap, didn't she? I probably had mere seconds to put a stop to this before the smaller head was taking charge.

"You mean like some kind of fake dating bullshit?"

She shook her head again. "No. Proper dating. All the perks of having a girlfriend without any of the hassle."

"How is hanging out with you not going to be a hassle?"

Her smile didn't quite hide the apprehension in her eyes. But then I was distracted when she huffed a self-conscious laugh and I blame the way it made her shift slightly for the effect it had in my pants.

"You won't have to be polite or charming," she told me. "You can just be your normal grumpy self."

"So in what way would this be real dating?"

She leant against me and I had to stop myself from letting us fall backwards. What the hell was she doing to me? "We'd be exclusive, we'd go on dates, we'd kiss and…other stuff."

"Other stuff?" I knew someone who was interested in this other stuff and he was fighting for control.

She nodded and I was finding it hard to reconcile the Avery I knew with the veritable sultry goddess in my hardening lap. "Like I said, all the perks."

"And I'm supposed to teach you how to…not be good?" Fuck, I was losing higher brain function fast.

"Just treat me like you'd treat those girls you don't know."

A strangled attempt at a laugh left me. "I am not treating you like them."

"Why not?"

"Uh. Firstly, because I wouldn't date any of them. Secondly, because tonight is not ending with me fucking you anywhere." God, what was happening to me?

She leant to my ear and whispered, "Are you sure?"

If she kept that up? No. Not for long. Needing some control back, I picked her up and flipped us so I was lying

61

over her. I watched her watching me carefully and wondered why this was so important to her. Currently more important to me though was the effect her under me was having on me.

"And this does nothing for my self-control."

"What?" she asked, a smile on her lips.

"Nothing," I muttered as I looked down at her. "You want to date me?"

She nodded.

"Just as I am. I don't have to do anything but somehow teach you how to not be so good?" Although how I was going to manage that, I had no idea.

But she nodded again. "Just dating you will probably be enough."

I wasn't sure if I should take that as a good thing or a bad thing. And I know what I'd said; one date and that was it, one kiss and that was it. But I wasn't thinking straight and there was something weirdly addictive about her. The fact that I could be my usual arsehole of a self and she still sought me out? It didn't hurt she kissed the way she did. I was just going to be a mistake, so there was no way this would last.

So whatever the flimsy premise, I was in.

"Okay." I nodded. "Consider me your boyfriend."

Her victorious smile finally found its way back into her eyes and I guess I didn't hate it. "Great."

"If you talk anymore, I am going to kiss you again, though."

Her eyes shone brighter in the moonlight. "Really? You're

already bossing me–"

Oh, I'd warned her. And I didn't bother reminding her. I just kissed her and thought that maybe it wasn't going to be the worst night of my life after all.

Five: Avery

Miles certainly hadn't kissed like Davin kissed. Miles had been better than Tom, but Davin put them both to shame and then some.

When Davin kissed me, it felt like he couldn't get enough of me, like he wanted to kiss me for kissing me and not just because I just happened to be there. He felt like heat and passion and it was sexy. It made me feel sexy and it made me kiss him back the same way.

When Miles had kissed me, it had been nice but the comparison made me realise that Miles had never turned me on just from a kiss – or even just the idea of kissing him. In fact I was starting to wonder if Miles had been what turned me on at all.

But sitting next to Davin on the beach and just *thinking* about kissing him again turned me on. And I couldn't help but sneak looks at him while he was staring at the water. It was dark now, with only the moon and distant streetlights to see by, but still early enough in the year that it wasn't cold.

"What?" he asked, still staring at the water.

"What, what?"

"I know you're staring at me, what?"

I buried my face in my knees. "Nothing."

"Really?" he scoffed. "Now you shut up?"

I rolled my head to the side to look at him and smiled. "I'm starting to realise you like the quiet."

As he looked up, there was that hint of a smile on his face but never the actual thing. "You're starting to realise? And here I was thinking I'd made it clear on Tuesday?"

I laughed awkwardly. "I'm naturally…sociable."

"I'd call it annoying. But you're not wrong."

We sat in silence for a bit longer.

Even when he said rude things I couldn't not be amused by him. There was something about the way he said it that made me believe he wasn't being completely serious. Plus I just really admired the way he felt comfortable saying whatever he was thinking. I couldn't do that. But I wanted to do that. I *needed* to do that. Which made Davin the perfect one to help me tank my rep.

And I could understand why a guy who barely talked to another human being would find me annoying. I was just hoping to change his mind. If I didn't, he might decide not to help me anymore. If I did, it was a pretty sure bet that I wasn't too good anymore.

"So… *This* is a date, huh?" he mused after a while.

"What?" I asked.

"This. Is this what the rest of our dates will be like, then?"

"Some of them."

"And the others?"

I shrugged. "We could stay home and watch movies–"

"How does that help you trash your reputation? Are you planning to become less good by mere osmosis?"

"What's that?"

"Used colloquially it means that by just being around me you'll become less good."

That was exactly the thought I'd had when I came up with this idea. "Well, I am quite confident that that would work."

"Of course you are."

I huffed. "Ideally we go out, if there were places you actually enjoyed being. But we date. We just spend time together and see what happens."

"See what happens? What are you planning? Murder-suicide pacts? Joining a cult? Devil worship?"

"Why is everything doom and gloom with you?"

"Why is everything so nauseatingly bright with you?"

I smiled at him before I looked back to the water. "I was more meaning we could talk, get to know each other…" I petered to a very self-conscious stop.

"That other stuff you mentioned earlier?" he added wryly when it was clear I wasn't going to continue.

"Yes. That." I hadn't been going to mention it because I really wanted to try that now. But I also didn't want to look like a total ease and I already had sand all through my hair after he'd seriously kissed me last.

That had never been me before. I'd never been the girl who wanted to do any of that stuff. Not like this. Obviously my plan was working. I'd just kissed Davin and already I felt less sweet and innocent than I'd been before.

No… That was stupid. Wasn't it?

"How long were you planning on this mistake, then?" he asked.

"Don't know. Until one of us gets bored?"

"And if I said I was already bored?"

I didn't like that idea. I didn't want him to be bored of me. Although I didn't know why. I just wanted his help. Right?

"Are you?" I asked, aiming for casual and not sure I hit it.

He scoffed. "No. I'm not sure I could be bored with you around. Uncomfortable? Yes. Bored? No."

"I make you uncomfortable?"

He shifted so his arms were leaning on his knees. "My own company makes me uncomfortable, Avery. Don't go thinking you're special or anything."

I laughed. "Oh, sure."

We sat in silence for a while longer and I watched him. There was a tenseness to his shoulders as he ran his hand through his hair and looked over the water that made me want to reach out to him. But I wasn't actually quite so naïve that I thought it would be okay to ask him if he was okay.

"Wow," he said finally, quickly as though he was really feeling that discomfort. "You actually managed – what? – a whole ten minutes of not talking?"

"I thought I'd give it a go. I like observing people different to me."

"So I'm some sort of social experiment?"

I looked at him with a frown. "I wouldn't call it that."

"No. I'm sure you wouldn't." He huffed. "So the guy who hates everything social and experimental has found himself combining the two into one tortuous package." He turned his head to look at me and I was struck by something in his eyes. Then he shrugged and looked away again. "Gran always said I was a sucker for punishment."

****

Saturday was Best Friends' Day! So I was excited about that as well as telling Blair all about my date with Davin.

The date had ended with a very steamy kiss in his car when he'd dropped me home. I'd figured why not start acting like his girlfriend with a kiss good night, and what had started out intending to be relatively innocent had definitely not ended that way. Not that I'd minded at all.

At nine on Saturday, I got out of bed and got ready to meet Blair. I had a tiny moment of sadness sneak in when I came across the dress Blair and I had bought for me to wear for the now-cancelled first anniversary date. I ran my hand over it for a moment and wondered where it had all gone wrong. I wondered what I'd done wrong.

But then I remembered I hadn't done anything wrong.

I hadn't done anything but be the person I thought people would like. Well, all that person had got was dumped by a guy she thought she loved but who, in actual hindsight, treated her like everyone else treated her. Because without my rose-tinted glasses on, it was plainly obvious that Miles had probably cheated on me because he thought if I ever found out that I'd forgive him. He, like everyone else at school, seemed to think he could walk all over me and I'd take it.

Davin wasn't like that. Sure he didn't even bother trying to hide the fact that he thought I was an idiot. But at least he didn't think I was any more idiotic than he thought everyone else was. To Davin, there was nothing special about me. I was the same as everyone else in his life. He looked down on me – literally and figuratively – and talked down to me like everyone else. But I saw something more in his eyes when he looked at me, something contemplative like he was actually paying attention to me and wasn't just dismissing me.

I liked being me. But I wasn't going to be that doormat again. I wasn't going to let it be okay that my boyfriend cheated on me for any reason. I wasn't going to let anyone talk down to me again. I was going to be fierce and never again was anyone going to be able to say that Avery St John was too good.

As soon as I worked out how…

"But that's where Davin comes in," I reminded myself with a smile as I hurried down the stairs.

69

"Morning, sweetie," Dad called as my foot hit the floor.

"How did you know it was me?" I asked him with a smile as I stuck my head into the kitchen.

Dad grinned at me. "Because neither your mother nor your sister would be up this early on a Saturday and be so light on their feet."

I giggled. "Ebony *does* have a tendency to sound like a baby elephant first thing."

Dad nodded. "She does." He looked me over like he'd only just actually looked at me. "You look nice. Where are you off to?"

"It's Best Friends' Day. So I'm going to pick Blair up and we're going out!"

Dad's next nod was a little vague as he frowned over his crossword. "That's nice, sweetie. Have you got enough petrol?"

I did have to think about that one. "I think so."

"Okay. Let me know if you need me to fill it up."

"I am capable of filling up my own petrol tank, Dad."

He looked up sharply, his bright blue eyes blinking behind his rimless glasses. "Oh…" he said slowly. "Of course you are, sweetie." He gave me a weird smile. "Say hi to Miles for me."

"Blair," I reminded him. "Miles and I broke up."

Dad's eyebrows narrowed in confusion. "Did you?"

I nodded. "He dumped me."

"Oh. I'm sorry, sweetie. I know how excited you were

about that Perfect Couple thing."

"Uh… Sure."

"Are you okay…with it?" he asked awkwardly and I had to at least be grateful he was trying.

"I will be," I told him honestly.

"Should I…have a talk with him? Man to man?"

Great. So even my dad didn't think I could do anything for myself! Offering to fill up my petrol was one thing. But offering to…what? Have a go at my ex for me? I really wasn't that useless, was I?

"No. Thanks," I answered. "I…sorted it."

Dad smiled at me with surprised pride. "Okay. Well I did always like Miles. But it's his loss. You're perfect to me, sweetie."

I couldn't help but smile back. "Thanks, Dad. I'll, uh, see you later."

"You home for dinner?"

I nodded. "Yeah. Blair…has plans."

When I was supposed to be having my first anniversary date, Blair had planned to go out with her family for her sister's birthday. She'd offered to avoid it – it just being Grace and all. But I told her she should spend her sister's birthday with her.

"Okay. See you tonight." Dad hummed as he went back to his crossword and I headed out to Mum's car.

I drove very rarely. As rarely as possible. It's not that it scared me…really. I just felt safer in other people's hands.

But I figured that Best Friends' Day deserved me pulling my weight on the driving front. Plus Blair hadn't been able to get a car for the day.

I carefully pulled out of the driveway and got myself to Blair's house only five minutes later than our allotted time. So she was ready and waiting for me when I got there and jumped into the car with an enthusiasm to rival mine. But that was why we were best friends.

"So," she started as I pulled away and headed for the mall, and I swear it was the last time she took a breath for what felt like ten minutes. "How was your date? Was he a gentleman? Was he *not* a gentleman? Did you kiss him? Oh! Did you sleep with him? Was he hot? Was he good? Did he *you know*? Did you go skinny dipping? What did you eat? Did he agree to be your boyfriend? Is he going to trash your rep? Are we officially not good girls anymore?" She finally took a breath as she grabbed my arm. "Did you get…arrested?"

I smiled at her as I kept my eyes on the road. "It was…nice."

"Nice?"

I nodded. "Actually really nice. We talked and had chips and…" She gasped in excitement as I paused. "We did kiss."

"Ohmigod," she squeaked. "How was it? Was it good? Was he good? All the stories say he's good!"

I laughed. "Where do those stories come from anyway? I've never seen him hook up with anyone from school?"

I felt Blair shrug. "Dunno. I assume someone's hooked up

72

with him. He just looks the type who'd be good at it. Don't you think?"

"When have you looked at him long enough to know he looks like he'd be good at it."

Before that week, I certainly hadn't looked at him long enough to wonder if he'd be any good. There were rumours – there were always rumours – but I suppose I'd never really stopped to form an opinion about it. About whether he was actually as good as the rumours said, I mean. I'd sort of just added the rumours to everything that made him perfect to be the guy who helped me trash my rep.

"I haven't. But someone must have. People say he's good. Is he good?"

I nodded. "Yeah. He's good."

Blair and I laughed.

"Was he, like, *sexy*?"

"It was pretty sexy, yeah."

She nodded like she knew about these things. "Grace says all Byronic guys are sexy."

"What's that mean? Byronic?"

Blair seemed to think about it for a moment, then shrugged. "I dunno. But apparently they're like really good in bed. Attentive good. Like they care or something. They enjoy your enjoyment? I dunno. I couldn't really keep up."

"Is Davin Byronic?" I asked.

Blair nodded. "Grace says so."

"How does she know?"

"Dunno."

"Huh," I mused.

"So…" Blair nudged me playfully. "He's probably good in bed."

I laughed. "Let's just wait and see what happens, yeah? He might not want to sleep with me."

"He's a teenage boy. Doesn't he want to sleep with everyone?"

I giggled. "What's our excuse?"

"We're teenage girls."

"Oh. So it's the teenage part that does it."

"Well, duh." She paused, then asked, "If he wanted to sleep with you, would you sleep with him?"

I thought about that. I *was* attracted to him. Really attracted to him. The idea of sleeping with a guy who seemed a little more…dangerous than Miles was exciting. And sleeping with Davin was unlikely to be considered 'too good' behaviour. Plus it was normal to have sex with your boyfriend if you both wanted it, right? We were in a day and age when it should be perfectly acceptable to be sexually active and women to be empowered by sex, right?

I just had to see if Davin brought out any of those things in me. Because that would definitely shed my goody-two-shoes image.

"Yes, I would," I answered finally. "Besides, I want to see if it actually is better with a bad boy."

We collapsed into giggles as we pulled into the mall

parking lot and the great car park search began. We finally found one under cover and made a beeline for our favourite café for some start of day refreshments so we had enough energy to complete a proper full day of shenanigans.

We shopped and ate and laughed and talked and took a bunch of pictures, and by the time the shops closed at five it felt like time had passed too quickly. But the only place still open was the cinema and Tunza Fun. We didn't have time for a movie and neither of us were any good at any of the games in Tunza Fun. So I took Blair back to her place and headed home. Where I checked in with Davin with a quick text – being my boyfriend now and all – and sorted the washing basket Mum left on my bed every Saturday afternoon.

"Avery!" I heard Ebony yelling as I sorted my socks from my undies, and I knew she wanted something.

"Yeah?" I called back, smiling.

"Can you *please* tell Dad that you're happy to have steak for dinner," she pleaded, swinging into my room.

I looked at her as I refolded the jeans I'd just inadvertently unfolded. "Steak? Two nights in a week?" I teased and Ebony glared at me.

It suddenly occurred to me that Ebony was the St John that Davin would probably like better were she a few years older. Ebony was a tomboy and a grump. Where I wanted to be a part of everything, she was totally happy by herself. Where my wardrobe was full of colour and flouncy materials, hers was jeans and t-shirts and a couple of jumpers for the rare occasion she got cold – even in the midst of winter. Where I smiled at the drop of a hat, you had to earn a smile from my little sister but you felt amazing when you did.

But despite our differences, we were close and I loved her a lot.

"Come on, Ave. Please?" she wheedled.

I sighed over-dramatically. "I just don't know, Ebs. It's Saturday–"

"You can have free choice on the movie," she said quickly and I gave her a wicked grin. To which she frowned. "You knew I'd offer…" She frowned harder. "Ugh. Deal?" she asked begrudgingly.

I nodded as my phone went off and I picked it up. "Deal."

"You saw her *all* day. What could you possibly have to talk about?" she said in disbelief.

"Oh, it's not Blair," I replied absently as I read the message.

Davin:

Going out. I assume I'm supposed to ask
what you're doing?

I smiled to myself and typed a reply.

Avery:

Movie night with my sister. You?

"Who is it then?"

I wasn't surprised Ebony sounded suspicious. I had quite a lot of friends at school, but not many that I texted with regularly.

"My boyfriend," I told Ebony with a smile.

Ebony frowned again. "You're really not so stupid that you took Miles back are you?"

"What do you know about it?"

"Enough that if I was bigger, I'd give him a beating."

I rolled my eyes at her. I loved that she was protective – honestly, she acted like she was the older one most of the time – but the last thing I needed was my little sister beating up my ex. And I could see her doing it.

"No. I don't want Miles back."

Ebony looked confused, then brightened again. "Oh." Then frowned. "Really? That guy you went out with last night?"

I nodded. "Yep."

"He's your boyfriend?" She looked like she was trying not to laugh at me.

"Ye-es...?" I said slowly. "Do you have a problem with that?"

She shrugged. "Just doesn't seem your type is all."

"I'm trying something different. Sticking my toe out of my comfort zone."

Ebony had been looking impressed, now she just looked judgmental. "Is this some kind of stupid social experiment?"

I opened my mouth, then closed it again because wasn't that exactly what Davin had called it? She nodded knowingly.

"Yeah. I thought so. Poor guy."

"It's not like that. Davin's just helping me trash my reputation."

Ebony looked me over like I'd lost my mind. "And I felt sorry for him before…"

"What is that supposed to mean?"

"Well anyone who is forced to spend time with you deserves sympathy–" I stuck my tongue out at her and she repaid the favour "–but you want him to what?" She snorted. "What are you doing that for?"

I shook myself out. "Because I'm sick of being Miss Goody-Two-Shoes. I want to be normal–"

"Ave, no one will ever look at you and think 'normal'."

"Well I want them to."

"What do you even count as normal?"

I paused for a moment to collect my thoughts. "You know… Normal."

"You have no idea, do you?"

I opened and closed my mouth indignantly a couple of times. "I do too."

"Give several examples."

"You know. I don't want people to treat me like an idiot. I want to be able to make normal decisions and people not be surprised or think I've gone mad or something."

Ebony scratched her head, quite clearly thinking I was talking a load of nonsense. "Uh huh. And what's so good about being normal anyway?"

"Why don't you leave my dating decisions to me?"

78

She shrugged. "Fine. Whatever. I need to go tell Dad steak is on anyway."

Ebony left me in a weird sense of grump and I wasn't quite sure why. I tried to shake it off as I finished with my clean clothes, interrupted now and then from a text from Davin. Texting with him was just as easy as talking to him in person was.

Davin:

Dinner with my grandmother.

Avery:

Is that a Sunday night thing?

Davin:

Why would it be a Sunday night thing?

Avery:

Because some families do that. Don't they?

Davin:

I assure you I wouldn't know what families do or don't do.

Avery:

So it's not a Sunday night thing?

Davin:

It's an it happens thing.

But while I tried to get answers out of Davin, something about Ebony's words gnawed at me. Maybe if I hadn't been quite so good, I'd have worked out what it was.

Six: Davin

I blindly grabbed at my phone, which was rudely making noises other than my alarm at such a godforsaken hour of the morning.

I'd expected it to be my grandmother. She was the only one who'd be brave – or stupid – enough to risk contacting me before midday on any given day. But when I picked it up, I saw it was Avery and a bunch of good morning wank in text message form that I didn't even bother looking at. I dropped my phone on my chest and sighed, looking forward to another twenty minutes of sleep.

However, sleep was fucking elusive because I had this niggling feeling in the back of my head telling me to open Avery's damned message. I lay there, staring at the ceiling in the near-darkness, willing myself to relax and just get those damned eighteen more minutes of sleep.

"Avery doesn't actually expect a response. Does she? She's not quite so delusional as to think I'd be functional now?"

I told myself I could just lie there quite happily and

remember the feel of her under me, on top of me. Jesus, I didn't care where she was as long as I got to feel her again.

My eyes flew open as I realised that the best likelihood of that came from reading and replying to her goddamned messages.

"Just this once," I promise you.

I pulled the message centre open and the 'good morning' was accompanied by a picture of her quite clearly already her usual peppy self. She looked as pristine as she always did. Hair in perfect curls that tumbled over her shoulders. The parts of her uniform I could see were clean, ironed and worn just like the kids in the prospectus photos wore it. She was annoyingly perfect, ridiculously perky, and I was torn between feeling like I'd chugged a bottle of caramel topping and like I was desperate to kiss her again.

"How does a girl who looks like that…kiss like that?"

I scrubbed my hand over my face, thinking it was probably past time I shaved. But I decided that if I was going to be awake too early, then my time was better served mainlining caffeine so I had some defence against the tornado of sucrose I knew Avery would be.

I managed to get the bottom half of my uniform on quite easily. Although I struggled with my belt for a moment. Then I dragged on my shirt, tie and blazer. I didn't bother doing any of that up yet, but at least I was in the required amount of uniform for when I finally stumbled out of the house.

As I lurched to the kitchen in search of coffee, I dialled

my grandmother's number.

"What's wrong?" was her panicked answer.

I mumbled somewhat unintelligibly, cleared my throat, and tried again. "Nothing."

"Well why in God's name are you calling me this early? Scaring your poor, frail, old grandmother near to death, Davin!" she chided but I could hear the smile in her voice.

"Poor, frail and old my arse," I told her, almost smiling myself as I turned on the coffee machine.

"You sound awful. Are you not sleeping again?" she asked.

"I just woke up. Give me a fucking break."

"I'll give you a fucking break when you learn some proper manners, young man," she said sternly. Gran only swore when I did and it was her way of telling me to clean up my damned mouth.

I sighed. "My manners are fine. Thank you. My inventive use of language is merely proof of my advanced grasp of the nuances of linguistic semantics."

"And what ridiculous so-called study told you that?" she snorted.

I frowned and was glad she couldn't see me. "I was awake and thought I'd ask if there was anything I can pick up on my way tonight."

"And were you going to ask? Or just tell me you were going to ask?"

"Talk about semantics," I muttered. "Is there anything I

can pick up on my way tonight, Gran?" I asked her in the insincere sweet tone I'd been practising with Avery lately.

"I could use some more milk and Flint's out of tuna."

Flint was Gran's cat. I was pretty sure he was older than me and we'd never got on. Not in the years I'd spent two out of every four weeks at Gran's, and not now that I was old enough to stay at home by myself and gave the stupid feline more space.

Cue expository backstory.

My dad worked in the mines. Fly in, fly out. Two weeks on, two weeks off. After my mum…died, I stayed with Gran for the weeks he was gone up until a couple of years ago when Gran said I could stay home, but I had to have dinner with her at least eight times while Dad was working.

No one said no to Gran. I particularly didn't say no to Gran. Not after everything that had happened and everything she'd done for me. So I went to her place for dinner a minimum of eight times in the fortnights Dad was away and I did whatever I could to show her I appreciated her.

"Oh. And my script is ready to pick up at the chemist if you're going to Newton."

I nodded. "Yeah. I need a refill, too."

"Davin." Gran's tone was a stern warning. "Tell me you're pre-empting the end of your previous script and haven't run out…"

"I'm pre-empting the end of my previous script and haven't run out, Gran."

83

"For all that's holy, Davin! There's a ruddy reason you're on those–"

"Gran. It's fine. I had the last ones last night. I'm good."

"Promise?"

"Yes."

I heard her sighing in relief. "All right. I should let you finish getting ready for school. I'll see you tonight?"

"Yep. See you tonight. Love you," I told her.

"I love you, Dav. To the centre of the Earth and back," she replied.

I nodded and hung up, stretching my neck agitatedly as I finished making my coffee.

I found one of Dad's travel mugs to put it in, bundled up my bag and fell into the car at my usual quarter to nine. But at least I had caffeine this time. That got me through first lesson without envisioning dousing the room with the fire sprinklers. It got me through to second lesson where I nodded semi-politely at Avery as I passed her on my way to my usual seat, and then through Mrs Weaving's ability to make even Math unbearably boring.

At some point in the lesson, I heard Avery's voice but hadn't been paying enough attention to know what she'd answered or what the question had been.

I watched Mrs Weaving smile at Avery and I saw the emotions play out on the teacher's face. "Good try, Avery." You couldn't quite call it condescension in her tone. Condescension implied a complete lack of sympathy. Mrs

Weaving had a lot of sympathy for Avery. But it didn't stop her from speaking down to her.

So there was this new small part – miniscule really – that was suddenly annoyed at the way people treated Avery. And Mrs Weaving was just one example. Avery was definitely no Rhodes Scholar. In fact I'd be thoroughly surprised if her grades were better than a C average. And I knew it was the teacher's job to – you know – teach us. But I wasn't sure that gave them a pass to treat her like there was no hope for her academically.

And it wasn't just teachers.

In case you hadn't noticed, Avery was one of those truly kind and warm-hearted people. It was disgusting really, but that didn't make it any less true.

Until I was forced to feel a modicum of responsibility masquerading as care for her, I hadn't realised that I already knew how people treated her: the girl who asked Avery to take her form to the principal's PA for her because she didn't have time, her so-called friends who dismissed every idea for the formal she came up with, the teacher who left her to clean up the art room because she was good that way.

I'd had no idea that I knew any of this stuff. But snippets of this treatment from over the years came to me as we walked down the hallway to Home Group – while she and Blair excitedly chatted about I didn't want to know what – like some ridiculous montage running through my head.

I was sure I hadn't been part of any of those scenes, but I

guess I'm supposed to inherently know her Before character, right? Because she's the popular girl and it makes total sense that the school loner has all the helpful expository knowledge when it comes to her. Because, you know, it would just be fucking weird if she told you all this herself and I guess there isn't time to do all the individual scenes to show not tell – besides, who doesn't love a time-saving montage?

Once in Mr Boyle's classroom, I gave Avery another nod and went to my seat. She and Blair sat in their usual seats, sneaking looks back to me now and then as our Home Group teacher did the roll and reminded us that our jumpers were going to be arriving on Friday, then dismissed us.

"Davin, can I talk to you a moment, please?" Mr Boyle called as students headed out to lunch.

I nodded resignedly and sat back down in my seat, waiting for him to get on with whatever it was I was being held back for. Mr Boyle took a perch on the desk in front of mine and waited until the last person had filed out of the room.

He sighed and looked me over. "What can you tell me about Mrs Nichol's computer, Davin?"

Ah, finally. That had taken longer than I'd expected. "If it's anything like the rest of the machines in this school, I'd say it was at least three years overdue for an upgrade, sir."

Mr Boyle looked like he sincerely wished he didn't have to be the one dealing with me and the feeling was definitely mutual. "And what can you tell me about the screaming goat that keeps popping up on her screen?"

I shrugged. "Not a lot, sir. I hear it's a popular video among the children, though. Perhaps Mrs Nichol is trying to recapture her lost youth?"

Mr Boyle looked at me, thoroughly unimpressed. "I'm going to have to give you detention for this, Davin."

I leant forward and gave him a contentious look. "Are you now? Why me, sir?"

Mr Boyle sighed again, slightly more exasperatedly like he knew exactly what he was in for and debating the sanity in even starting it. "IT has no idea what was done to Mrs Nichol's computer, Davin–"

"I wouldn't think that was a great shock to anyone, sir."

His glare got harder. "Regardless. That doesn't leave a lot of room for speculation."

"So you just assume it was me?"

"You are the only person in the school remotely smart enough."

"But you have no proof it was me."

"I don't need proof it was you. Everyone knows it was you."

"I was under the impression our country worked on the supposition of innocent until proven guilty, sir."

"Mitchell College is not the Australian judiciary system, Davin. Detention. Friday."

"I'm sorry, sir." I sat back in my chair and crossed my arms. "But I see no way you can enforce detention for a crime you have no proof I committed."

I felt the fact I did commit it was irrelevant.

My Boyle actually grunted in frustration. "Mrs Mack will see you in detention on Friday afternoon, Davin. Unless…?"

"Really? What am I? Five?" I ask you as I frowned at his blatant attempt to engage me. "All right, sir. I'll bite," I said with sarcastic excitement. "Unless what?"

Mr Boyle saw right through my sarcasm somehow and I knew he wanted this conversation over with as much as I did.

"Unless the goat disappears from Mrs Nichol's computer. I don't care how it happens and I don't care who's responsible. No goat equals no detention." He dragged himself off the desk like I'd just aged him twenty years. I seemed to have that effect on people. I liked having that effect on people. It meant people expected less of me and I was under no obligation to perform.

"Well, sir. If I ever determine who's responsible, I'll be sure to let them know." I got up and picked up my books.

"You do that, Davin," he replied wearily, dismissing me with a wave of his hand as he went back to his desk.

I gave him a sardonic grin as I left and found Avery waiting for me outside the classroom. "What are you doing?" I asked her.

She looked confused for a moment. "Waiting for you."

"Why?"

She smiled, but was still confused. "Uh. Because we're dating. It's what you do."

So leaving the same room as the same time wasn't

88

enough. Now we were expected to wait for each other as well?

"More social mores," I huffed.

That one sailed over her head. "Social whats?"

I rolled my eyes. "Customs. Traditions. Obligations."

She nodded. "Oh." Then I got a huge hit of that unfailingly nauseating sweetness. "Yes."

My nod was somewhat less enthused as I flashed her a split-second humourless grin. "Brilliant."

She followed by my side for a while. I wasn't sure where she thought we were going, but I was going to my locker. But I didn't have the energy to try to dissuade her. I avidly ignored people staring as the Queen of Pep trotted presumably quite happily along beside the Lord of Malcontent.

"What's Byronic mean?" Avery asked finally.

"Characteristic of Lord Byron or his poetry," I replied dourly as I pulled open my locker.

"Who's he?"

"Is this for an English assignment?" I didn't think we were doing poetry until second semester.

"No. Blair mentioned it the other day."

"In what context did Blair *mention* Byron?" I replied in total surprise.

"Byronic *guys*," she said like it was really important.

I snorted despite everything in me feeling utterly disappointed with such an emotional display. "What?"

"Byronic guys. Grace said all Byronic guys were sexy."

I stopped what I was doing and looked at her. "Who's Grace?"

"Blair's sister."

"The one into the whole Goth thing?"

She looked surprised for a moment. "You remembered."

I shrugged as I went back to swapping my books over. "Was I not meant to?"

"No. I just… I'm surprised. Anyway, Grace apparently said you were Byronic and all Byronic guys are sexy."

I froze as dread seeped into my soul. "Oh. Hell no."

Did that actually just happen? Were you aware of this? Fucking Jesus. No.

I was not going to be the Byronic Hero here. Fuck that for a joke. No.

I was not going down in history as yet another Heathcliff, an alternative Darcy, Dorian #5782, one more Gatsby (all right, I'm reaching now). And if anyone had the audacity to compare me to Edward-fucking-Cullen, I might just prove you all right and off myself.

"What's wrong?" Avery asked me.

I looked at her like she really should have known. "I am not the Byronic hero," I told her, my tone icy.

She cocked her head to the side as she pulled her phone out of her pocket. I watched her fingers play over the screen and waited to see what in the ever-loving hell she was doing.

A crooked smile lit her lips and she giggled. I still didn't care for it, but it did starkly remind me of a slightly more breathy laugh she'd given on Friday night while I had my lips on her neck and my hand up her skirt. That I hadn't minded quite so much.

"You are definitely a Byronic hero."

"Why didn't you just look it up in the first place?" I slammed my locker, trying to work out how many Byronic heroes actually managed to get out of these situations whole and without the added inconvenience of a love interest.

"Grumble all you want, Davin. But it's all here. Cynical. Arrogant. No respect for authority. Moody. Intelligent. Mysterious. Sexy. The only thing missing is self-destructive impulses and a past trauma."

Well. Fuck.

She had me.

And neither of those last two things were missing. I had self-destructive impulses perfected like it was my native language and past trauma in spades. Not that the shiny happy beacon of annoying buoyancy next to me needed to know that.

"But in good news…" she continued. "You're capable of redemption, heroic behaviour and deep affection."

I had a sinking feeling about where all this was going and I maintained I wasn't having a bar of it.

"Oh. That's the good news? So pleased," I muttered.

She giggled again. "Come on. Let's go find Blair."

"For what purpose would I possibly want to find Blair?"

91

"To hang out with my friends."

"Oh. Of course." I nodded then stopped. "No."

Her hand was suddenly in the middle of my chest and I found myself with my back against the locker behind me, looking down at this smirking minx in front of me. I watched in almost disbelief as her had ran up my chest slowly and I felt my heart thud inside it.

"Please, Davin. It'll just be you, me, and Blair."

"Threesome from hell?" I ask you, trying to picture that and how dreadfully colourful it would no doubt be.

Another giggle and she took my hand and dragged me after her. I had very little choice but to follow and arguing would have been far too much effort. I knew people were still watching us carefully, trying to work out what was going on. But no one stopped us, no one said anything. As far as they were concerned, I was probably in trouble for something again and Avery was delivering me to Mrs Mack.

"So… What would you say your super power was?" she asked me as we walked and I could not believe I was putting myself through this. Even the way she kissed was surely not worth it.

"Super power?"

She nodded excitedly and I grimaced.

"Superheroes aren't real. I have no super powers."

"Fine. What are you *really* good at? Other than computers and dark humour."

"Is this some mandatory dating protocol or something?"

"What?"

"This getting to know each other bullshit."

"Yes."

I sighed and stretched my neck. "Okay." I thought about it. "I twomble. If there was an Olympic medal for twombling, I would get gold. Every time. Hands down."

She snorted. "You what?"

"Twomble. It means to abruptly leave an awkward situation without saying a word."

She was trying – and failing – not to laugh at me. "I'd bet you'd just twomble out of life if you could."

I shrugged. She wasn't totally wrong. But I'd been on the other end of that and, previous threats aside, I wasn't going to do that to the two people who cared about me. "I'd certainly twomble out of here if I thought you wouldn't notice."

"I *would* notice, though."

"Why do you think I'm still here, then?"

"Because we need to plan another date!"

How did we get onto that? I hung my head back. "One isn't enough?"

She laughed and I did not want to look at her again, but I did when she said, "Of course not."

I glared at her. "Fine. But if we have to actually go on dates, then there's going to be a point to them." Was there? Oh good.

And, oh! I was so close to a frown there. But it was just

confusion on her face. "A point? Well, duh. The point is to get to know each other and for you to show me how to not be good."

I liked how she always phrased it that way – never 'be bad', just 'be not good'.

I'm lying. I did not like it. I'd had no idea there was a distinction, why there needed to be a distinction, or how said distinction was being made. It was stupid.

"Exactly. So we have to date? Fine. But you have to learn one lesson on every date."

I did not expect her to be excited by that. I really should have known better. "Like a *lesson* lesson?" she asked and I nodded.

"You want me to teach you how to...be not good, then we're doing this one lesson at a time."

"What kind of lessons?"

I blinked. "Right. Keep your panties on." Because I had no idea. Yet. I'll work it out. "Enjoy the surprise."

She beamed and I wished I had my sunnies. How could someone's face hurt my eyes?

But while I was busy pondering that, she stopped, pulled me down and kissed me. I rolled my eyes, but... All right, I got into it...a little. With my eyes closed, I could almost forget how inanely excitable she was.

She finally pulled away and I did *not* just nearly follow her for more. That was not a thing that happened. But she had this look in her eyes and she bit her lip as she half-smiled at me and I didn't know what was happening.

The question was, was that bite of her lip just for the benefit of the people around us? They were certainly looking at us and whispering. Did she think she was succeeding in trashing her reputation? And if that's all it was, why did I feel a little conflicted about that? After all, that was the whole point, wasn't it?

"Okay." She nodded. "Lessons. I look forward to it."

Who was this girl with that sexy, playful look in her eyes? Avery St John wasn't supposed to know the meaning of sexy let alone pull it off to the point I was fighting to control a boner in the school hallway. And I'm not sure she knew she was doing it. Because the next second, that annoying pep and vigour was back and she bounced off, still dragging me behind her.

How the fuck was I supposed to come up with lessons? Short of just corrupting her entirely and having her streak across the oval – note to self: do not even suggest that, there was no telling if she'd take me up on it – I had no idea how to teach her how to 'be not good'.

All I knew was how to be bad.

Seven: Avery

The idea of dating Davin was thrilling. The actual act of dating Davin was... Well it wasn't boring but he was less eager than even I'd expected of him. He'd managed to wangle out of hanging out with Blair or anyone else on Monday, or any other day. And we only really talked by text or between lessons. But he still kissed me in a way that seemed to ignite my senses and he hadn't refused another date.

On Wednesday, the school knew we'd been on that one date and they'd seen us talking in the hallways and that, but I wouldn't have definitely said that anyone knew we were actually going out. But Blair and I put that to rights when Molly and Krista were sitting with us in the Common Room at Recess.

"How are you...? You know? Dealing?" Molly asked, her eyes darting to Cindy on the other side of the room.

Blair scoffed as I shrugged.

"She's fine with her new boyfriend," Blair told them and I saw them look at each other in interest.

"New boyfriend?" Krista asked.

Molly leant forward. "You don't mean Davin Ambrose?" she asked like it was scandal of the year.

Blair nodded. "The very same."

I saw a newfound respect in Molly's and Krista's eyes.

"Really? Why?" Molly asked as Krista said, "I didn't think he dated."

"Well, he dates Avery," Blair said proudly and I smiled.

"How did it happen?" Molly asked.

I smiled coyly. "I decided I wanted to try something...different."

That had their attention.

As the unofficial force behind the school's rumour mill, Molly and Krista were the people to tell something if you wanted the rest of the school to know something.

"You mean better?" Krista asked.

"Less vanilla?" Molly offered.

Damn. I wished I'd thought of putting it that way. I was going to need to talk to Davin about hurrying along those lessons.

But I pretended that was exactly what I'd meant as I looked up and shrugged innocently, which was all the 'yes' they needed.

Molly sniggered. "And *is* he better?"

"Is he better?" I scoffed, like that was so obvious it didn't even need to be stated.

"And..." Krista looked around. "It's official? He's your

boyfriend?"

I nodded. "Yes."

The girls looked like they were about ready to burst with the excitement of spreading the news around. Luckily for them, the bell for third lesson went and Blair and I slowly picked ourselves up as Molly and Krista hurried out.

"Step four is well under way," Blair said with a smirk and we giggled as we headed for class.

"Goodbye, little Miss Goody-Two-Shoes," I answered.

As we went through third and fourth lesson, it was already obvious that Molly and Krista had done their jobs. Kids looked at me differently. Some seemed to think it was a joke and some didn't seem to know what to think. Miles frowned when he saw me and for a moment I imagined jealousy on his face.

Unlike usual, when Davin walked into Home Group he made a beeline for me. He dropped his hands onto my desk and his semi-vague glare seemed a little harder than usual.

"Do I want to know why the school is talking about how I kiss better than Miles?" he asked, looking between me and Blair like Blair might have put me up to it.

I looked up at him with a smile. "Because you do. Isn't that great?"

He looked like he seriously couldn't care less and had no idea why anyone else did. "It's infantile. Why does it matter?"

I didn't know why it mattered. Only that it did matter.

"Because—"

"You want to use me to make Miles feel like shit? Fine. But don't pretend that's not what's happening here. Even you're not that idiotically naïve." He gave me a scathing look, pushed off the desk and walked out of the classroom.

"Davin?" Mr Boyle said as they almost collided in the doorway.

I jumped up and started following Davin.

"Avery?" Mr Boyle looked at me as I paused in front of him.

"Uh… I should… See if he's okay?" I said uncertainly.

Mr Boyle was understandably confused, but nodded slowly. "Sure. I'll mark you both off as present…"

I nodded my thanks and ran out after Davin, calling his name.

He stopped halfway down the hallway and swung around to face me as reluctantly as possible. "What, Avery?" he snapped.

I hesitated as I looked him over. His eyes were hiding behind his hair and glasses as usual. He towered above me in his uniform that looked almost too big, and I wasn't sure if he'd lost weight or had got it to look like that on purpose. His face was as usual an unimpressed, expectant expression with his mouth held hard. Only he looked like all he expected was disappointment.

"Davin, I'm sorry…" I started rather lamely.

"For what?" he asked like it mattered little for what or that

I was sorry.

"For… If you felt like I was using you to hurt Miles."

"Well, you are. Aren't you?"

My hands fiddled in front of my body. "Not Really… Not on purpose."

"You just expect me to somehow make you not so good. That my bad boy qualities will, what? Rub off on you?" he asked. "You want me to get you arrested? You want me to corrupt your innocence? You want me to put you in detention? What exactly is it you want from me, Avery?"

I swallowed hard, super glad that it was Home Group and there was no one in the hallways to see us…

Did this count as a fight?

"You know I've never actually been arrested, right?" he continued. "I don't know where the rumour came from. But I haven't. The most severe detention I've served was under Mrs Mack. I do stupid shit out of acute boredom and I stick to myself for a reason. I don't play well with others."

"I… I want you to help me tank my reputation, yes. But… Davin, I actually like spending time with you, too…"

He blinked like I'd completely surprised him. "Excuse me?" It was like the idea that someone could enjoy his company was unimaginable.

"I know you're grumpy and…well, rude. But you always say what's on your mind and you stick up for yourself and you're funny and smart…" I looked at him, hoping I hadn't put him off the whole idea. "I want to be like that."

For once, the great Davin Ambrose was speechless. He ran a hand through his hair, for a moment raking it off his face and I was struck by the fact that it wasn't just his touch or what came out of his mouth that made him sexy. He was actually attractive under there.

He cleared his throat awkwardly as the familiar sounds of students starting to move came from the classrooms around us. "Lessons, then."

I nodded. "Lessons. One lesson per date."

He ran his tongue over his teeth. "And you want another date this weekend, I suppose?"

"I think that would be appropriate," I replied.

A few students started filing into the hallway so I moved closer to him.

"Fine. But I'm not dating you in anything resembling public again so soon. You want to hang out and get to know each other, you can come to my house."

I was intrigued. "Okay. When?"

"Friday night."

"Oh, meeting the parents already?" I teased and his face was even more emotionless than usual.

"No." He looked down at me and there was a shine to those hypnotic green eyes. "My dad won't be home. Fly in, fly out at the mines. It'll be the middle of his two weeks on."

"Home alone, then?"

He gave a slow, seductive wink. "Just the two of us."

I took another step towards him, catching my lip in my

teeth for a second. "Isn't that the whole point of this little exercise?"

I almost thought there was a hint of respect in his eyes and I grinned up at him. I watched as his eyes darted around the hallway behind me for a moment, then he looked back at me and nodded once.

"Fuck it," he said before pulling me to him and kissing the ever-loving heck out of me.

One hand was on my cheek and the other was firm on my hip. I reached up on the tippest of tip toes and my arms went around his shoulders. A few people around us cheered the way you did when someone made out in the hallway – not that I'd ever made out in the hallway before – and I thought Davin was going to pull away. But instead, he just pulled me closer and deepened his kiss. His hand slid around onto my arse and he held me tight against him.

My nose bumped his glasses, but he didn't seem to care as his fingers trailed down my leg and found the bottom of my skirt. I could feel him collecting up the material in his fist and I laughed against his lips. Our eyes opened and we looked at each other, and I was totally not bothered by the fact that probably every person in the hallway was watching us avidly.

"What do you think that's doing for my reputation?" I asked him.

His eyes were shining bright as he answered, "Exactly what was intended."

"So that was all in aid of trashing my rep?"

"What else would it have been?"

"I don't know. Because you wanted to?"

"Me want to kiss you? Why?"

"Enjoyment?"

"Did you enjoy it?"

I nodded at him and I saw a flash of heat in his eyes.

"So you'd want me to do that more often?"

"Please, be my guest."

"Are you supposed to be my all-consuming passion?" he asked.

"So you're admitting you're a Byronic hero?"

"Never."

"You sure?"

"You seem to know a lot about it considering you didn't even know who he was two days ago."

"I did some research."

"Did you now?"

I nodded.

"What for?"

I looked him over. "I thought it might help me understand you better."

He scoffed. "Because I'm a character in a novel, written specifically as the Byronic hero, and have no other traits, emotions, or motivations?" He paused, then muttered, "Don't say anything," the way he did like he was talking to someone else.

I pulled out of his arms and smiled at him ruefully. "At least I'm trying."

"What about me suggests I ever plan to?"

I started walking backwards away from him, giving him a shrug. "A feeling."

"You can keep those to yourself!" he called as I turned and hurried off to find Blair, assuming she'd be at our lockers.

I hurried around the corner a little quickly and bumped into Cindy Porter of all people.

"Oh. Uh…sorry," I said with an awkward smile.

"No. It's fine," she replied with an equally awkward smile.

We stood in awkward silence for a moment until I burst out with, "So, uh. Hi?"

"Uh. Hi," she laughed self-consciously. "How are you?"

"Uh. I'm fine. Fine. You?"

She nodded. "Also fine. Uh…" She pointed behind me randomly. "So, Davin?"

I nodded and, "So, Miles?" just popped out and I stamped down any excitement I felt at pulling off even passive-aggressive.

She had the decency to look legitimately sorry. "It…just happened."

I nodded slowly. "I don't blame you."

And I didn't. It wasn't Cindy's fault that Miles had cheated. Sure, I could argue that a girl shouldn't sleep with another girl's guy. But when it came down to it, Miles was the one to blame for the way he'd treated me. Cindy and I belonged to the same circles, but we weren't close and she owed me nothing.

Cindy breathed a heavy sigh of relief. "Oh, thank God. I was so worried you'd hate me or we couldn't be friends anymore. But of course. You're Avery," she said like that explained everything.

I smiled at her sweetly, though I felt a little bit of Davin's sarcasm had rubbed off on me, and didn't say what I actually wanted to say to her. "Of course. I'm Avery," was what I did reply before she nodded happily and flounced off.

Because I was Avery. I didn't have the courage to say what I was really feeling. I was the push-over who forgave everyone everything because I wanted to be kind and nice.

"Not for much longer," I promised myself.

Eight: Davin

Avery wanted the Byronic hero to sweep her off her feet and trash her reputation by – among other things – making out with her enthusiastically at school? Well it was unfortunate she'd chosen me. But for whatever godforsaken reason, I went along with it.

For good measure on Thursday, I 'anonymously' – because let's be honest, everyone *did* know it was me – distributed a few of the popular kids' less savoury photos and added a screaming goat to it for good measure. But I had been somewhat behaved and removed the screaming goat from Mrs Nichol's computer. Although that had more to do with the fact that I'd told Avery I'd meet her in the carpark after school on Friday and I wasn't willing to face whatever punishment in the guise of fun she'd put me through if I ended up in detention instead.

Why I was pandering to this infinitesimal walking rainbow, I didn't know.

And when I pushed her into her locker and kissed her the way I assumed only a bad boy would kiss her only to have her respond in a way that had me wishing I'd never started anything in the school hallway to begin with, I didn't care.

Neither did I care that people were actually risking whatever wrath they thought I had by looking at me more often than usual. Like I've already told you, I didn't have a reputation to ruin. Naturally I had a reputation – it was high school after all – but I didn't fucking care if the student populace thought it was weird the loner kid was suddenly dating Miss Popular Nice Girl 2017. I didn't care that the other popular arseholes were suddenly taking more than a vague interest in my life. Because unlike the rest of the non-popular kids, they didn't intimidate me.

"Hey, Davin?" one of the aforementioned popular arseholes called while I was at my locker.

I did what I usually did when I heard someone call my name. I ignored them.

"It *is* Davin, right?"

I slid my eyes left to find a girl with bright red plaits leaning on the locker two down from mine. I was sure my expression told her exactly how I felt about being interrupted. Her look of superior smugness became ever so slightly less smug.

"Uh. So, I figured if you were dating Avery now that you'd want to know about the party on Saturday…" She seemed to be waiting for an answer. When I didn't give one, she continued, "Or whatever…?"

I put my last book away, slung my laptop bag strap over

my shoulder and slid my headphones around my neck before shutting the door. I opened my mouth like I was going to answer her, then closed it again.

"'Cause I mean, you're like invited or whatever."

I turned to face her and looked down on her, putting one hand on my headphones.

"I can assure you I don't give a fuck," I told her before I pulled my headphones on and walked away.

But I didn't get far before Avery stopped me with a hand to my chest and a frown on those usually upbeat features. I knew she'd seen me talking to the redhead. That frown alone made my day. Knowing I put it there was just icing.

I waited to see how long it was going to take her to realise I had my headphones on and blissfully couldn't hear a thing she was saying. The corner of my mouth was just starting to quirk up weirdly when her frown became a sardonic glare and she totally did just stamp her foot at me.

She reached up and I didn't stop her pulling my headphones down around my neck.

"What?" I asked her.

She wasn't impressed with me and I loved it. "You could be less rude."

I shrugged. "I probably could. But socialisation credits, Avery. I don't get more just because I'm helping you trash your rep now."

"Krista is my friend, Davin."

"What is it about me that made you think I'd care?"

"You're my boyfriend now!"

"I thought the agreement was I could be my usual grumpy self?"

"Well…yes. But I didn't think–"

"I'm supposed to be the bad boy, Avery." I took a step towards her and her back hit the locker behind her as her eyes widened. "I can't do that *and* be polite to your friends." I dropped my lips as close to her ear as I could get without folding myself in half. "Or did you think this was going to go some other way?" I whispered and I felt her shiver.

Suddenly this whole ruining Avery St John's reputation thing was becoming interesting. It gave me a whole new excuse to be rude to people and not have to hide my disdain. My grandmother spent enough time reading about bad boys that I knew exactly what was expected here. Add in some Byronic flair and I was pretty sure I'd have this one in the bag. Helping Avery meant I got to be me, just without having to tone down how much I hated most everything in this fucking hell hole.

I pressed against her and she bit her lip as she looked up at me.

"So you don't want to come to the party on Saturday, then?" she asked, a hint of teasing sneaking through.

"I think I'd rather wear a yellow blazer to school next week."

She tried to hide her laugh, but she failed. "Okay. Not coming to the party then."

"No."

"But a date tomorrow."

I nodded. "I avoided detention for it and everything," I said with sarcastic joy.

"Only just, I'll bet."

"Exactly what are you suggesting, Avery?"

She giggled. "The goat was a nice touch."

I blinked slowly. "I'm sure I don't know what you're talking about."

She was having trouble taming that smile and there was something about it that I didn't absolutely, completely, entirely hate. "I'm sure you don't."

"Mr Ambrose!" came the very familiar, dulcet shriek of our vice principal, Mrs Mack. "Will you stop harassing the other students?"

Avery sniggered as she looked to Mrs Mack, then back at me. "Yes, Davin. Will you?"

"Not likely," I told her before crushing her to the lockers and kissing her hard.

Her arms wound around the back of my neck as she melted against me and I momentarily forgot every heavy thing that weighed me down. All my past, present and future issues faded into inconsequentiality as she kissed me back the way a good girl really wasn't supposed to do.

Once again I was left wishing I hadn't started this at school. I wanted to be very far away from the school hallway where there were a shit tonne of eyes on us, not in the least the vice principal who already had the same amount of time for me as I had for most other people on the planet. I wanted Avery somewhere I didn't have to think about being respectable. I wanted her somewhere I could really show her what it was like to be not good.

But I didn't actually think most of that at the time, I was too busy being wrapped up in everything that was Avery to the point even whatever sickly sweet perfume she wore did more to turn me on than it did turn me off just then. Until…

"Mr Ambrose! This is a school corridor, not a red-light district back alley!"

Avery pushed me away gently, still with a barely suppressed smirk on her face. She licked her lip self-consciously and turned to my nemesis.

"I'm sorry, Mrs Mack," she said in that nauseatingly sweet tone. But of course, the majority of the human population think that sort of thing's adorable so Mrs Mack's expression softened somewhat in the face of it. "We…We didn't mean to…"

Avery put her hand on my sternum softly and I looked down at it like I wasn't sure what it was or what it was doing there.

"Is everything all right, Miss St John?" Mrs Mack looked her over like I'd been beating her senseless rather than just kissing her.

Avery nodded. Her face was that perfect mix of innocence and naiveté that made people think she was incapable of higher brain function. "Yes. Fine. Uh…honeymoon period, you see."

"Honeymoon…?" Mrs Mack looked between the two of us in shock.

Avery nodded eagerly. "Yes. Davin and I are dating."

Had I actually remembered how to laugh, I might have at the look on Mrs Mack's face. The tall, stern woman was not one to be messed with. She looked like she'd attempted to style herself after Miss Trunchbull – and if you don't know who she is, go and rent *Matilda* or however you young people watch movies these days – although she was younger, prettier and had less a propensity for bullying minors. But in the face of Avery's overwhelming virtue, she was having trouble reconciling the idea that that very same virtue and I were dating.

"Young love, huh?" I added and Avery elbowed me surreptitiously.

Mrs Mack's eyes narrowed as she looked at me. "Indeed. Might I suggest you refrain from overly amorous displays in the corridors in future, Mr Ambrose?"

"You can certainly suggest it, ma'am," I replied.

Mrs Mack took a deep breath, but just walked away like it was taking every ounce of her strength.

Avery whacked me in the chest and I looked down at her. "What?"

"I thought you were avoiding detention?"

I shrugged. "She's given up detaining me of a Friday

afternoon for a bit of lip. You on the other hand…"

"Me, what?" she asked.

"You want a lesson? That right there? Stop that."

Avery looked legitimately confused. "Stop what?"

"With the doe eyes and radiating…goodness."

"What doe eyes?"

"She doesn't know she's doing it," I tell you. Although, I'm sure you'd already figured that out. Avery looked around for a moment. "We'll…work on it. Okay?" I told her. Because I could totally work out how to make that into a proper lesson at some point because I was quite clearly a professionally trained behaviour therapist and this sort of thing was totally normal and safe.

She nodded, giving me a wide smile. "Okay. Sure."

I shrugged my laptop strap back onto my shoulder properly and cleared my throat. "I'm going to…" I pointed down the hall.

"Just don't get detention this week, yeah?" she teased and I gave her a condescending look.

"I'll let you do whatever you goddamned want and expect the same in return. Thanks."

She grinned and it was more of that wry and calculating again. I gave her a terse nod and started to walk away.

"Davin?"

I turned back with a sigh. "Avery?"

She tapped her cheek and – *"Seriously?"* – I gave her a questioning look to which she just gave a single nod. I sighed heavily, decided to rebel by kissing her lips instead of the proffered cheek, and stalked away, hoping I could avoid her for the rest of the day.

I managed in person – my phone was less lucky – and got to Gran's a little after five – *"Segue."*

"Gran?" I called as I let myself in. Flint meowed at me as though my appearance was a heinous violation of the tenuous treaty we had employed and I nodded at him. "Flint."

"Davin, that you?"

"No," I called back as I headed for the kitchen to put the shopping away and check whatever was in the oven. I noticed Flint followed me as though he hoped I was purveyor of tuna again.

"You know, one day someone else is going to say that and I'm just going to let them wander around my house until they murder me," Gran said idly and I turned to see her walk into the kitchen wearing a wry smirk.

Gran was still tall. Not as tall as me, granted, but she was still a fiercely formidable woman. She'd given up dying her hair three years earlier and made the sudden and dramatic change to a silver shot through with dark grey that she wore in a loose bun. I'd inherited her green eyes, though she kept hers behind tortoiseshell rims. She always wore trousers and a jumper and, when we were at home, her ugg boots.

"Unlikely." I went to her and let her give me a hug and kiss my cheek. "Flint will shred their skin to ribbons first."

"No, dear," she replied. "That's just you."

I rolled my eyes. "Thanks."

She pushed me to arms' length and looked me over. "You look good."

"I look no different than I did last night. Or the night before. Or the night before that."

"So? I can't tell you that you look good now?"

I huffed as I pulled two glasses down from the cupboard and went to the fridge. "You know you can do and say whatever you want." I sounded epically pissed off, but the statement was no less true for my lack of warmth.

"How was school today?"

"No update?" I said with a ghost of a smirk as I poured her gin and tonic.

"Not today. But you'd know that. Unless they just didn't catch you?" she sniggered.

I passed her glass over and went to pour myself a water. "I am a model pupil, Gran. I don't know what you're talking about."

Gran snorted and I looked at her through the hair hanging in my face to see her smiling widely. "On paper, sure. So," she pressed. "What tests did you ace?"

"None today."

"Have you got *any* news?"

"I'm sure I have plenty of news. It highly depends upon your definition of news."

"At this point, I don't care. If I don't have to drag it out of you with the force of a two tonne truck, then I'll be happy to

115

hear how many times you made use of the little boy's room today." Gran glared at me over the rim of her glass as she took a demure sip and I sighed as I put the water jug back in the fridge.

"Fine. I have a...girlfriend. Happy?" I asked while I wasn't facing her.

A very uncharacteristic noise that was close to a squeal popped out of my reserved yet loving grandmother. By the time I'd turned to look at her, she'd composed herself. "A girlfriend?" she clarified nonchalantly.

"Don't get excited. It's nothing special."

"Davin," she chastised firmly.

I shrugged as I led the way into the family room. "What?"

"You know you don't treat a woman like that."

"That's not what I meant."

"Good. Because I don't care what scars lie in your past, young man, nor how deep they run. No grandson of mine was brought up to disrespect a lady."

I waited for her to sit before I did. "It's not like that."

"Then you explain to me what it's like before I remind you of the proper behaviour. Emphasised by my foot up your backside." Gran was frowning hard and I sincerely wished I hadn't brought up anything about Avery.

"She's–"

"The cat's mother?" was delivered seamlessly.

I glared at her and huffed "–called Avery," I finished, my tone telling her to can it if she wanted any more details. "And

116

she's...unique."

"For a boy so smart, your vocabulary has certainly deserted you tonight, hasn't it?"

"Avery is...a vivacious, genuinely compassionate young woman. Her outfit choices, while making me thoroughly nauseated, would lift your soul to new heights. She constantly sees the good in people and refuses to be anything but an optimist."

Gran nodded solemnly. "Well I suppose that explains how she ended up with you."

"Your encouragement, as always, prompts me to excel," I told her wryly.

She laughed. "Your account was intended to make me think the two of you were poorly matched. You and your firm understanding of linguistic semantics," she teased, "ensured that. Don't go pretending otherwise."

"It's not like I...hate spending time with her."

"You're attracted to her," she said simply, no doubt having no delusions about what went through my mind when I thought about Avery.

To quote a brother in Byronic-arms, "She's handsome enough."

Gran snorted. "A glowing review by all accounts." She put her glass down. "But she deserves better from you if you're going to date her, Davin. If you don't like her that way, then don't string her along."

I was fairly sure that Avery wouldn't take 'I'm just not

that into you' as a reason for ending our social experiment. As far as she knew, I saw zero redeeming qualities in her or the time we spent together, and she seemed quite happy with the arrangement the way it was.

"If you knew Avery, you'd know that was not a problem."

"So she knows you well?"

"Better than I'd like."

Gran nodded. "All right then."

When I realised she was looking at me expectantly I sighed, "What?"

"I suppose it's too much to ask that your grandmother meet your girlfriend?"

I knew it would hurt her if I said no. But neither did I want her meeting the saccharine goodness that was Avery St John and falling in love with the tornado of liveliness only for it to end. I wasn't sure how I felt about it from the position of Avery meeting my grandmother either. I had a sinking feeling that they'd be enamoured with each other. A part of me wanted to be a part of that. But when Avery's reputation was ruined and we went our separate ways?

I didn't say anything for long enough that Gran nodded. "I understand, dear."

"No," I said too quickly, pained by the dejection in her voice. "It's only new. We'll see how it goes. All right?"

Gran smiled warmly and the heaviness left my heart for a moment. "Wonderful."

Yeah, was it?

Nine: Avery

Davin did his best to avoid me at school unless he was kissing me in the middle of the hallway. He also made sure he radiated hostility to anyone who came near him except me. But he answered almost every message I sent him and he was waiting for me after last lesson on Friday to drive me to his house for our date.

He spent the whole drive there in silence, his eyes focussed on the road like that gave him an excuse to not look at or talk to me. I covered his silence by waffling the long-winded story about the time the St Johns drove to Melbourne and Ebony's car sickness set off mine. I was under no delusions that Davin was actually interested in the story, but once I'd started I couldn't stop and he didn't stop me at any point.

Eventually, Davin pulled into the driveway of a nice little place with a sweeping lawn out the front and some rose bushes in neatly manicured sections of garden. I looked over it as he parked and wondered what his home life was like. The house was nicer than I'd have expected given the way he acted at school.

"Okay." Davin cleared his throat as he swung out of the car and I followed him. "So, my house."

"It's nice," was all I could think of to say, and it's not like I was lying.

"Sure." He unlocked the door and held it open while I ducked under his arm and inside. "I'm going to change. Make yourself at home."

He started heading off and I looked around. "Bathroom?"

He paused and looked back at me. "Already?"

I clucked my tongue. "I was also going to change. If that's okay?"

"You can change in my room."

"Bathroom's fine."

He nodded and pointed to the right. "Through there."

"Thanks."

We hovered for a moment where I thought he was going to say something else, then he gave a curt nod and walked off. I wandered through the kitchen and into the laundry, off which was a half-bathroom.

I changed and headed back out to find Davin in the kitchen in a very similar outfit to the one he'd worn on our previous date, minus the shoes. He was staring almost contemplatively at the fridge and only turned when I dropped my bag on the floor at the end of the kitchen counter.

"Taste the fucking rainbow," he muttered as he looked me over, then sighed. "You want anything? Drink? Something to eat?"

I shook my head. "No thanks. All good."

He nodded and went back to looking in the fridge. "I usually have pizza when Dad's gone. That okay for dinner later?"

"You have pizza every night for two weeks?"

He closed the fridge and fixed one of his patent stares on me. "I'm not usually home when he's not."

I felt my cheeks flush and looked down for a moment. "Oh."

"Jesus," he huffed. "No. I'm usually at my grandmother's. I get to sleep at home, but I still have to have dinner with her most nights."

So it wasn't just a Sunday night thing, then.

I looked up and smiled at the thought. "Really?"

He shifted like he was uncomfortable. "Really."

"You're close with her then?"

Davin looked almost surprised by that question. "Yes. Most days we're in the same room."

"I didn't mean it like that and you know it."

He shrugged. "We…keep an eye on each other."

He didn't say any more and I didn't really know what to say. So we both stood in silence for a while. I tried to think of something to talk to him about. I hadn't had this problem the weekend before. I'd been fine coming up with things to talk about, even if he hadn't really said much back. But for some reason, I was finding it more difficult just then.

121

"So what's today's lesson?" I finally asked him and he looked at me like he'd been hoping I'd forgotten all about it.

"Lesson?"

"It's a date, so doesn't that mean a lesson?"

"Today's lesson is for me," he said sourly after a pause.

"How does that help me be not good?"

Davin sighed, walked towards me, lifted me onto the kitchen counter behind me, and planted his hands on either side of me. "How am I supposed to know how to make you less good if I don't know what makes you so good in the first place?" he asked me.

"Huh." I looked him over and tried not to get distracted by his proximity. "Good point."

He nodded once, apparently not at all affected by my proximity. "So?"

"So, what?"

"When Miles called you too good, what do you think he meant? What do you want to change? What makes you too good?"

I thought about it. "I've never been drunk!" I said quickly.

"Okay…" he said slowly, definitely surprised. "Well that one's certainly easy enough to change. Next?"

"People treat me like I'm stupid."

"Sure. But we can't do anything about that unless we change the why," he said slowly. "So why do people treat you like you're stupid?"

"Because…I'm always happy?"

"Why would that make them think you're stupid?"

I didn't know. I just assumed it played a part. I shrugged, feeling like I was letting him down.

"Ignorance is bliss?" he offered and I frowned in confusion. "People assume happy people are too stupid to grasp reality, which is why they're so happy all the time. No sense of understanding means no worries."

I nodded. "So I need to be...depressed?"

He rolled his eyes. "We're making you less good, not turning you into me. No. You just need to show people you do understand the things that go on around you. Provided you do understand them of course," he added ruefully.

"I think so," I grumbled.

"I think so, too. What else makes you too good?"

"Um...I always forgive people?"

He nodded thoughtfully. "Some would call that a positive attribute."

"What would you call it?"

"In the wrong circumstances, being a pushover."

"The wrong circumstances?"

"Learn to stand up for yourself."

"How?"

"Well I suppose that all depends on why you don't in the first place."

"I guess I don't like to upset people. It's not nice."

"Is that why you let Miles get away with cheating on you?"

"I *had* thought it was just a kiss."

His eyebrows rose. "And that's better?"

I bristled. "I thought I was being kind."

"And I guess you were. To him. What about you?"

I blinked in surprise. "What *about* me?"

He nodded like I'd just revealed everything he needed to know.

"What?" I asked

But he shook his head like he wasn't going to divulge whatever he'd just worked out and said, "Come on. What's next?"

I sighed, trying to think of what else. "Miles and I...never messed around in public."

"I'm not sure that's a defining feature of being not good."

"Well I'm pretty sure *not* doing it is a defining feature of being too good."

He cocked an eyebrow at me. "Fine. I'm going to need you to clarify 'messed around' and 'public' for me then."

"I thought you were good at English. Like stupidly good?"

His eyes widened for a second and he ran his tongue over his lip. "I just feel as though our definitions are probably a little...different."

"Why?" I laughed. "What's your definition?"

"Sex. In front of other people. Everything on show."

"Oh..." I breathed.

"Oh," he agreed.

There was just a slight difference in our definitions then.

"And have you had sex? In front of…other people?" I asked him.

"Was that one question or two?" he huffed an almost-laugh. "Yes. I've had sex. No, not in front of other people."

I nodded slowly. "I…just meant that Miles and I hadn't really even ever hooked up at a party in front of other people…"

There was a ghost of a smile on his face as his eyes searched mine. "And yet we've definitely made out in the school hallway."

I nodded quickly, feeling a smile on my lips. "We did do that."

As he looked me over, his expression became more thoughtful. "Why didn't you and Miles hook up in front of other people?"

I frowned. "What do you mean?"

"Exactly what I asked."

I dropped my eyes and wriggled a little where I sat. "I…I don't know."

"Did you feel uncomfortable?"

"I don't know. I guess I felt a little…weird about it."

"Weird how?"

I looked up at him quickly. "Why does it matter?"

His eyes burned straight into mine. "Because you have boundaries."

"You're supposed to be teaching me how to not have boundaries," I reminded him.

"There are boundaries even I won't cross, Avery. You set the rules and I follow them."

"That doesn't seem fair. What about what you want?"

"By all accounts, you're the girl who didn't feel comfortable kissing your long-term boyfriend at a party. Whereas I'm the guy who'd have no problem fucking you in the disabled loos the first day we met. Ergo you set the rules, Avery," he said firmly, "and I follow them."

"I want you to teach me to break the rules," I told him, equally firmly.

Because I did. I wanted him to kiss me. I wanted him to do more than kiss me. I was still adamant I was never having sex at school. But I didn't shy away from fantasizing about it for a second. I didn't shy away from fantasizing about a lot of things when it came to Davin.

When Davin looked at me the way he was looking at me just then, his eyes all hard and bright and serious and...heated, it sent a thrill through me no other guy had caused before. I got goose bumps. My stomach squirmed in anticipation. I felt restless.

Davin's hand gripped my knee for a moment, then started to slide up my leg torturously slowly. He took a step forward so he was standing between my legs, his eyes never leaving mine. His other hand trailed my hairline and down my jaw until he was cupping my neck. I swallowed hard and was pretty sure if he didn't kiss me soon I was going to launch myself off the counter at him.

126

"If you want me to push the boundaries," he said carefully, his voice low, "I'm going to need to know what they are…"

My boundaries with Miles had been pretty standard, I guessed. We pretty much exclusively kissed and, if we were alone, he'd say something like, "Do you want to?" and I'd say yes and then we'd have sex.

The Goody-Two-Shoes Avery never started anything. Even when I wanted to. So what would the less good Avery do? Davin already had his hand under my skirt. I could do something like that.

A nervous tingle shot through me, but I tried to keep it together. I ran my hand over the front of his jeans and watched his eyes flash with a singular sense of satisfaction. "Kiss me and find out," I said, hoping I sounded sexy and not like I was constipated.

"Avery, I–"

I put my finger on his lips and shook my head.

He took a deep breath. "Sure. Why not? I'm fluent in body language," he said against my finger like he was giving himself a pep talk.

Then he took my wrist and guided my arm around his neck before pulling me to him and kissing me hungrily. His hand was splayed high on my thigh under my skirt and I took the opportunity to wrap my leg around his hip and tighten my arms around him, bringing us closer together.

"I don't get it," he murmured against my lips.

"Get what?" I asked, only pulling away from him far

enough to catch my breath.

"This. I touch you and…you respond instantly. There's no hesitation, no shyness, you just go for it."

"Is that…bad?"

He shook his head adamantly. "Fuck no. But it's not exactly the behaviour of a girl who's too good."

"Are you stereotyping now?"

"Haven't we been doing that this whole time?" he said and it was obviously not directed at me, but I answered anyway.

"I guess."

"I'm just confused, Avery. In the school hallway you're one person, in my arms another. I've got to wonder if you really need my help after all."

I ran my hand up his chest and bit my lip, knowing if I didn't say the right thing now then I might lose my chance to shed my goody-two-shoes image. "The girl who climbs in your lap and bites your lip isn't me, Davin–"

"Well who is she? Because unlike Miles, I don't cheat."

"I appreciate that." I smiled. "I guess she is me, but I can only be her with you. Put me in front of anyone else and I'm just good little Avery."

"I've got to say I'm kind of pleased to hear that. What with good little Avery being my girlfriend and all."

I batted him gently. "Good little Avery is the girl you despise. Good little Avery is the girl everyone pats on the head and tells to have a nice day. Good little Avery lets boys cheat on her and does nothing about it."

He looked me over, a softer look in his eyes than I remembered seeing before. "I don't despise you, Avery..."

"No? Name one thing you don't hate about me?" I asked, feeling a wry tilt to my lips as I ran my hand over his jeans again.

He looked up at the ceiling like he was praying for strength. "I don't hate that."

I took his cheek in my hand and pulled him to me for a kiss. Things heated up quickly to the point I thought that maybe the kitchen bench wasn't the place for that anymore.

"Bedroom?" I breathed against him.

He seemed confused for a moment, then nodded. "Bedroom. I have one of those. Yep."

He hopped me off the counter, took two steps, then kissed me again like he just couldn't wait. After a moment he pulled away quickly, shook his shoulders out like he was trying to get a grip, took my hand and pulled me after him.

I had to say it made a nice change to be dragged after him for once.

I barely paid attention to the hallway he led me down and I had no time to look at his room before he'd turned, picked me up, crushed his lips back to mine, and then I found myself lying on his bed with him over me.

The thing I liked about the way Davin kissed me was that he explored. He explored with his hands and his lips, just touches all over my body like he was trying to commit it to memory. And it was hot. The skim of his fingers over my stomach as his lips brushed my throat sent little flutters from my tummy and straight down, demanding more but also happy if he took his time.

And take his time he did. It was like some kind of pleasurable torture until finally his fingers skimmed up the inside of my leg, pausing just shy of my undies. But that was the only thing that paused as he deepened his kiss before trailing it down my cheek.

"You don't have to stop," I panted and he looked up at me.

Whatever my hands had been doing had pushed his hair off his face and I got my first proper look at the whole package. There was a little stubble on his jaw that explained the slight heat in my skin, his skin was smooth and pale from what I suspected was no time in the sun, and his eyes…they shone so brightly as he looked into mine.

"On only the second date?" he asked with a note of teasing, but I suspected he was actually just checking I was okay with it.

"Second base on a second date. Seems appropriate to me," I replied, failing to keep the smile from my face.

"So does that mean I'm heading for home on our fourth date?"

"That's terribly presumptuous," I giggled.

"I'm just doing the math."

I winced. "Why would you do that?"

"What?"

"The math?"

He cocked his head to the side. "Because I like Math."

"What? How? Why?" I laughed.

He shrugged and I felt his fingers tracing lazily over the skin on my inner thigh. "I don't know. I like it. I'm good at it. It makes sense."

I sighed. "I'm awful at Maths."

"Well your boyfriend can help with that. But first…" There was almost a smile on his face.

"But first what?" I asked.

His hand skimmed up and dragged gently across my undies. I took a shallow breath and tingles shot across my body. My legs parted ever so slightly further and there was the hint of a smirk in his eyes as he looked down at me. I smiled and brought his face back down to mine.

He kissed me slowly as he rubbed his hand over me, and I fought not to arch the whole way into him and make his access more difficult. His touch was somehow gentle and firm at the same time and everything in me started thrumming warmly. He seemed in no hurry to get me anywhere. It didn't feel like he had anything to prove. He just played with me until I took a sharp breath when he hit a perfect spot.

Then it was like we were playing a different game entirely. His focus changed, his touch more precise, his kiss less leisurely. And I felt that sweet, tingly coil tighten in me. I breathed harder as his kiss moved back to my neck and I fisted his hair in my hand.

There was nothing hard and fast in the way I finished. It was a slow build up until it broke over me. My hand tightened in his hair and my leg tensed around his hip. I released a breathy laugh as his touch became lazier again before his lips came back to mine and he ran his hand up my body to grip my waist.

As I kissed him, I ran my hand down his body between us and found him hard.

"You don't have to, Avery," he said against my lips.

I nodded and started undoing his jeans. "I know."

I bit his lip and I ran my hand over him and he groaned.

"Avery…"

"Shh…" I told him before deepening our kiss and focussing on my hand keeping a steady rhythm.

We got caught up in his t-shirt enough that when he finished it somehow managed to catch most of it. He huffed a rough chuckle when he realised as he pulled away from me.

"Lucky," he said as he looked down.

I giggled and he looked up at me, his hair still swept off his face. "Yeah," I answered. "Lucky. I'm, uh… I'm going to wash my hands…"

He nodded. "Good idea. I'll change my shirt," he huffed another almost laugh, "and meet you out there? We can order dinner?"

I bit my lip as I looked him over. "Sure."

He pulled me to him and gave me a quick kiss before jumping up and going to his wardrobe. I got up and smoothed my skirt as I headed out to the bathroom.

I looked myself over in the mirror and couldn't wipe the smile off my flushed face as I cleaned up.

I had actually started sexual activity and it had been met favourably. And it had been... It had been different than with Miles. The whole encounter had felt effortlessly natural. Something about it was more exciting. Sexually exciting. Good little Avery had never just suck her hands down Miles' pants, but I'd wanted to touch Davin. I'd wanted to feel him.

Being with Davin had felt... Dirtier seemed such a...corny description. But it felt like the right one. A good dirty. The kind of dirty that made your heart flutter and your skin tingle, and gave you the urge to just lie down with that ridiculous smile on your face while you played it out in your head over and over.

As I walked into the kitchen, I saw him sitting at the breakfast bar. I sat next to him and we ordered pizza. There was a bit of an awkward moment for a bit where I was tempted to just crawl into his lap – as nearly physically impossible as that would have been – and hope he got me off again.

But I thought getting to know him a bit better was a better plan. Physical intimacy was all well and good, but he was my boyfriend and it was probably good that I know more about him than what he liked in the bedroom.

"So what do you do for fun then?" I asked. As soon as it was out of my mouth I realised how awkward it had sounded, but there was no taking it back.

He looked over at me. "You mean apart from what just happened?"

I flushed and looked down to hide my smile. "Yes. Apart from that."

"I read. I game. I watch TV and films."

I could do movies. "What's your favourite movie?" I asked excitedly.

"Probably *Fight Club* or *Pulp Fiction*."

I wrinkled my nose, having never heard of either of those. "What are they?"

"Films."

I gave him my most unimpressed look. "I'd worked that out."

"I'm not allowed to talk about Fight Club."

That made no sense. "Why not?"

"You've never seen it, have you?"

I shook my head. "No. Are they old?"

"Older than us."

"You like all that old stuff, then?"

He paused for a moment like he was working out what to say. "You could say that."

"I could say a lot of things. Wouldn't make it true," I muttered, finding myself both loving and hating the way he was so caged off.

"Okay. Fine. Yes. I appreciate things that came before my time. Books. Films. Music. There is some really great

134

material out there."

"Games?"

He shook his head as he got up and headed over to the fridge. "Not really. Those are better off being more recent. You want a drink?"

"Uh, sure. Something cold?"

"I've got cola or lemon."

"Lemon, please."

He got the lemon soft drink out and the milk then went over to turn the coffee machine on.

"You're having coffee now?" I asked him.

He looked up at me through his hair like that was the stupidest question any person could ask. "Yes."

"Doesn't it keep you awake?"

There was an almost humoured shade to his face, but I'm not sure what about it made me think that. "How many guys do you know who can go all night without a little pick-me-up."

I felt my cheeks flush and I looked at my hands resting on the bench.

"Did you want one?" he asked.

I shook my head and laughed. "No, thanks."

"Thank God."

I looked at him. "What?"

His eyebrow rose the way it did when he thought I should know the answer. "Because you manage to bounce off the walls without any assistance."

"Maybe it'll make me all grouchy like you?"

"Caffeine doesn't work that way."

I thought of another thing to ask him. "How about–"

"How about we talk about boundaries?" he interrupted, walking over to me and propping me back up on the kitchen bench. I had to admit it made for an almost perfect height difference, or lack thereof.

I frowned. "I thought we already did."

He nodded slowly. "We started. You distracted me."

I smiled, remembering that distraction fondly. "Okay. So what else about boundaries?"

"I want to know more about those boundaries. No distractions allowed."

"What do you want to know?"

"Over the panties was fine. How about under them?"

I pressed my lips together before I nodded. "That would be fine."

He nodded once. "If I took them off?"

I nodded again. "That would also be fine."

"What if I filmed us?"

I'd been ready to agree to almost anything he was going to suggest, but I hadn't expected that. That was quite the jump.

"What? No!"

A smile lit his eyes. "Good."

I blinked. "What? What do you mean good? Why good?"

"Well, I was going to up it to a live sex show next."

"Why?" I asked, horrified at the thought.

"Because I wanted to see where you'd stop."

"There's quite a leap from taking off my…undies and recording us, Davin."

He nodded. "True. But that doesn't change the fact you have very clear boundaries."

I frowned at him. "You know, I'm starting to think this boundaries thing was to distract me from me asking you about yourself…"

He shrugged. "We said one lesson per date, didn't we?"

"I thought the lesson for this date was for you?"

"Well I came up with one for you."

"What is it?"

"The fact that boundaries don't just exist in a physical relationship. Boundaries also exist between friends and family."

I frowned again. "What has that got to do with me refusing to do a sex tape?"

"There was going to be a segue. You sort of ruined it so I skipped ahead."

I readjusted my seating on the bench. "Okay. So the lesson is there are boundaries with friends and family? So what?"

"My point – the lesson – is that you have to set these boundaries so people don't walk all over you."

"I have…boundaries," I said slowly.

He looked me over sceptically. "Do you, though?"

"I…could have boundaries."

He gave a single nod. "You could. Let's work on that."

I just nodded and he went back to finish making his coffee. Once he was done, we took our drinks into the living room and tried to come up with ways for me to establish boundaries while we waited for the pizza.

Ten: Davin

Avery spent the whole next week trying to convince me to pick another date activity. I tried to convince her that she could just come over again. I'd certainly had a pretty decent time considering I was technically on a date. But she wouldn't be dissuaded.

I'd eventually just yelled, "Fine. Cinema!" at her. Which earnt me a wide smile until I insisted she pick the film. There was another day or so of arguing over the fact that if I picked the cinema then I should also pick the film. Once I'd pointed out that picking the cinema as an activity had been tiresome enough, she said she'd surprise me.

I was dreading it, but still had almost twenty-four hours before I had to worry about that. In the meantime, I had to get through the end of dinner with Gran and my cousin.

"Boys, stop that or you'll get no dessert!" Gran snapped.

I shoved Nate away and glared at him. "He started it."

"That's what you always say, Davin." Gran gave me a look and I wasn't sure if she was on my side, on Nate's side, or on the side of less violence at the dinner table.

I looked at my cousin and we both knew he was always the one who started it. He was just never going to tell dear old Gran that.

At a couple of years older than me, Nate wasn't exactly what most people would call a good influence. But he and his friends were the closest I came to having friends of my own and, when I felt inclined to have a modicum of social interaction, they were the people with which I chose to have it. Being Nate's cousin, there was a sense of removal from the actual centre of their friendship group and no one really cared if I did or didn't turn up. If I did, great. If not, no big.

"That's because he does always start it. Why don't you give me his dessert to teach him a lesson?" I huffed.

"Well…" Gran looked me over and raised her eyebrows. "You could do with the extra calories."

I rolled my eyes while Nate sniggered beside me. "I'm not underweight."

"A boy your height needs more meat, Davin. It's a fact."

"It's not a…" I muttered as Nate laughed, "When you join me in the men's leagues, you'll probably lose the lankiness."

Gran gave him one of her scathing looks. "Whereas boys like Nathan could lay off the crisps while they're sitting on their backsides doing nothing all day."

I came as close as I ever did to grinning at Nate as he gasped at Gran. "And what do you think he does all day? He's not some star athlete or anything, Gran," he said as my phone vibrated and I pulled it out of my pocket. "Oh, look. Nerd

140

boy's got friends," he teased.

"Oh, is it Avery, dear?" Gran asked only half-innocently and I froze.

"Who the fuck is Avery?" Nate asked, then I heard the slap of Gran's hand hitting the back of his head and his subsequent "oof".

"Davin's girlfriend."

My eyes slid up and caught Nate grinning like an idiot at me. "No, shit. Little Dav's got a girlfriend?"

"You watch your mouth, Nathan. Or Davin might get your dessert after all."

"Hang on," Nate said in disbelief. "Are we really just going to sit here and accept Davin has a girlfriend? Since when does Davin do girlfriends?"

And Nate would know.

At not yet eighteen, it wasn't like I could go out to the local pub and pick up a girl when I wanted some company. And excuse me for thinking that apps like Tinder seemed like more hassle than they were worth, presuming it was a simple matter of faking my age to get an account in the first place.

So when I'd wanted company, it was found at a party hosted by Nate, one of his friends, or one of their many acquaintances. This had left me with a fairly small pool of prospects and I'd had a couple of girls I hooked up with semi-regularly. But that was pre-Avery bursting into my life and forcing me to taste the rainbow. Not that I actually minded being stuck with nothing but her rainbow for the foreseeable future.

"It was about time he did someone," Gran muttered and Nate's snort was less small laugh and more giant, barely contained explosion. "Oh, for pity's sake. You know what I meant, Nate!" she huffed and he laughed again.

"Shut up," I snapped.

"No, mate. That's great. I mean, Freya and Lara will be devastated. But good for you."

I looked up at him in annoyance as Gran asked, "Who are Freya and Lara?"

Before Nate could answer, I replied, "Why don't you ask Nate about Nova, Liv and Ash?"

Nate groaned at me in annoyance and I gave him a self-satisfied look.

Gran looked us over and I could see her debating in what direction to take this. Finally she held up a hand to us. "I don't even want to know what you boys get up to. But I will remind you there are consequences for your actions, boys. Just remember that."

I nodded solemnly. "Yeah, Gran. We know."

"Good boys." She kissed me on the head, then Nate, and headed back into the kitchen.

"You want to keep your mouth shut in front of Gran," he hissed at me.

"Speak for your fucking self!" I hissed back.

"Why didn't you tell me you've got a girlfriend?" he snapped.

142

"Why the fuck would I have told you?"

"Because I'm the best friend you have."

I shook my head. "It's not like that."

"You're going to explain yourself after we leave here or I'm going to smack it out of you."

"That threat only works for Gran because we both know she wouldn't actually smack us to save ourselves," I shot at him.

Nate cocked his head. "Well that's true."

"Gran, you need a hand?" I called as I got up. "We don't talk about Avery! Ever," I muttered to Nate as I passed him.

I shook myself out as I pushed my way into the kitchen and Gran passed me the oven mitts.

"Make yourself useful and take the dish out," she said. "And while you're at it, you might think more about opening up to people."

"Like how she just slid that one in there?"

I did as she instructed. The first bit at least. "I have a girlfriend. How much more open do you want me to be?"

Gran scoffed haughtily. "And how much does she know?"

I actually nearly dropped the dish. "Excuse me?"

Gran nodded at me, her displeasure with me showing in her face. "You told her everything then?"

"Fu–" I stopped and took a breath. "No. Of course not."

"Why not?"

"Because she doesn't need nor want to know."

"Are you embarrassed about it?"

143

Embarrassment was not an emotion I had ever associated with my past. "No."

"So why not tell her?"

"God's sake, Gran! We've been together for about two weeks," to say nothing of the lack of permanence we had, "she doesn't need to know."

"And how long until you decide you've been together long enough? Hm? One year? Two? Ten?"

"Why does this matter to you so much?" I yelled.

"Because you've closed yourself off for eleven years, Davin. If you're going to open up to anyone, surely your girlfriend's an excellent place to start!"

"Our relationship's not like that–"

"So you just fuck each other and call it dating?"

I was completely taken aback. This wasn't Gran. Not the Gran I knew. I took a deep breath. "Can I at least wait and see if we've got what it takes to last?" I asked shakily. There was no lasting for me and Avery, but I could take some liberties with the truth if it was going to make Gran feel better.

Gran crossed her arms. "And how long do you think that's going to take?"

I shrugged. "I couldn't tell you. How long does it take to fall in love, Gran?"

Everything about her softened and I realised there had been a touch of vulnerability in my tone. Enough of a touch that I couldn't hide it and I couldn't take it back.

"It takes as long as it takes, dear," Gran said. "If it's meant to be, you'll know."

"Will he, though?" Nate answered, his teasing good-natured for once, and I looked behind Gran to see him hovering inside the door with a sympathetic smile on his face. "This is Davin we're talking about."

I huffed a rough laugh and Nate cheered in victory. "Ha! That was almost a smile! We'll crack that emotionless shell yet."

"Us or Avery, dear?" Gran asked him, throwing us both a superior look as she dished up dessert.

Nate and I finished up our dessert, then drove back to his place. We were going to Freya's to have some drinks and hang out for a while, and Nate's house was closer. So we were walking to Freya's and I was going to crash at Nate's after.

"All right," Nate started as we walked. "Jokes aside, tell me about this girl then."

"I said we're not talking about her," I reminded him.

"Come on. It's me. Tell me about her."

I'd known Nate since I was born – I was delighted I didn't remember the first few years so it felt like less time – and he was right, he was the best friend I had. So I knew he wasn't going to give up until I told him. I also knew he wasn't going to mock me pitilessly. For the most part. Telling him was going to be less hassle than him hounding me to tell him.

"Fine. Avery St John."

Nate shoved his hands in his pockets and looked up at the sky. "Name rings a bell, but I don't really remember her."

Gran had forked out the unnecessary hundreds of thousands it had cost to send both Nate and me to Mitchell College. She was probably lucky she only had the two grandchildren. But then, knowing Gran she probably would have found a way to send an entire sports team worth of grandchildren to Mitchell College if she'd had them.

I pulled my phone out of my pocket and scrolled through it until I found one of the pictures Avery had sent me. I passed him the phone and I couldn't tell by that noise if he was impressed or laughing.

"The face definitely rings a bell. Her?"

I nodded as I took my phone back. "Her."

Now he was definitely laughing. "How the hell did a loser like you land her?"

"She's no great catch herself, thanks."

"Fuck," he spluttered. "If that's the way you talk about your girlfriend, I'd hate to think about what you say about Mrs Mack these days."

I grunted in annoyance.

"Oh, watch out," Nate sniggered. "Your emotions are showing."

"Fuck off."

"No. No," he said, trying to contain his laughter. "Sorry. Talk to me."

"There's nothing to talk about. She wants me to help her

tank her rep."

"You *chose* to help another human being?"

I shoved him. "She's...persuasive."

"Ah," he breathed. "She showed you her tits."

I shoved him harder. "No. I'm yet to see her tits, actually."

"What?" His step faltered for a second, then he hurried to catch up. "You've been dating two weeks and you've still not seen her tits?"

"Is that okay?" I asked sardonically. "I wasn't aware there was a time limit on breast unveiling."

"I'm just surprised. You must really like her."

I turned a hard glare on him and he held his hands up in defence.

"All right. You *don't* really like her?"

"She wants me to teach her how to be not good."

"You mean be bad?"

"No."

"There's a difference?"

I nodded. "There's a difference."

"That's the stupidest fucking thing I've ever heard."

"See?" I tell you.

As we walked up to Freya's front door he looked at me. "Okay. So how are you supposed to do this?"

"We go on dates and I teach her something."

He snorted. "Sure. Like what?"

I shrugged my shoulders. "She's just a little lacking in confidence, I've just got to help her loosen up."

Nate barked a laugh and I smacked him even before he opened his mouth, yet that didn't deter him from sniggering, "Yeah, I know what kind of loosening you want to do with her." I smacked him again for good measure. "I don't remember her ever having a problem with confidence."

"I don't know how to explain it–"

"What? The cunning linguist," He winked at me and I rolled my eyes, "can't explain it?"

"Very clever. How long have you been holding onto that one?"

"Months. I've been waiting months to use that."

I nodded. "I'll bet. I don't know. She's full of energy and confidence like ninety percent of the time. Then…she'll just be hesitant about something. She won't say what's on her mind or she'll get embarrassed if she did. I don't know what it is about her."

"She a virgin?"

"No. Not that that should have anything to do with it."

Nate nodded. "Calm down. I just wondered if maybe her hesitation came from it all being new."

"What would you know about it?"

"About as little as you, mate."

"Fuck off."

We both had girls we saw regularly. However, where Nate liked to think he was the great Casanova of our time, he liked to imply I was merely a whore. I didn't like to remind him that Casanova was really just a whore until he fell in love.

148

"Well, there you slackers are," Freya said as she pulled the door open. "You bring me some of Gran's cobbler?"

"Nope," Nate said, totally pleased with himself for being a dick.

"Pleasure to see you, Davin," she said to me and I knew it had more to do with the fact that she wanted to annoy Nate.

"Yeah. You, too."

My phone went off again and I pulled it out to see another message from Avery.

Nate chuckled as Freya closed the door behind us. "Oh yeah. Dav's got a girlfriend now."

Liv, Vinny, Lara, Zac and Beau were all there too, and they all looked at me in various states of humoured surprise.

"Is he shitting us?" Lara asked.

I shook my head. "No."

"You've got a girlfriend?" Beau asked.

I nodded. "Fact hasn't changed since the dipshit mentioned it."

"Good for you, Dav," Zac said with a smile.

"She nice then?" Freya asked.

"She's…" Nate sniggered. "She's very nice."

"You bringing her over then?" Vinny asked.

I scoffed. "Uh. No."

"Why not?" Zac passed me a beer.

"She'd take one look at us and realise she's with the wrong bloke?" Vinny grinned.

I thought about that and the likelihood was low. "Actually

the opposite probably. If she survived the culture shock."

"You've got a lot of faith in her." Vinny's face told me exactly what sort of girl she was and what sort of fun he'd like to have with her. But Vinny was mostly talk when it came to girls. Especially the ones we didn't know.

"You remember that little girl in Dav's year with the blonde pigtails who used to bounce around everywhere?" Nate asked as he sat next to Liv and put his arm around her.

"That Saint chick or whatever?" Freya asked as she dropped next to Nate.

Nate nodded. "That's her."

"The fuck you see in her?" Lara sniggered and I knew she remembered Avery well.

I shrugged, not really sure about that myself. Something about her had got under my skin. I didn't totally hate being around her, even if her incessant buoyancy often made my skin crawl. For some reason I was averse to the way people dismissed her or made fun of her, and Nate's friends were no exception. But I wasn't going to tell them that she was a legitimately nice person who was kind to me even when I was my grumpy self and that she deserved better than she got.

"She's probably just a good lay," Beau said.

"He's not even seen her tits," Nate told them.

"Okay. Can we stop with this shit now?" I asked, trying to keep the full annoyance from my voice. "Where's Nova?"

"She had shit to do. Apparently." Nate shrugged like it was no big deal, then he buried his nose in Liv's neck and she

150

laughed.

I fell into the empty arm chair and sipped my beer while we did the usual things we did. Well they all got up to the usual things we did, and I did the usual drinking and chatting and beating everyone but Freya on the console. And they all noticed.

"You're serious about this girlfriend business then?" Zac said while the others were basically all paired off.

I drained the rest of my current beer and gave him a nod. "Sure."

He chuckled. "You don't sound so sure. But you keeping your hands to yourself tonight makes you sure look it."

"I'm spoken for now, mate. Excuse me if I take that shit seriously."

Zac looked around the room where Nate was hooking up with Liv, but the others had gone looking for some private time. "Nothing wrong with that. I guess I'm just surprised that you were the one to settle down first."

I rubbed the back of my head. "You're not the only one."

Zac laughed away the semi-seriousness we'd fallen into and nudged my shoulder. "Come on. I'm still betting I can beat you one day."

"Not likely."

I followed him over to the TV and we set to, not really paying attention to whatever it was Liv and Nate were getting up to behind us.

Eleven: Avery

Davin walked towards me on Saturday evening and I had to admit I felt a little flurry of excitement at just the sight of him. He was in his usual dark jeans and scruffy black Converse, with a non-descript tee under a non-descript jacket. He had his hands shoved in his pockets, his shoulders were hunched, and he was scowling as he looked around. But as a package, it did something for me.

"More florals?" he asked, totally unimpressed as he pulled his sunglasses down to look me over – it was still early enough in the year that the sun wasn't quite down yet.

"I'm very impressed you know what floral is," I told him with a smile.

"I'll bet." He pushed his sunglasses back up his nose. "Right. What torture in the guise of entertainment have you got planned for me today?"

"Something from this century."

"The horror," he mono-toned. My smile widened. "Oh, God. I'm going to hate it, aren't I?"

I shook my head. "No. I think you'll love it!"

"Impossible."

I would not be deterred. "No. I think you'll be really pleased with my choice."

"Go on, then."

"*Ready Player One.*"

He blinked and I did an internal victory dance at having surprised him. "You picked what?"

I nodded. "I thought it sounded just like you."

"What? It sounds incessantly annoyed by a small fairy creature straight out of Wes Craven's most depraved nightmares?"

I laughed, having no idea who Wes Craven was but I got the gist. "Sure."

I took his hand, noting his protest was limited to an eye roll – progress – and dragged his totally unenthusiastic person into the cinema complex.

"Okay," I said as we walked in. "Dinner choices?"

"Well, Grill'd is the closest," he said unenthusiastically.

I smiled. "Great. I love burgers."

He pulled off his sunglasses and swapped them out for his normal glasses. "I'm yet to find something you don't love."

"I'm sure you can find something," I said as I led the way to a table.

"I find that very hard to believe," was his dry reply as we sat down.

"All right, you can have a free one. I don't like spiders."

"Shame you live in Australia then, isn't it?"

"I happen to quite like it."

"Even though everything wants to kill you?"

"Not everything wants to kill me."

"It's not personal or anything."

I laughed even though there was nothing about his face that suggested he was joking. "No. I'd like to think it's not."

He looked around as he took a deep breath. "What do you want then?"

I looked over the menu and tried to decide. "I think I'm going to have a…crispy bacon and cheese today."

"Come here often then?"

"Blair and I enjoy it, yes."

He nodded as his eyes skimmed over the menu. "Okay. Drink?"

"I think lemonade."

"You think lemonade?"

I nodded. "Lemonade. What about you?" He stood up and I frowned in confusion. "Where are you going?"

"To order," he said simply, pulling his wallet out of his pocket.

"You don't have to pay for me."

"Of that I'm aware. And yet…" He shrugged lazily.

"I'll get the tickets then."

He shrugged. "Suit yourself. Be back in a tick."

I watched him walk away and realised I'd never really watched him walk before. He looked sure and confident as he manoeuvred through the few people crisscrossing around the restaurant. I watched him order and took note of the interaction. He wasn't the hunched over guy he was at school. I wondered what was different about school and here that had him acting so differently.

"Want a drink to go with that straw?" he asked me as he came back to the table and I realised I'd been chewing the end of a straw as I watched him.

I smiled as he sat back down, sliding my drink over to me. "Thanks."

He nodded. "No problem."

"Can I ask you something?"

"I'm not sure how I'd stop you." He was looking around and I wasn't sure if he felt the need to keep an eye on the people around us or he didn't want to look at me.

"At school you kinda hide…"

"Not a question, Avery."

"Fine. Why do you seem to be hiding at school?"

"To avoid human interaction."

"Just how many socialisation credits do you have a day?" I asked him.

The corner of his lips twitched, but he sniffed and any sign of a smile was quickly gone. "I've had to borrow against future credits since we started dating."

"So why don't you feel the need to hide here?"

He looked at me, his eyebrow quirked in surprise. "What?"

"You went over there and ordered with total ease and

confidence."

"I'm not shy, Avery. I dislike social contact. There's a difference."

"So you don't want to talk to people at school who you know, but you'll talk to strangers?"

"Strangers only talk to you as necessary. Attending the same school breeds an assumed familiarity that leads to unnecessary discourse–"

"You just don't want to be nice to people."

He blinked. "Excuse me?"

"Are you afraid people will like you?" I asked as I took a sip.

He scoffed. "If anything, I'd prefer to avoid the unfortunate circumstance in which they do."

"I like you."

A range of emotions flickered through his eyes as he looked at me, his bottle of Coke halfway to his mouth. "You don't know me."

"I know you enough. You're smart, you're funny, and you're interesting. You think I'm an idiot, but instead of talking down to me or dismissing me you try to teach me… Whether it's needed or not."

He leant over the table towards me. "You like what I do to you."

I mirrored his lean. "I like that, too."

"Why me, Avery?" he asked softly.

"Why not you?"

"That's what you said the other week. I want to know why me."

I looked at him and said the first thing that came to mind. "Because it didn't matter if you laughed in my face. I didn't care what you thought and I had nothing to lose. Plus you're mysterious and moody and in trouble all the time, I figured if anyone could trash my reputation it would be you."

A single eyebrow rose on that stony face. "I'm flattered you thought so highly of me. Does the use of the past tense mean you care now?"

I paused before I answered, not quite sure how to answer, let alone how I felt. "I... I don't *not* care...?"

He nodded thoughtfully. Finally, all he said was, "You know I don't laugh, right?"

The waiter came over with our burgers in hand. "A pork and pine?"

"Thanks." Davin nodded and the waiter put it down.

"And the chilli addict." The waiter put the other board in front of me and my eyes widened in terror.

I looked up at Davin and there was this glint in his eyes as he popped a chip in his mouth. I frowned at him and there went that ghost of a smile on his face.

I opened my mouth, closed it and turned an awkward smile on the waiter.

"Thanks," I said.

"Everything okay?" the waiter asked.

I nodded quickly. "Yep."

Nope. Big nope. I couldn't get through the slightly spicy twiggy sticks when Dad accidentally bought them at the shops. How was I going to get through a chilli addict burger?

"You sure?" the waiter asked and I looked to Davin again.

It felt an awful lot like the waiter was waiting for me to complain.

"What did you do?" I hissed at Davin.

Davin shrugged. "I certainly don't remember you ordering a chilli addict, Avery," he said meaningfully.

"Oh, you didn't?" the waiter asked and his tone was far too innocent for me to think this was a total accident.

"It's fine," I said with an awkward laugh.

"Are you sure?" the waiter asked.

"Yes. It's no problem. Thanks."

Davin had a chip on its way to his mouth, but he dropped his hand and looked at me pointedly. "Lesson. When someone brings you the wrong order, you are allowed to say so. You don't just have to eat something you didn't order."

"Yes," I hissed, leaning closer to him like the waiter wasn't going to hear me then. "But they didn't mess up, did they? You set me up."

Davin's nose scrunched in a way I was starting to wonder was him suppressing a smile. "No. I merely ordered you an extra burger and asked this nice young man to bring over the wrong one in the hopes you wouldn't let it go."

I frowned at him. "You paid for an extra burger?"

"That is irrelevant."

"No it's not!"

"It is. Explain to the nice young man that this wasn't the burger you ordered."

"Davin," I hissed.

He leant his elbows on the table. "He knows there's a purpose to this and you're still not going to say anything to him?"

I looked up at the waiter with an apologetic smile before I glared at Davin again. "No. I don't want to make a fuss."

"You wanted lessons. And I've paid for you to make the fuss. So make it."

I huffed at him, then looked up at the waiter. "I'm really sorry about this. But…" Even knowing the waiter was in on this, something was holding me back from saying it. I cleared my throat, widened my smile, and tried again. "This isn't what I ordered."

The waiter was looking between us with a knowing smile. "So sorry about that. What did you order?"

I threw one more glare at Davin. "A crispy bacon and cheese. Please."

"I'll bring it right out."

"Thank you."

The waiter picked up the chilli addict and left.

"That wasn't so hard, was it?" Davin asked.

It was terrible. But as embarrassing and awkward as it had been, I also had a sense of accomplishment. I wasn't sure if I wanted to tell Davin that or if he needed berating for setting it up in the first place.

"That was mortifying. How did you even get him to agree to that?"

"I told him it was foreplay."

"Davin!" I yelped, then looked around in embarrassment.

"Relax. He was quite happy to play along. I told him my girlfriend was amazingly wonderful but needed a little help being assertive."

"You told him I was amazingly wonderful?"

"That's what you take from that?" he sighed. "But yes. I did."

I smiled and we moved onto general chit chat as we ate. Well I moved onto general chit chat. Davin wasn't exactly any more talkative than he usually was, but he didn't seem quite so closed off as usual somehow either.

When we went to buy tickets, he let me buy them but then beat me to paying for the drinks and popcorn, saying, "You can pay next time."

I was already practically elbow deep in the giant popcorn tub as we found our seats and Davin helped me catch it as I sat down.

"We just had dinner."

"So?" I asked, my mouth full of popcorn.

"And you're not full?"

I shook my head as I swallowed. "Me? It's a rare occurrence."

He looked mildly surprised. "Good to know."

160

"Ebony's worse."

He nodded. "Great."

As the pre-movie ads started rolling and the lights went down, I realised the cinema was oddly empty. But I was distracted by remembering I needed to put my phone on silent.

We got all of about ten minutes through the movie before Davin put his arm around me. And it was another five or so when he bent his head to kiss my neck. His breath on my skin tickled pleasantly and I instinctively shied away a little at the same time my head tilted to give him better access.

"What are you doing?" I whispered, trying not to giggle.

"Either tell me to stop, or relax," was his hushed answer.

"Are they my only options?"

He pulled back to look at me. "How many options do you want, woman?"

"How many do you have?"

"Two. I have two options. Take it or leave it."

I knew how he felt about me laughing at him, so I tried not to. "I choose option three."

"There isn't an–"

I shut him up by kissing him. His hand went to my cheek as he kissed me deeper and everything in me responded, until I remembered we were in a movie theatre.

"You're missing the movie," I told him.

"We'll rent it later," he replied, his flippant tone telling me exactly how much he cared.

I laughed, but he soon distracted me with kisses as his hand trailed down my body. When he slid it up under my skirt, he didn't stop and I felt his thumb rub between my legs. It sent an oh-so-amazing shiver up my spine and I didn't want him to stop, but…

"Davin!" I hissed.

"What?" I could have sworn I felt a smile against my lips. But that was ridiculous because Davin didn't know how to smile.

"We're in public."

"Hardly."

"What if people see?"

His lips skimmed towards my ear as his thumb kept moving over me. "There are two other people in here and they're paying less attention to the film than we are. They're not going to see anything."

The way I was leaning into him, he'd know I didn't want him to stop. But my mind was warring with my body.

"Do you want to be that good girl forever?" he asked teasingly.

"Another lesson?" I asked wryly.

"If you like." Goose bumps chased across my skin as his breath tickled my neck. "Let me teach you how to let go…"

Now I knew that if I had wanted to stop and I'd told him that, he would have and he would have been fine with it. But I didn't want him to. I wanted Davin to bring me out of my good girl shell, so why not let him finger me at the movies?

I knew why I wouldn't have done it if Miles had suggested it. I wouldn't have done it because there would have been no reward for the risk. Which is to assume that Miles would have got me so worked up that I'd be near desperate for release anyway.

But Davin wasn't Miles. Davin made me feel things that Miles never did. And there *was* something sort of enticing about knowing we could get caught, but also knowing it was unlikely.

I mean, we totally still could... Which was scary. But it was unlikely. Which was less scary...

And Davin knew what he was doing down there, so the reward for the risk would be definitely worth it. Besides, good girls didn't get fingered at the movies because they were too shy and innocent. And I was going to not be too shy and innocent anymore.

So when Davin looked at me, his nose bumping mine as he waited for my answer, I kissed him hard and spread my legs just a little wider so he wouldn't misinterpret the message. Davin swapped his thumb for his fingers and increased the pressure. I felt my back arch towards him and my fingers threaded through his hair.

By the time my hips were rocking in time with the movement of his hand, he slid it into my undies and stroked me up and down, slowly at first, then building gently in speed. As the tingling spread through me, our kiss grew more heated and I know a moan or two escaped me.

His fingers stroked all the way down and he paused, his finger tracing gently around me. We looked at each other and I felt like he was asking permission. If he was asking what I thought he was asking? God, yes, I wanted it. The previous weekend had been great and all, but I was more than ready for the next step.

His lips were back on mine as he slid his finger into me slowly, in short slow thrusts, each one deeper until I felt the heel of his hand massaging me. It felt so good as his finger pumped slowly in and out. My hips moved with his rhythm, meeting him halfway. I felt my orgasm growing and I was desperate for it at the same time as I didn't want that pleasurable feeling to stop.

Now was really not the time to think about how Miles had never made me feel like that. But I couldn't help it. Miles had fumbled his way around down there and not known what he was doing. But it was like Davin had the roadmap to my body and he knew exactly what to do.

As my breathing came shorter, Davin's finger thrust faster. I moaned softly and I could have sworn he smiled against me again.

Then his lips were back to my ear as he said, "Don't make me gag you, Avery."

I didn't trust myself to keep quiet if I spoke, so I just took his face in my hands and brought his lips back to mine.

The pleasure built and I tensed as my orgasm hit me. My teeth caught his lip as I fought to stay silent, but he had me shaking, it had hit so hard. I just held him tight, tense and my eyes shut as I rode it out.

Finally the shakes subsided. I relaxed again and I opened my eyes to look at him.

No one had ever looked at me like that before. I wasn't sure what it was exactly, but it sent a skitter of something quite nice through my chest.

Davin ran his fingers softly over me a couple of times. "How did that feel?"

"Amazing," I laughed quietly. The reward had been more than worth the risk.

There was a crooked tilt to his mouth that was almost a smile. "I didn't mean physically."

"Oh." I smiled self-consciously. "Saying 'bad' feels kinda corny…"

He ducked his lips back to my ear as his hand slid up my body firmly, turning me on all over again. "Everything about you is corny, baby. Don't stop now."

I grinned against his cheek. "Fine. It felt bad."

He pulled back, whispered, "That's my good girl," and gave me a wink before rearranging us so I was leaning against him with his arm around me to watch the rest of the movie.

I didn't know what it was about Davin. He was rude. He was crude. He was bossy and arrogant. But it all just made me want to spend more time with him. Maybe it was me naively thinking that I was cracking that cold exterior, breaking through those seemingly infinite defences. Or maybe it was just that there was something else about him too that I hadn't quite put my finger on yet.

We got through the movie without any more distractions and he even deigned to walk out holding my hand.

"What did you think?" I asked him and he nodded slowly.

"It wasn't bad."

"That's almost a positive review coming from you."

He huffed like he was trying not to smile. "Sure." He rubbed the back of his head. "So, did you have plans now?"

I shook my head as I took a sip of my drink. "Nope."

He looked around like he wasn't sure if he wanted to actually come out with what he was thinking of saying or not. "Do you want to come back to mine?"

I looked at the time on my phone. "At half eleven?"

He nodded. "At half eleven."

"Some people might think you're asking me to stay."

He shrugged. "You can if you want. Dad's not home until late tomorrow."

I looked him over as I thought about it.

I'd stayed over at Miles' place and he'd stayed at mine before. Only once when there hadn't been parents home, though. Even then I didn't think Mum or Dad would have a problem with it. They knew I was honest with them and they – so far – trusted me.

"Okay. Let me call my parents."

He shrugged like it didn't bother him and I dialled my mum's number, thinking she'd be the most likely to answer.

166

"Hey, sweetie. How was the movie?" she answered.

"It was good."

"Good. What are you up to now?"

"I was thinking maybe I could stay at Davin's tonight?" I started.

"Did you now?" I could hear the smile in her voice.

"I did. Would that be okay?"

"Would staying at a boy's house I've only met once before be okay?" Mum teased and I laughed.

"His dad's not home, so I get if that's a no."

As I turned around aimlessly, I caught Davin's look of obvious surprise and I grinned at him.

"His dad's not home all night?"

"Correct."

"Have you two had sex?"

"Mum," I whined. "Now?"

"I think that would count as child pornography, Ave. I wouldn't suggest it."

I sniggered. "I'll keep that in mind."

"If we were to say yes, what time will you be back tomorrow?"

I looked at Davin. "I don't know. By midday?"

Davin's eyebrow rose then he shrugged like he'd assumed he knew what I was talking about.

"Ave wants to stay at her boyfriend's house tonight," Mum said, presumably talking to Dad.

"This isn't Miles, is it?" I heard Dad ask.

"No. Davin," Mum replied.

"And you've met him?" Dad asked.

"I have. Once when he picked her up. He seemed nice. He had a bit of a stunned mullet thing going on though."

I smiled at Davin as I listened to their conversation, slightly muffled from wherever Mum had put the phone.

"We did let her have sleepovers with Miles," Mum added.

"They'd been dating for a while before we did that," Dad said thoughtfully.

"That's true."

"She's trustworthy, though," Dad said. "She always makes good decisions. And she's always honest with us."

"That she does. She's our good little Avery."

I grimaced in annoyance and Davin threw me a questioning look, but I just shook my head.

"Which is why we never have to worry about her," Dad said.

"So what do you think? Yes or no?"

"I'm all right with it as long as he comes to dinner next week."

Mum didn't say anything for a moment, then I heard her say, "Okay. Deal." There was a scruffling noise, then she was talking to me again. "Did you hear your dad?"

I nodded. "I did. I'll let Davin know he's coming to dinner next week." Davin turned back to me quickly from looking around, his eyes narrowed and full of barely contained anger.

"I'm expected to do what?" he asked.

But I was listening to Mum. "Great. Have a good night – be sensible – and we'll see you tomorrow. Love you, sweetie."

"Love you too, Mum. Love to Dad." I hung up and gave Davin a single nod.

"Dinner?" He looked at me in utter disbelief.

"Dinner." I nodded.

"With your family?"

"Yup."

"For just having you over for one night?"

"You've got it."

"You could have lied to them and spared me this."

I nodded. "I could have. Although I didn't know they were going to go with the dinner route."

"But you knew it was a possibility?"

I shrugged. "Not really. But I'm not surprised by it."

"Dinner?" he clarified as if it might have changed.

"Dinner."

"And you didn't lie because…?"

"Because then they wouldn't trust me and I wouldn't get to stay at your house any other time."

"There might be more times…?"

I nodded. "If I tell them the truth and you meet them for dinner."

He sighed and looked like he wanted to argue more. But all he mumbled was, "I don't know what's happening anymore," then looked at me. "Okay. Fine. You stay over and

169

I will go to dinner with your family."

I grinned as I took his hand and started leading him to his car. "Great. Oh, can I borrow a t-shirt to sleep in?"

"Yes. I think I've gone insane," he said then cleared his throat. "Sure. Why not."

Twelve: Davin

On D-Day, the day I lost my Meet the Parents virginity, I told Avery I'd go home and get changed and be at her place at about seven.

"Do you own something…less black?" Dad asked as I almost fell into the kitchen while concentrating on doing up my belt. It was his week off work and it would have been impossible to get out of the house without him seeing me.

I looked up at him and there was no way you could say we weren't related. I had my mother's eyes, and her genes combined with Dad's to make sure I wasn't going to be anything but idiotically tall. But everything else was just Dad. The dark hair, the nose, the square jaw, the five o'clock shadow by midday if I bothered shaving of a morning.

"Most of us call that grey," I responded.

"I'll take that as a no then."

"No. By all means. I have different colours in my wardrobe. I have midnight black, jet black, raven black, onyx, coal, obsidian–"

"Okay," Dad chuckled. "I get it. Just black." He flipped

the page in his newspaper and took hold of his coffee mug. "I guess it'll have to be good enough to meet your girlfriend's parents."

I huffed. "Avery's under no delusions about who I am. If it's good enough for her, I'm sure her parents won't give a fuck."

Dad chuckled again and I could see by the look that crossed his face that he was about to enter reminiscing mode. "To think, the girl who accidentally doused half the school in glitter at that stupid talent show four years ago would end up your girlfriend."

"Laugh it up," I grumbled.

"No, Dav. I'm glad you're getting out of your comfort zone."

"No one's getting out of anything," I told him. "I've chosen a specific girl to vent my hormonal frustrations with and she insists on us going on actual dates. To wit, I am required to meet her parents. There's nothing more to it than that."

There was plenty more to it than that. For example, I was trying to help her trash her reputation. So far I wasn't sure that we were succeeding. Another example, I could be venting my hormonal frustrations much more efficiently with her. But I neither expected nor needed that.

"Well, you've got me convinced," Dad said with a grin and I ask you, *"Why do parents insist on treating their children like…children?"*

172

"You say something, Dav?" Dad asked as he flipped another page of his paper.

"Never mind. I need to go."

"You coming home tonight?"

"Does it matter?" I huffed and Dad gave me an annoyed look. I sighed. "Yes."

Dad nodded. "Good. If I'm up, I'll see you then."

I waved my head noncommittally, a poor facsimile of a nod, picked up my keys and headed out.

It wasn't exactly that my dad and I didn't get along. But he'd really only seen me for half my life. It was sort of difficult to impose true paternal authority when you were gone half the time, and it certainly hadn't been easy to keep up a close relationship. Add to that the fact that eleven years ago I'd become difficult to get close to, and Dad and I didn't have much of a father-son relationship to speak of.

I loved him and he loved me. He took the (good-natured) piss out of me more often than not and I begrudgingly let him. But I didn't go to him with my problems and he didn't expect me to. Most days when he was home, we behaved more like roommates who had developed a fondness for each other due to a relatively close proximity.

I folded myself into the car, realising too late that I was probably supposed to take wine or chocolate or something with me when I met my girlfriend's parents.

"But how will I maintain my bad boy image if I do something so...thoughtful?" I ask you.

I threw the car into reverse and reminded myself that meeting my first girlfriend's parents wasn't that big a deal. It wasn't like I wanted or needed their approval to feel good about myself or to date their daughter. There was zero concern that I might feel good about myself and it's not like dating Avery had become the main event in my life or anything. She was nothing but a vaguely entertaining, temporary affair which alleviated some of my current boredom.

And I kept that notion firmly in my mind as I drove to her place and forced myself to walk to the front door like a calm, normal human being. I took a deep breath as my finger hovered over the doorbell, then I just went for it. I heard the tone echo through the house and the familiar noises of people inside reacting.

The door opened and Avery's mum Heather was standing there beaming in her three-quarter chinos and pale blue shirt. Like Avery, she had blonde hair. Although, hers looked more dyed than her elder daughter's. She also had blue eyes and her smile still didn't quite reach them, despite the nice show she was putting on.

"Davin!" she cooed and I thought I could see where Avery got that horrifying sweetness. "So nice to see you again. Come in. Come in. Avery!" she yelled and I winced as I stepped in. Heather closed the door behind me. "We're in the living room." So I headed for the living room.

In the living room was a man with short ash brown hair, a

174

cropped beard, and blue eyes behind rimless glasses. He wore dark navy trousers with a white shirt, tucked in, top button undone, and sleeves rolled up. His posture commanded authority and demanded attention the way only a teacher could.

"Davin, this is Phil," Heather said happily.

Phil met me in the middle of the room, his hand outstretched. I took it and saw him sizing me up as we shook. A master at the game, he gave away no indication of the conclusion to which he came.

"Davin. Nice to meet you. Avery's been talking about you almost constantly," Phil said.

"More's the pity for me then," I replied and wondered if he'd actually understood the joke.

"Davin," came Avery's voice behind me and I spun to see her coming up short just inside the archway, with Ebony beside her.

The two sisters were starkly different.

There was Avery in a figure-hugging maxi dress that looked like it was made of a thousand different pieces of material in different patterns and colours. Her hair was bundled into a messy bun with wisps of hair escaping around her face and her lipstick was even brighter than her usual bubble-gum pink.

Then there was Ebony. Her eyes and her hair were a few shades darker than Avery's and it seemed that wasn't the only thing about her that was darker. In grey denim shorts, a black singlet, and Batman Converses, with her hair in a plain pony tail, she was the total opposite of the shiny happy beacon beside her.

"Davin, you remember Ebony?" Avery said.

I swallowed hard and nodded, something about the smaller girl was terrifyingly off-putting even to someone like me. "Ebony. Nice to see you again."

Her eyes narrowed and she gave me a single nod. "Davin."

Heather giggled almost nervously. "Why don't we sit down? I'll get some drinks. Dinner's still a few minutes off. Drink, Davin?"

"He'll have anything caffeinated," Avery answered for me.

Heather looked at me questioningly. "Coke?"

I nodded. "Would be great. Thanks."

She smiled and ducked out. Phil took a seat in an armchair and Ebony sat on one of the couches. Avery came over to me and half held my hand, half bundled me to sit on the other couch and sat down beside me.

I didn't feel totally on display or anything.

"So, Davin," Phil started and I managed not to remind you out loud that no good conversation had started with, 'So, insert your name here'. "How was school?"

Well it could have been a completely worse start. I shifted slightly in my seat, trying to remind myself why the hell I was in Avery St John's living room to have dinner with her parents. The whole thing was fucking bonkers and I was, at

176

that moment, having trouble remembering why I'd agreed to this whole thing in the first place.

Oh yeah. There wasn't actually a reason besides furthering the plot.

"As far as a compulsory system of education, it was…fine," I said carefully.

Heather chuckled as she came back in with a tray of drinks. "That was a very good answer."

Phil's eyebrows rose. "You dislike school?"

I took a breath before replying, "Define dislike."

"Feel distaste for or hostility towards," Phil said with a wry smirk.

Avery leaned towards me. "Dad's an English lecturer at Adelaide Uni."

I nodded slowly. "That makes sense."

"In light of said definition, I'll repeat the question. You dislike school?"

I looked him clear in the eye and said, "I enjoy learning. I enjoy being challenged. But yes, I dislike school."

Phil looked surprised for a moment, then his smile was slightly warmer. "An honest answer at least. Does your dislike for organised forms of education mean you don't plan on going to university?"

"Dad!" Avery hissed.

But it was fine. "Barring any unforeseen incidents, I will be attending university next year."

"Unforeseen incidents? Like what?"

I shrugged. "I feel my death may have a negative impact on my ability to undertake tertiary education."

Phil huffed a small laugh. "I imagine it would."

"And how was your day?" Avery asked Phil, like she was desperate to change the subject. "Did you get your crossword finished?"

Phil nodded.

"Both of them?" Avery wheedled and Phil grinned.

"Yes. Both of them."

"Throw us a clue then, Dad," Avery said with a smile at him then me. "Let's see if they're so easy."

"With company?"

Avery nudged me. "Oh, Davin won't mind."

In her defence, Davin didn't mind at all.

Phil spread a slow glance over the room, an expectant smirk growing on his face as he picked up the paper beside him and looked over it calculatingly. "All right. 'Damp fog hides nothing'."

I looked around as Avery, Ebony and Heather all frowned in concentration and wondered about the sanity in answering. It's not like I cared if my girlfriend's parents liked me or not. But I was also loathe to pass up a time to prove my intellect.

"Moist," came out of my mouth before I'd even realised I was going to go with showing off.

Phil's expectant smirk turned impressed and he gave me a single nod. "Well done, Davin."

"What?" Ebony asked sceptically. "How."

"Care to explain?" Phil looked at me.

"Fog is mist. Nothing is zero. Hide zero, or 'o', in mist and you have moist for damp."

Ebony didn't bother hiding her scrutiny. "Are you like smart or something?"

I shrugged. "That's what I'm told."

Ebony waved her hand in her dad's direction without taking her eyes off me. "Ask him another one."

Phil smirked. "All right. Let me see... 'Wave cereal bowl'."

"Brandish," I replied after a few moments.

Phil nodded again. "So it is."

On the surface his tone was somewhat condescending, but if you listened deeper you could hear that it was surprise and quite possibly begrudging respect that I was sure he didn't want to show. I can't say I blamed him.

"How?" Ebony asked, leaning towards me with her eyes narrowed like she still wasn't convinced.

I leant towards her a little, finding the smaller St John rather amusing. "Cereal is bran. Bowl is dish. Brandish is a synonym for wave."

"Are you a reader, Davin?" Phil asked.

"In that I'm capable or that I choose to read for pleasure?" I replied and he smiled.

"I'd be very surprised to find you incapable, so I surmise you do in fact read for pleasure."

"I've been known to."

179

Phil nodded. "What are you reading now?"

"I finished *The Monk* again last night. Don't know what I'll pick up tonight."

Phil looked legitimately surprised. "Matthew Lewis?" he asked and I nodded.

"The guy from *Harry Potter*?" Ebony asked, looking between us.

"Not quite, Ebs," Phil said with a smile. "Bit before his time. Seventeen nineties, wasn't it?"

I nodded again. "Ninety-six."

The way Phil was looking at me, I had to wonder how he'd looked at Miles. What the hell was the distinction between me and the popular, charismatic, do-no-wrong arsehat in Avery's father's mind? I'd have been willing to bet that as soon as Miles walked in their front door he was simpering and going on about how special Avery was and how lucky he was to be dating her. I could picture it now, like I'd been there on that very night he was in my place.

Avery would have bounded down the steps in her horrifyingly bright wardrobe choice and he would have been in the midst of telling Phil and Heather how amazingly exceptional she was. He would have timed it just right so she'd hear but not realise he was saying it for her benefit. He would have appeared all self-conscious when she made it known she'd heard – because it was Avery and she would have been excited and thrilled by such a thing. Their conversation was probably full of all Miles' accomplishments and his hopes and dreams for the future while Avery gazed at him lovingly, Heather imagined their wedding, Phil thought he seemed a very upstanding sort of young man, and Ebony... Actually I doubted she much liked anyone, let alone Miles.

"So you like the Gothic texts?" Phil asked, pulling me out of my supposedly impossible flashback.

"I do."

"Are they the scary ones?" Ebony asked.

"They can be," Phil answered.

Ebony nodded. "I like those ones."

I felt the corner of my mouth tugging up strangely. "Colour me surprised," I said sarcastically.

She grinned. "What's your favourite then?"

"That would be like asking on which day of the week I prefer to breathe," I said suavely.

Ebony stared at me with wide eyes full of wonder and I had a feeling I'd won her over at the very least.

"A man after my own heart," Phil commented.

"Well Ave, sweetie. I think Dad's close to giving his stamp of approval," Heather chuckled. Under the smiles and welcoming tone, I noticed the way she still watched me warily. She was doing her job well: be supportive but cautious.

I felt Avery's hand slide under my arm and find my hand, her fingers threading with mine. I was surprised by the ease and comfort of the action but didn't let it show.

"He's prickly, but not so bad once you get to know him," she said warmly as she gave my hand a squeeze.

I looked at her, not quite sure what I was feeling. I was finding her pep and vigour slightly less annoying than usual, and this whole meeting the parents (and Ebony) thing wasn't quite the ordeal I'd expected. So far it seemed being my usual self was actually working out rather in my favour.

There was a buzzing noise from another room and Heather smiled. "That will probably be dinner."

Everyone stood up and I followed in awkward suit as much from Avery pulling me up by the hand she still held as of my own volition. I felt like Avery was going to say something to me but, as we walked to the dinner table, Phil fell into step with me and started talking to me.

"Have you read much Byron?" he asked and I looked at Avery like she'd orchestrated the whole thing. She grinned at me, but there was no indication the smile meant anything more than a shared joke.

I sighed. "Yes. Although, I've never been one for the Romantics. I prefer the Victorians."

"Really? Poe?"

"Le Fanu, preferably. *Carmilla* is a spectacular piece of work."

"I've always thought–"

"Phil, darling," Heather said gently but pointedly. "Do we want to not inundate Davin with your literary excitement *just* yet? Save that for at least the second dinner, hm?"

Fuck. There was supposed to be more than one dinner? Was this normal? Do most boyfriends have to have dinner with their girlfriend's family on the regular? Double fuck. Was I supposed to reciprocate? Was she meant to have dinner with my family?

I felt a nudge and collected my somewhat frazzled mind to look at Avery. She was smiling at me and nodding to a seat at the table. I dropped into it and cleared my throat.

"Uh, it's fine. Literary excitement I can reciprocate," I said, wondering if I looked as awkward as I felt.

"Oh, something you actually enjoy?" Avery teased as she sat beside me.

I gave her a look that quite clearly told her in no uncertain terms how I felt about her teasing me in front of her family. The last thing I needed was them thinking I was warm and fuzzy.

"*Carmilla*'s the vampire one, yeah?" Ebony asked, looking around the table from her seat across from me.

I nodded. "It is."

"I think I've heard Dad talk about it."

"I would imagine you have," Heather said as she started bringing plates to the table. "I didn't think there was another person besides your dad who liked Gothic books anymore."

Of course. Because it made total sense that I would share an interest with my love interest's father. Why not? It wasn't like that was totally coincidentally convenient at all. Brilliant.

"It's nice to see a young person who admires the classics,"

Phil said, smiling at me.

Holy shit-biscuits. Did I just get the approval of my girlfriend's father? Was that what just happened? Me? I was either doing something terribly wrong or terribly right. I just wasn't sure which it was yet.

"I'd admire the classics if you let me read them," Ebony grumbled. "I'm totally old enough for lesbian vampires."

I coughed only because something was in my throat. I in no way almost laughed at that.

"If you insist on describing it as lesbian vampires, then I don't think you are," Phil replied sedately.

"Why? What's wrong with lesbian vampires?" Ebony asked.

Phil looked at her like he knew there was a right and wrong answer here but had temporarily forgotten which was which. "Well...nothing–"

"Exactly. So why don't I get to read it? You know I can just get it online or probably in the library at school right?"

"You could. But that wouldn't make me think it any more suitable."

"Why not?"

Phil looked at Heather like he wanted her back up on that one, but she just smirked and shook her head. "No, dear. You're doing so well," she said.

"Davin?" Phil looked at me and I paused in raising my fork to my mouth.

"Yes?"

184

"What are your thoughts on it?"

I blinked. "I'm not sure I'm qualified to comment on your parenting choices."

Phil looked at Avery like I was a terrible help. "About the suitability of Ebs reading *Carmilla*."

Really? In what universe did I have any authority on the matter? I was a seventeen year old boy! But I rearranged in my seat and cleared my throat before I gave him an answer I presumed he was looking for.

"I think the argument that it vilifies female and homosexual desire has validity. But I don't think that needs to be read into it. After all, Dracula had a healthy dose of sexual desire for his victims. So in theory these stories were more about venerating the purity and prudishness considered appropriate of the time, and perpetuating the image so commented on by Wilde with *Dorian Gray*. In this day and age, the fact that Carmilla's preferred victim was female is merely a fact, rather than an issue."

Phil put his wine glass down and looked at me in astonishment. I was suddenly not so sure that being myself had been the best idea. Again, it wasn't like I cared if Avery's family liked me. But not having an argument with them or being thrown out of their house was probably preferable for our continued dating.

But instead of the debate I'd been expecting, I got the opposite.

"I'm impressed. Very few of my students now could

discuss sexuality in Victorian texts the way you just did," Phil finally said.

"You *do* seem to know a lot about sexual desire, Davin," Heather commented and Avery almost choked on her dinner.

I barely batted an eyelid. "I'm a teenager. It comes with the territory. If I can put it into even a vaguely academic framework then it just lets me sounds less degenerate."

Phil laughed. "Oh, I like him, Avery." He nodded to his elder daughter as he saluted me with his glass.

Avery grinned at me. "Me too."

A weird thing happened in my chest and I wasn't so sure about this boyfriend-girlfriend behaviour she was exuding. I knew this wasn't fake dating, but it wasn't totally real either. This wasn't a forever sort of thing. She'd get bored at some point because all she needed was lessons. And if the unthinkable happened and she gave me her heart, I had nothing to give her in return.

But I gave her a nod and the closest I came to a sincere smile in an effort to hide my uneasiness.

"So… Is that a yes or a no to me reading *Carmilla*?" Ebony asked the table exasperatedly and they all laughed.

"Find yourself a copy and you can read it," Phil answered and I made a mental note to pass my copy onto Avery the next day.

Thirteen: Avery

While Blair was hanging out with Molly and Krista in the Common Room, I went looking for Davin at Recess. I found him in one of the meeting rooms again, wearing his headphones as he read one of those thick, hardcover novels I was getting used to seeing around him when he wasn't on his laptop.

Before I even thought he'd seen me, he'd pulled a book out of his satchel on the table in front of him and held it out to me. I took it and realised I recognised the name as one he and Dad had thrown around the night before.

"What's this for?" I asked him as he pulled his headphones off.

"Ebony."

Davin had done something for someone else without being asked to do it. Something that didn't involve screaming goats. Something nice. Something for my little sister.

I blinked. "Is it the lesbian vampire one?" He nodded and I smiled. "Thanks. She'll be super pleased." I paused then amended, "Well as pleased as you'd be."

He leant his elbows on the desk. "I would be very pleased to receive a book."

"Ha! So there are things you like."

He shrugged as he leant back again, crossing his arms over his chest. "I never said there weren't."

"Things just don't include people."

"There are some people I don't…dislike."

I snorted. "Am I one of them?"

"Most of the time."

"Who else? I never see you hanging out with anyone at school."

"That's because I choose not to hang out with anyone at school."

"You could hang out with me."

"I could not hang out with you."

"You're very resistant to this."

"You're very insistent on this."

"I thought it might be fun to meet each other's friends."

"In no universe would meeting your friends be something I'd constitute as fun."

"Okay. So we start with me meeting your friends."

"I don't have friends."

"That can't be true."

"It is."

"But you told me once that you might meet up with a mate… And there was something about drinking and sex after that…" I frowned, not sure I had it right.

"I did let that one slip," he said, not to me. "He's less of a friend and more of an…acquaintance."

"An acquaintance you spend time with. Presumably a reasonable amount of time?"

Davin scrubbed his hand over the stubble on his jaw and sighed. "He's my cousin. Any time I spend with him is…" He paused.

"Obligatory?" I guessed.

"I was going to say something more along the lines of not for the purposes of spending time with him per se. If you get my drift."

I nodded. I did get his drift. "So he's your pimp?"

Davin spluttered as he sat up. "Uh. No. I pull fine on my own. Thank you."

I crossed my arms and looked at him. "Really?"

"Who was the one begging me to date them?"

I rolled my eyes. "I wasn't desperate to get you into bed."

"Past tense," he said with an almost cocky smirk on his face.

I felt my cheeks heat and I tried not to let my smile show. "Point is. I think it would be good for us to be around people. If they're your people, won't that help the cause?"

His eyebrows furrowed for a moment. "The cause being trash your reputation?"

I nodded. "Yep. Surely they have parties and stuff?"

He sat back again and looked at me like he was thinking it through. "You come to a party with my cousin and his friends?"

I nodded again. "It's perfect." I suddenly thought of something. "They are...like you, right?"

"Desperately seeking solitude and yet destined to be showered in all your...relentless optimism?" he asked dryly.

I huffed. "No. Mysterious and dark and broody and–" I grinned.

"Don't say it!" he warned.

"Byronic!" I said anyway.

He rolled his eyes and muttered, "Why did you let me go along with this?" But I'd stopped wondering who he was talking to at times like that because it was Davin and he did that sort of thing. He looked at me again. "You want to go to a party with my so-called friends?"

"Yes, please."

"That wasn't... I wasn't inviting you. I don't even..." He stopped and seemed to be thinking of something. "Vinny is probably doing something..." he muttered. "Nate and Zac would have a fucking field day..."

Oh, this was exciting. I already had three names of Davin's friends. That was three more than I'd had previously. Which also meant there were at least three of them. Which went to show that maybe he wasn't quite as isolated as he liked to make himself seem at school. Something much like the confidence, or at least willingness to be visible, I'd witnessed the weekend before.

"You could get me drunk!" I said.

Davin looked around quickly, although I had no idea who might be listening to us. "Jesus! Don't say it like that in public. Do you know how that sounds out of context? Fuck."

I gave him my sorry grin. "Oops."

"Yeah. Oops. Until you make those rumours true and I get arrested for...fuck knows what."

"Come on. It's fine. No one's going to care."

He looked at me as though saying he knew I wasn't that stupid. "I assure you that is in no way true."

"My parents loved you. It's been less than twenty-four hours and my dad can't stop talking about you. He thinks you're amazing."

His eyebrow rose, only evidenced by the way his hair shifted a little. "Sorry. What?"

I nodded. "Even Ebony said something nice about you. And she barely ever says nice things about me."

Davin looked unconvinced. "Seriously?"

It was true. Dad had raved about how great Davin was – how he was so intelligent and witty and funny. Ebony had hands down agreed with him. Even Mum had said he seemed like a very nice boy. I was really happy that my family liked him, but I also felt a bit weird about it. Mum and Dad had like Miles too, and that had turned out *so* well.

But they liked Davin...

That was good, right? But why was that? Aside from the obvious 'it made it easier to date him' thing, I could see no reason why I'd be so pleased my family liked him. It wasn't like I was going to fall in love with him or anything.

I nodded, turning my thoughts away from that. "So…a party with your friends…?"

He looked at me for what felt like the longest time. Finally, Davin growled and sighed. "Fine. I'll see what they're doing. I make no promises, though."

"Great." I smiled at him warmly. "This weekend?"

He blinked. "What did I *just* say about promises?"

"Would I have to ask Grace about the Goth thing? Or can I–?"

"Why? Is there a fancy dress party you're planning to irk me with after?"

I frowned at him. "I'd like to try to fit in with your friends."

"Not my friends," he said as he stood up from the seat and dropped onto the corner of the table.

"Obviously not *not* your friends though. It would be nice if they didn't hate me quite so much as you do."

"Don't hate you."

"Anymore." I thought of something. "What about baking something? I make excellent peanut butter and chocolate brownies. Well Ebony loves them and I feel like she's a pretty good judge of food. And not just my food. Plus she's picky as–"

Davin caught my arm gently and spun me to face him, then drew me closer.

"We're not counting this as anything close to a date, but

I've got a lesson for you."

I beamed. "Yeah?"

"Enough with the constant chatter, yeah?"

I blinked. "In what way?"

"In the way that you are constantly on. You're babbling about something as trivial as baking brownies for…a bunch of teenagers who I can promise you will love them but think you're insane to be bringing them."

My head tipped sort of sideways and he sighed.

"Look. Have you noticed those moments when I'm sitting quietly doing nothing?" he asked and I nodded. "Right. And have you noticed that other people can manage to get through more than ten minutes without blurting out the first thing that pops into their heads?" I nodded again. "Okay. So maybe just think about giving that a go."

"Not talking?"

"Not *not* talking. Just some quiet time. Reflection time."

I thought about it. "You mean like on the beach that time where we just sat and watched the water?"

He nodded. "Like that. Did you hate that?"

Usually I hated the quiet, it felt like something was missing. But that hadn't. That had felt…nice. "No. It was nice. Weird, but nice."

He nodded again as he ran his hand up my side. "Okay."

"And that will make me less stupid?" I asked.

His brows furrowed for a moment. "You're quite capable of deeper thought, Avery. You just need to be less busy and let yourself."

"Huh," I breathed. "I guess I could give it a try. Quiet's just always so…"

"Quiet?" he finished and I nodded. "Yeah. It's supposed to be."

I wrapped my arms around his neck, finding him sitting on the table to be a much more convenient height, and told him, "I'll think about it."

"Of course you will," he replied.

Then he kissed me until the bell for lesson three went. And even then we were a little late for class.

****

I gave a cursory stretch as I jogged down the stairs later that afternoon and saw Ebony coming out of the kitchen with a bowl of cereal.

"What are you doing?" she snorted as she looked me over.

"Going for a run."

She nodded knowingly. "Ah. Is it that time of the month where we pretend we're a healthy specimen of humanity?" she asked as she shovelled a spoonful of Milo cereal into her mouth, showing me exactly what she thought of my plan.

"I'm not a completely…unhealthy specimen of humanity…" I said indignantly.

Ebony shrugged. "No. I s'pose not. Is this because of a boy?"

194

"No it's not because of a boy. I just feel...twitchy." As though it emphasised or proved my words, my feet decided on a stationary jog.

"Well I can't tell you to give up the caffeine..." She looked me over like she'd be quite happy to point out every one of my flaws.

But I already had someone to do that for me. I didn't need my little sister jumping on the bandwagon as well. And thinking of Davin reminded me of a good way to distract Ebony.

I frowned at her. "Don't you have a book to read?"

Her frown somewhat brightened and I was reminded that she'd actually smiled at Davin the night before. "So I do," she said as she made her way up the stairs passed me. "Thank your boyfriend for me."

"What? No ridiculous commentary on the idiocy of my social experiment?" I teased her and she threw a wide grin back at me.

"Nah. I kinda like him." She scoffed. "He's so not your type. But somehow you two work..." She frowned in confusion, then shrugged and her and her cereal disappeared up the stairs.

I again rethought the whole my family liking Davin thing. Was my so-called teenage mistake not going to be a mistake after all?

I put my music on and headed out the door, starting out slow but then working my way up to a jog. As I felt my feet hit the pavement I relived the night before. It had gone surprisingly well considering I'd invited the school loner over for dinner with my parents.

Davin was the complete opposite of Miles. When Miles had met my parents he'd been full of warm smiles and nothing but compliments for the entirety of the night. He'd won them over with his effortless charm and both my parents had loved him from the moment he walked in the door.

Davin hadn't had that effect on my parents at all. I'd watched Mum's cautious interest through her excited exterior. I'd seen how unimpressed Dad had been when I'd walked into the room. But then Davin had opened his mouth and had won Dad over with more than just pretty words and an ability to say 'sir'. Davin had won him over with intelligence and nothing but his less than enthusiastic self.

To hear Dad go on about him, you'd think Davin was the smartest person he'd ever met. Knowing Dad, it was just the contradiction of Davin's outsides to Davin's brain. But there was still something weirdly exciting about the fact that my boyfriend had shown my father probably far less respect than he should have and yet Dad hadn't stopped talking about him.

Although, as great as that was for our continued relationship, I wasn't sure how conducive that was to the mission. I was debating again if it a good thing or a bad thing that my parents had warmed to him so quickly. And Ebony? I was pretty sure she idolised him. I was pretty sure she'd decided she was going to be Davin when she grew up. One look at her face while he was talking about sexual…something, something in those books had been enough to tell me that.

I slowed to a stop as I wondered if this was me doing it again.

Was this me focussing on those ridiculously trivial things instead of having quiet time? Was running even supposed to be quiet time? Runners in movies always went on about how calming it was, how it was the time they cleared their heads.

Part of me was somewhat inclined to think that clearing my head would be further proof of my idiocy to the wider population. But this was the bad boy's guide to being not good, after all. If Davin thought I could do with some quiet time, then I was going to give it a shot.

I turned my music down so it wasn't blasting in my ears and took a deep breath. The streets were relatively quiet outside the soft tones of the song. There was a lawn mower running nearby and a door closing. But otherwise it was your typical street in the eastern suburbs of Adelaide with very few people around on a Wednesday afternoon in early March.

"Are you all right, dear?"

I looked around and saw an older woman getting into her car in the driveway I'd stopped in front of. I smiled at her

"Yes. Fine. Sorry."

She smiled back at me, but it did look a little bit like she was worried about my sanity. I gave her a friendly wave and jogged off, trying out this new quiet time idea.

Trying not to think of anything was quite possibly the worst way to not think of something. Snippets of random bits of thought floated into my head one after the other as I tried to shut them out.

What was an idea for the formal theme that hadn't been done to death in every movie, book or TV show in history?

Was it really stupid to make brownies for Davin's friends?

Would Davin and I go to the formal together?

Did Miles ever regret dumping me for Cindy? For that matter, did he ever regret cheating on me in the first place?

What was Davin like in bed? Like in bed…

Should I ask him about actually helping me with Maths if he was so into it? God knew I could use the help.

I should probably call Blair and ask her–

I came to a thundering stop as I realised it wasn't working. My brain had zero interest in quiet time. I put my hands on my hips and took a deep breath.

"Quiet time. I can do quiet time," I said to myself. "Quiet time's not that hard, surely. You're turning into Davin – talking to people who aren't there…"

I took another breath and tried to find that feeling I'd had on the beach beside Davin.

I hadn't thought much of it at the time, but that had been an oddly thought-free, calm moment. I closed my eyes for a second and thought back to that date, trying not to get caught up in the making out portion of that date.

Because Davin kissed like…

I wrenched my eyes opened and tried again.

As I kept running, I breathed deeply and tried to focus on the feeling of sitting with him on the beach and just watching the waves tumble in and out along the sand. I remembered the slight breeze on my face, the smell of the salty air and I felt my heart rate evening out as well as it could mid-exercise.

And my brain just…stopped.

Not literally, obviously. Or I would have fallen flat on my face for a pavement facial.

But my mind quieted and the only thing that ran through it was the song in my ears, the thud of my feet on the footpath, and the rhythm of my breathing. And it was…peaceful.

I wasn't sure how it was supposed to make me seem less stupid to everyone else, but I did like it. I usually felt more antsy when I wasn't keeping busy, but this was nothing like that at all. It was absolutely…

Oh…I'd ruined it.

I slowed and took a deep breath, figuring I had plenty of time to practise.

Fourteen: Davin

I couldn't believe Avery had talked me into taking her to Vinny's. And for his birthday no less, which meant it was going to be big and busy and loud. Well big and busy and loud compared to our usual. Still that might let us melt a little into obscurity.

Vinny couldn't wait to meet her because he was under the misguided assumption that he could steal Avery away from me. Zac and Nate were just looking forward to meeting the girl that had finally made me settle down – like I was some guy in his mid-thirties who'd spent years whoring around and had finally met my match or some bullshit. And I'd avoided listening to anything Lara had had to say on the matter.

I'd organised with Nate to pick me and then Avery up. Which was potentially a terrible idea in hindsight. But by the time we were both walking up her front path, it was far too late to do anything about it and hindsight could fucking bite me.

I rang Avery's doorbell and threw one more look at Nate, warning him to behave himself. "I don't know why you didn't stay in the car," I muttered.

"Davin!" Phil cried as he opened the door. "How are you?"

I nodded. "Fine. Thanks."

"What did you end up choosing?"

For a moment I forgot what he was talking about. "Uh...I took the easy route and went with *Bleak House*."

Phil nodded as he stepped aside to let us in. "Excellent choice. This is Nate?"

I pointed at my cousin. "It is. Nate, Avery's dad Phil. Phil, my cousin Nate."

Phil stuck his hand out, "Nice to meet you, Nate," and Nate shook it.

"You too," Nate said and I wasn't sure if he was trying his damnedest not to laugh in the face of the farce I'd fallen into or if he was legitimately surprised at how nice Phil was being.

"Sorry. Sorry!" I heard Avery say and looked up to see her basically skipping down the stairs. "I'm here and I'm ready." She grinned at Nate. "Hi."

Avery had put on this pink pleated skirt with a cropped, ribbed white singlet that was, for her, reserved but was still going to make her stand out among Nate's friends. Don't get me wrong, I was all for her being herself, and the easy access didn't hurt either. But I'd be lying if I said I didn't feel a little apprehensive about introducing Avery to everyone. Or about everyone meeting Avery. I wasn't sure if I was worried they'd corrupt her or she'd corrupt them.

Based on the look on Nate's face, it was going to be the latter. I elbowed him and he cleared his throat.

"Uh, hi."

"Thanks for picking me up."

He shook his head. "No worries at all. You ready?"

She nodded and grabbed a bag from next to the hall table. "All good to go."

I held my hand out expectantly and she passed me her bag with one of those wry smiles.

"I'll drop her back tomorrow, Phil," I said with a nod to him.

"Sounds good. You lot have a good night."

"We will. Night, Dad!" Avery sang as she picked another smaller bag off the table and headed outside.

"Night, then," I said.

"Night, boys," Phil called and shut the door behind us.

"So…he just lets *you* take his daughter, knowing full well she's staying over at your place tonight?" Nate hissed at me as we followed Avery to the car.

"Yep."

"And he just let her stay over last weekend even though they knew Uncle Don wasn't home?"

"Yep." I nodded. *"Convenient, huh?"* I ask you.

"Wow. And where do I find myself one of these manic pixie dream girls?" Nate asked as we came up to Avery at the car.

"Fuck off," I muttered. *"We are not doing that, okay?"*

I was going to have to admit – only in the privacy of my own mind – that I was fairly stereotypical Byronic. But Avery wasn't just some manic pixie dream joke. For starters, she wasn't teaching me jack shit. I was not going to learn to embrace life or its infinite mysteries or adventures. I would rather relive my mother's final moments than accept that Avery St John was just another manic pixie dream girl with zero added depth.

"Dav?" Nate nudged me. "You right?"

I cleared my throat. "Sure." Because starting out the night you introduce your insanely optimistic girlfriend to your cousin's rather more pessimistic friends by thinking of your mother's death was the perfect plan by any stretch of the imagination.

Nate unlocked the car and I put Avery and her bag in the backseat. And as soon as Nate and I had our doors closed, she was talking and it was obvious that my free lesson hadn't sunk in.

"So, whose party are we going to?" she asked, her voice more chipper and happy than I thought I'd heard it in a while.

Surely she wasn't actually that excited about going to this party? Why the hell would she be so excited about this? Unless of course she was forcing it to cover anxiety?

I almost turned to check on her.

"It's Vinny's birthday," Nate told her when I didn't reply.

"Did he go to Mitchell, too? Was he in your year?"

I felt Nate throw me a look, but I stared stoically out the

window and pretended that the current events weren't happening.

"He was," Nate said.

"You were…two years ahead of us?"

"Naw," Nate cooed and I heard Avery giggle. "You remember me?"

"Sort of. I don't think we ever talked or anything."

I tuned out to whatever they insisted on talking about as we drove to Vinny's dad's place – the dad who felt guilty for leaving his mum so Vinny got free reign there. When we got there, we left Avery's bigger bag in the car and I took her hand possessively as we walked to the front door, which was weirdly out of character on my part. The music was already audible from the street. It wasn't vibrating us out of our skin or anything, but I knew it would be pretty difficult to hold a conversation at a normal timbre once we got inside.

Nate opened the door and Avery looked at me in surprise.

"Oh, yeah," I said lazily as I kept a firm grip on her hand. "Degenerates don't lock their doors."

She looked around as though it was new to her. I found that very hard to believe. But then maybe the cool kids just sat around and played Scrabble at their parties or something.

"It's the same," she said, almost like she was disappointed.

"There you go."

"What?"

"Nothing," I told her as we headed down the hallway.

"Hi, Mr Duncan," Nate called as we passed the sitting room.

Vinny's dad looked over at us with a smile. "Hi, boys. Head on through. You know the drill."

Nate nodded like he was an awful lot cooler than he actually was and we continued on down the hall until we got to the back room where all of Vinny's parties were held.

"Nathan!" Vinny called as he saw us and started threading his was through the people.

By all accounts, it wasn't his biggest party. But he liked to keep everyone as squashed into one room as possible, with any overflow heading outside, so it felt in his words cosier. I gagged every time I thought about it.

"Vincent!" Nate called back as Vinny met up with us and they hugged.

After Nate finally let him go, Vinny turned to us and gave Avery the cockiest half-smile I'd ever seen on the little fucker's face.

"And this must be the gorgeous Avery," he said and I rolled my eyes at him.

Avery chuckled. "Now I know you didn't get that off Davin." She spared me a half-glance. "He wouldn't dare call me gorgeous."

"He might not. But I wouldn't make the same mistake." Vinny oozed about as much charm as a pile of fetid flesh. But Avery was smiling and giggling like she was totally falling for it.

"That's very sweet," she said coyly as she wrapped her other hand around my arm.

"Vinny here's got delusions you'll realise you're with the wrong man," Nate said and I'm adamant I didn't growl at him. Because human beings didn't actually do that.

"Will I now?" Avery asked.

Vinny nodded. "We can all be as broody as Dav here. But," he winked, "we're a fuck load more fun too."

Avery's smile would have lit up the room had I been so ridiculous as to think such a thing. "I think Davin would say I'm fun enough for the both of us."

"You wouldn't be wrong," I grumbled.

Vinny sniggered. "Let's get you a drink."

Nate and Vinny followed the way to the drinks table and set about getting beers for all. Nate took his and dropped onto the couch beside Ash, putting his arm around her as she put her leg over his.

"Don't forget Avery's beer," he said, pointing at Vinny.

Avery bounced on her toes. "Yes, please. No more Miss Goody-Two-Shoes. I'm getting drunk."

Ash laughed. "I think I like her, Dav."

"Avery?" I heard Nova and I looked up to see her walking in from the hallway.

"Hi!" Avery said with her trademark wide smile.

"Hey!" Nate cried, totally oblivious to the glare Nova was sending him. "You know her?"

Nova looked around with a derision that made me jealous.

"Of course I know her. She's best friends with my sister."

"It's Grace," Avery said like it made total sense. "Remember. She's into the whole Goth thing."

"Wait. What?" I blinked. "Grace? Wait. Grace, Grace?"

"Say my name one more time, Davin," Nova dared me, her eyes narrowing.

"I thought you were Nova?"

"Nova comes from Donovan," she said nonchalantly, looking around.

"Donovan's her last name," Avery said helpfully.

I looked at Nova. "But your real name is…Grace?"

Nova looked at me and shrugged. "Yeah. What of it?"

I shrugged, knowing better than to cross Nova. Something Nate could learn a thing or two about if he didn't want to lose her for good. "No. Nothing."

"You're right nothing." Nova turned to Avery. "What are you doing here?"

"I'm…" Avery pointed at me as she finished swallowing her mouthful of beer, "Davin's girlfriend. I thought it would be nice to meet his friends."

Avery seemed not at all concerned that her best friend's older sister was at my cousin's party. But I suppose she thought it made sense since she'd know they were in the same year at school.

Nova scoffed. "Dav doesn't do friends, Ave. And he doesn't do girlfriends." There was a touch of sympathy in her voice and she frowned at me. "It runs in the family. Behave.

207

You get me if these arseholes give you trouble."

"Nova, come on!" I said as she walked away.

"What did she mean by it runs in the family?"

I took Avery's arms and made her look at me. "Yes. I didn't used to...do girlfriends. But for you I'll do girlfriends, babe." I paused and winced at my choice of words "A girlfriend. I'll do *a* girlfriend. You. I'll do you..."

I stopped because she was giggling at me. I still didn't care for it in the traditional sense, but I was getting used to it. I actually wasn't sure what was worse, that I was becoming used to her inanity through mere exposure or that it tried to distract me with other things we could be doing.

"What?" I asked, focussing on the fact she was laughing at me to take my mind off the idea of other things.

She shook her head. "Um... I was actually more thinking..." She bit her lip like she was trying to get her laughter under control. "Is Grace sweet on Nate?"

I looked over her head to where Nate had his arm around Ash and sighed. "I think Nova's as...sweet on Nate as she could be sweet on anyone." Who called it being sweet on someone anymore?

"And he doesn't like her back or he's just a butthead?"

I looked back at her. "Pretty sure it's the butthead one."

Avery was smiling at me, full warm and open. Those blue eyes shone brightly as they looked at me carefully. It was as though it wasn't just our conversation that made her smile but something else she was looking at. Given she was looking at me, I couldn't have begun to imagine what that was.

Finally she sighed. "No wonder she's in such a bad mood all the time."

"Nova?" I scoffed and she nodded. "You think Nova's...Nova because Nate's a fucking idiot?"

Avery nodded as she turned to look at Nate. "If I really liked someone and he didn't notice, I think I'd want to wear black and yell at everyone too."

I actually didn't believe it. I refused to believe that there was a situation in all of the world where Avery would choose to wear black and yell at anyone. Even after whatever we were doing here, I couldn't see any future where that happened. For fuck's sake, her first real boyfriend had cheated on then dumped her and the gnat of positivity had put her singular focus to exceptional use by inducing me to date her to trash her image. Whether she saw it or not, she was the kind of person who thrived to spite adversity. She wasn't the sort to wallow with us at the bottom of the muck. I just had to find some way to show her that.

But Vinny's party wasn't going to be the place for that. As much as I was supposed to be teaching her how to be not good, the only thing I succeeded in doing was getting us both drunk. Although it took me a hell of a lot more imbibing that it took her – thank fuck she drank slower than me.

I'll give you the basic rundown of the majority of the night and let you fill in the blanks with your imagination.

"After all, I'm sure you'll be far better at it than me."

Avery was noticeable no matter where she was the whole night. She was somehow one of the shortest people in the room and yet you couldn't miss her. It was like she'd become a literal beacon so I could always find her and keep an eye on her.

She talked to almost everyone and, despite the fact that I had known all these people to laugh at Avery's kind in the school yard, they all took to her. Some of them took longer than others. But when she hit a bit of a roadblock, she just had some more to drink and persevered. She made people smile I'd never seen smile before. Half the time I lost sight of her, I heard her laughing with someone else before I had time to worry about what she'd got herself into.

I watched her listen avidly to stories that Beau and Zac told about the time they'd 'borrowed' the Coles trolley and ridden it down the hill to race the wheelie bin Nate was riding. She asked Ash and Liv where they got their clothes from as though she was legitimately looking for fashion advice and I saw Freya actually send her something I later found out to be a link to whatever makeup tutorial they'd been discussing.

Everything Avery did, everyone she talked to, she looked a half a heartbeat away from clapping her hands in pure joy. It did not suit the dim, grungy feel of the place whatsoever and still she seemed to be having the time of her life. I didn't understand it. There wasn't even a muttering of mockery behind her back. No one called me out on the great joke I'd sprung on her like the time Vinny had brought a similar girl to one of these. It made no fucking sense.

It was typical Avery, but on steroids. She talked at twice her normal rate, laughed at least twice as loud, and she whirled around the room with more optimistic outlook than I think I'd ever seen on her. Except for the few times I caught her eye and there was something else there.

"I'm starting to think she's definitely overcompensating for something."

As these things inevitably unfold, we get to sometime later which finds a few of us sitting down, drinking beer and just talking.

"So," Lara said as she dropped beside Avery on the couch and I kept a watchful eye on them. "Riddle me this, Goody-Two-Shoes? Why is it guys get weirded out if you touch yourself when the girls in pornos are doing it like all the time?"

I nearly choked on my beer as Avery replied completely innocently and thoughtfully, "I actually couldn't tell you. I wasn't aware of either of those things."

"Really?" Lara asked, throwing a look to me and I glared at her.

"Davin?" Avery said as she looked over at me.

The innocence on her face hit me. Until I saw that look in her eyes. "Yes, Avery?" I asked warily.

"What do you think?"

"About what?" I asked her, very aware that there were a

fuck tonne of eyes on me all of a sudden.

Avery leant forward, leaning her elbows on her knees as her eyes ran over me questioningly. "If I touched myself, would you get weirded out?"

Well that all depended, didn't it. That all depended on us having sex in the first place. And that depended on whether I walked away after or not. I wasn't nearly energetic enough to be a one and done type – all that meeting new people and needing to be charming all the time just seemed like too much effort. But it wasn't like I usually hung around after the deed was complete.

With Avery I wouldn't be able to walk away.

I was just yet to determine if that's because she wouldn't let me or I wouldn't let myself.

"You know what, babe?" I said smoothly, flicking my hair out of my eyes. "Either I'm not getting the job done or you just want to? Have at it." I gave her a wink as I drained the rest of my beer.

Lara looked at me pointedly. "It wouldn't bother you? You wouldn't feel *inferior*?"

I shrugged, knowing exactly the game Lara was playing and wishing I'd never set Avery or myself up for it. "No. Why would it?" I put my empty bottle on the table next to me and stood up. "I'm into whatever gets her off." I walked over and held my hand out to Avery. "And you know that, Lara."

Avery's beer-saturated brain seemed to be trying to piece things together, but she took my hand and I pulled her away before Lara could say anything more. As I found us a quiet corner – all right, bathroom – and closed the door, Avery burst into giggles. It was obvious I'd succeeded in the date's lesson because those giggles were a lot less put together and more spluttery than her usual.

"You okay?" I asked her. "You've been acting like you're on speed all night."

She nodded, but nothing about that made me change my diagnosis. "Yeah. No. I'm fine." She giggled but it didn't sound quite as jovial as usual. "No. I'm good. Why?"

"I just… Something's off."

She frowned a little like she was having trouble thinking. "No. I just… I want your friends to like me."

My breath caught and I coughed to cover that. "I appreciate that, babe. But remember how we talked about some reflection time?"

"I've been trying that whole quiet time thing. I've been running and…I'm not really sure it's working though."

I had no idea what she was talking about. "What? Running? Why?"

She shrugged. "I kind of like it. I mean I only did it once. But I wasn't sure how else to have quiet time."

I still didn't know what she was talking about. "Is this the thing we talked about the other day?"

She nodded. "Yeah. You said I needed less talking."

I was feeling like maybe I hadn't been as articulate as I'd intended. "I only meant that maybe take a breath before you

213

open your mouth, babe. Like just give yourself a second to think about what you're saying instead of just blurting it out…"

"Huh?" she looked up at me in confusion.

"Well…" I thought how best to explain it since I'd obviously done a piss-poor job before. "You don't have to fill every silence. Silence is okay. I was just saying you should take a breath before you open your mouth. I didn't mean… Running?"

She pursed her lips and wrinkled her nose while she thought. "But I kind of like it. I think."

"Jesus. Why?" I huffed.

She shrugged again. "I dunno. Being quiet is kinda nice. Even if it's not what you meant."

"Okay. Well mindfulness is a great skill. But no. That wasn't what I was trying to get you to do."

"So…you want me to take a breath before I talk?"

I nodded. "Yes. If you have a thought, just take a deep breath and see if you still feel like blurting it out."

"And if I do?"

"Then go for it, babe."

She smiled. "Awesome."

I coughed to cover the laugh I didn't almost huff. "So… Uh, sorry about Lara before…"

She looked at me for a second, her eyes calculating. Until…

"Ohmigod!" she squealed as her hands flew to her mouth.

"You and Lara?"

I gently tugged her hands from her mouth and rolled my eyes. "Yes."

Avery looked at me closely, almost like she was having trouble seeing. But surely she wasn't *that* drunk? It was her first time drunk, but I didn't think she'd had that many…

"She's jealous. Of me." Avery pulled back and blinked. "No one's ever been jealous of me before."

"You don't know that," I told her. I also found that very hard to believe.

She nodded in that very sure way that drunk people have. "I do know that. Even Cindy Porter wasn't jealous of me. She just took Miles out from under me."

I felt a niggling twinge in my chest and I swallowed. "Babe…I'm sure–"

She huffed and waved a hand. "You know, I thought I cared. Then I thought I didn't care. But then…then I just realised that I cared the way you do when someone else gets the last pair of neon green pumps in your size at the Myers sale. It wasn't Miles I felt bad about losing. I can't actually remember a single real thing about him I liked. I just felt stupid I'd wasted my time on him and especially after I'd let him get away with cheating on me! Why did I do that?"

She looked up at me and I felt it in a place I didn't know I had. She wasn't upset, she wasn't angry, she was just confused and annoyed. I ran my fingers along her hairline and a small smile lit her face, utterly transforming it.

215

"I don't know," I told her. "But you deserved better."

She nodded. "I did, didn't I?" Her smile became more crooked and she seemed to search my face for something. "But you…"

Oh fuck. "But me, what?"

"I know why I like you."

That was unexpected. "I'm sure you knew why you liked Miles at the time as well," I replied stiltedly.

She scrunched her face up like she was thinking. "I'll tell you what I would have told you a few months ago if you'd asked me why I liked Miles."

"Be still my beating heart," I droned. "I can't wait."

She giggled. "No–"

"Are you sure you don't want to try that big breath before speaking thing now?"

Her smile did not warm me up inside. "I would have told you because he was hot, he was popular, he was good at sport, and we were going to be voted best couple again this year."

"Aren't you pleased we got ourselves into this?" I ask you.

"Sh." She batted me gently. "You, though. I like you. I like you because you make me laugh. You actually listen to me even though I know you hate it. You're interesting in one of those fascinatingly morbid sort of ways. You don't pretend…anything with me. You don't pretend I look nice. You don't pretend to like my friends. You don't pretend to be someone you're not so my parents will like you. But then

216

they like you anyway…"

Maybe having her blurt out what was on her mind wasn't the worst thing in the world?

"I think we should get you some water," I told her softly, refusing to acknowledge my heart fluttered a little in my chest or that my stomach flip-flopped a bit.

She shook her head. "No. I'm okay. I think. I just feel chatty. Is that normal? I'm meant to be doing the breathing thing. Or is this just drunk? Is that what drunk does?"

I was not just about to smile. "Yeah. That's what drunk does, babe."

She grinned up at me. "So we should get you drunk!"

I coughed and it wasn't to hide a laugh. "I think you'll find I'm adequately south of sober."

"So why aren't you chatty?" Her frown was actually sort of cute.

"Eleven years of denying I have emotions," I said, then realised maybe I was a little chattier than usual.

She blinked at me. "What?"

I lifted her up onto the vanity behind her and shook my head once. "Nothing."

And this time I didn't just kiss her to shut her up. Even I couldn't pretend I did. I didn't know why else I'd kiss her. I just knew that I wanted – needed – to be close to her.

Nothing had changed from our first date. All her colour and happiness still annoyed me to no end. But I was done telling you or me that I hated being around her. There was still that same weirdly addictive thing about her that I still hadn't put my finger on. I was in no way going to start enjoying or appreciating life – you couldn't pay me with all the first editions in the world to do that – but I didn't want her to stop wanting me.

And even if I had any idea how to tell her that, I wouldn't. So I just kissed her instead.

Fifteen: Avery

"How big even are your feet?" I giggled.

"What?" he asked as he opened the front door and shushed me inside.

"You shoes are huge. I could totally use one as a ski."

"You could not use one as a ski."

"I could."

"Even your feet aren't that tiny."

"They're pretty tiny. I can buy kid's shoes you–"

"Davin?" came a voice I didn't know.

I pulled up short and Davin walked into the back of me. There was someone standing in the semi-dark hallway in what looked like a dressing gown.

"Dad." Davin cleared his throat. "I didn't think you'd still be up. Did we wake you?"

He shook his head. "No. I'm just on my way back to bed. Have a good night?"

I felt like there was a very obvious elephant in the room and that elephant was me.

"Yeah…" Davin started. "Yeah, it was… Uh. This is

Avery." Davin put his hand on my arm.

"Hi, Mr Ambrose. It's lovely to meet you," I said, pretty sure I'd nailed the whole sounding totally sober thing.

"Please call me Don," he said and I heard the smile in his voice that suggested maybe I didn't sound as sober as I thought I did. "It's very nice to meet you too, Avery. You kids have a good rest of your night. But not too good."

"Oh, no," I laughed. "I'm trying to not be too good."

"Avery," Davin hissed as Don chuckled.

"All right then. Well I'll see you both tomorrow sometime."

"Yep. Night, then."

"Night, Don," I called as he turned and headed to presumably his room.

"Okay, Miss Not-Too-Good. Let's get you into my room."

I snorted. "Oh, you do know how to charm a girl."

Davin muttered too low under his breath for me to hear as he steered me to his room and I threw myself backwards onto his bed. His bed was soft. I liked it.

"Make yourself at home," he said sardonically.

"Thanks. I have."

"For all that's…" he grunted. "Okay. Water for you."

I sat up quickly and didn't even feel dizzy. "I'm fine."

"And you'll be better with water. Go nowhere. I'll be back," he said pointing his finger at me like he actually expected me to probably go exploring his house in the dead of night with his dad home.

I snorted at the thought.

"What now?" he asked, pausing in the doorway.

"Your dad's home. I forgot your dad was going to be home."

"He is. You can meet him properly in the morning."

"Do you think he liked me?"

Davin had been about to walk out again and paused. "I don't see how he couldn't, babe," he said softly then hurried out.

I grinned to myself and decided now was a brilliant time to get into my pyjamas. I shuffled to the end of Davin's bed and grabbed my bag off the floor where Davin had dropped it. As I pulled off my singlet, I noticed that one of Davin's Converses was lying just out of reach. I threw myself off the bed and picked it up.

"What are you doing?" Davin asked.

I brandished his shoe at him. "Seeing what size your feet are."

He rolled his eyes. "And what did that tell you?"

I looked at the sole of it. "Twelve. Is that normal?"

"What do you consider normal?"

I looked up at him from my position on the floor. "Average?"

He held his arms out, a glass of water in each hand. "What about me says average, Avery?" he asked. "I'm not yet eighteen and already over six foot."

"You do look very tall from down here."

He sighed, put the glasses down and held his hands out to me. "Why is your top off anyway?"

I looked down. "Oh. I was getting changed."

"I'll give you some privacy."

I laughed. "Nearly thirteen years of changing with the other girls at school, I think I can manage without you seeing whatever it is you think you're not supposed to see."

His eyebrow rose slightly. "Of course you can."

I grinned and went to my bag to pull out my nightie. I pulled it on, pulled the old 'thread the bra straps through the sleeves' trick, kicked off my heels, and pulled off my skirt. "Ta-da."

"Ta-da indeed," he said simply, but I was almost sure there was the tiniest of twitches in the corner of his mouth. "Mine is slightly less impressive."

He pulled his button up and t-shirt off in one smooth motion before dumping them in the corner of the room. I don't actually remember what happened after that because the boy had been hiding a mighty fine body underneath all those loose-fitting tops. He was a touch on the lanky side, but most of that was due to the fact he was just unrealistically tall. But his muscles were defined. I'm talking 'I understood the concept of wanting to lick it' defined.

My eyes didn't seem to know if they wanted to stare at his abs or check his face to make sure those abs were actually attached to Davin and I hadn't inadvertently ended up in someone else's bedroom.

"Are you having some kind of fit?" he asked and I stopped freaking out long enough to notice he was now wearing nothing but a baggy pair of tracksuit pants.

"I don't think so."

He looked mildly pleased. "Good."

I walked over to him and pushed his hair out of his face.

"What are you doing now?" he asked as he pulled his head out of my reach and took hold of my wrists.

I looked him over and nodded. "Yep."

"Yep, what?" he asked, bringing his face into my view for a moment.

"You're hot."

Davin looked as unimpressed as I'd expected him to look. "Uh huh."

"No. I mean it, you're hot."

"Avery," he started as he picked me up and put my legs around his waist, "it may shock you to learn this, but not everyone cares about being attractive."

"Objectively maybe," I said as I wrapped my arms around his neck. "But don't you want someone to find you attractive?"

"I'd like to think sincere attraction is based on more than just the physical alignment of one's features," he commented dryly.

I huffed a rough laugh. "Tell me you find more about me attractive than the physical alignment of my features," I teased.

"If we were going solely based on your physical features, I'm not sure I could stand you."

"Well aren't you pleasant," I laughed.

He rolled his eyes. "I more meant that you cover yourself in such gaiety that I would never have bothered looking at you twice."

"So why is it you did look at me twice?"

"Because you have this look in your eyes that makes me very interested in what's going on in that mind of yours."

"Plenty of people would tell you there's not a whole heck of a lot."

He nodded. "Plenty of people would be wrong, Avery."

He kissed me hard and I pressed myself into him, feeling a happy little flutter in my chest. I was under no delusions that Davin Ambrose was falling in love with me. But it was just possible that he was going to get something positive out of this as well. Could it be that the self-professed Lord of Malcontent would find himself a little less closed off after all?

That or he was so keen on getting me into bed that he was willing to pull out any even remotely corny line it took.

But when we fell onto his bed and he tucked us under the covers, he didn't try anything else. We kissed, we touched, we explored the same way we'd done before. The only difference this time was that we were properly in bed. But neither of us seemed in any rush to move it onto the next level. I didn't know if I was giving off the not ready yet vibes

224

or if he wasn't quite as interested in me as he'd made it seem so far.

I fell asleep quite contentedly and far more comfortable than the previous time and woke up with his arm over my waist.

I grinned at I looked at his hand, feeling rather pleased about something. Until I realised I had a really sore head and my tummy didn't feel so great.

Davin had made me drink plenty of water before we went to sleep, promising me that it would help stave off a hangover. Although all it seemed to do was make me need to pee about four times before I actually fell asleep.

I watched Davin's hand twitch in his sleep, barely discernible in the very little light getting around his curtains. I ran my fingers over the cord of thread he always wore on his wrist, over his hand and traced the silver ring he wore on his middle finger.

I felt him shake his head and mumble something, then his arm tightened over me like he was stretching before his hand ran lazily over my hip as I felt his lips on my shoulder.

"How are you feeling?" he asked and I stamped down any excitement the gravelly tones of his 'I've just woken up' voice gave me.

"A little…" I wasn't sure what word described it.

"Seedy?" he offered.

"Seedy?"

I felt him nod against me as he seemed to snuggle into me

like he had no plans to get up any time soon. "Yep. Mild hangover. Little risk of actual vomiting, but you'll feel like it for a while."

"Yep. That sounds like it."

"Ah, you'll be right, babe," he said, sounding like he was falling asleep again.

"You going back to sleep?"

"Do we need to be anywhere?" he asked.

"Well, no…"

He grunted. "What's the time?"

"You can't look?"

"Nope."

I smiled as I reached for my phone on his bedside table. "About ten to twelve."

"Will not getting up until midday kill you?" he muttered.

"No. I suppose it won't."

"Excellent."

He pulled my back tighter against his front and I felt his breath steadying as he fell asleep again. I lay there for a little while, just enjoying the idea of waking up with my boyfriend like that.

"Woah."

I sat up suddenly and Davin yelled in surprise.

"What's wrong?" he mumbled quickly.

I shook my head. "Uh, nothing."

"Freak me out why not," he said, rolling onto his back and rubbing his hand over his face.

"Sorry."

"Nah, it's fine." He sat up resignedly and breathed out. "I need coffee."

I watched him get out of bed, telling me heart to return to normal. Because I couldn't afford to think about how nice it was waking up next to Davin. Could I?

"Avery?"

I looked up. "Yeah?"

"You…want a cup of tea or anything?"

I nodded. "Yeah. That would be great, thanks."

He nodded as well and I was pretty sure he could tell something wasn't quite right. "Okay. I'll meet you in the kitchen?"

"Yep. Be there in a minute."

"Okay. Good."

He walked out slowly and I took a deep breath before I got up.

"You don't like *like* him, do you?" I mumbled to myself as I pulled my track pants on under my nightie.

"No. Of course not," I chuckled awkwardly in reply as I pulled my hair into a wayward bun as best I could with my fingers and no mirror.

I huffed another breath and walked into the kitchen.

"…me at the appointment with Dr Mills?" Davin's dad was asking.

"No. She said she wanted to see you. But you don't need to come in while I'm discussing the darkest parts of my soul or whatever bullshit we're calling it," he answered quickly.

"Davin, the therapy helps. You know–"

Davin dropped the mug he was holding as he turned and saw me standing in the doorway. I opened my mouth, then snapped it shut at the look on Davin's face. It was pure fury mixed with something I'd never seen on Davin's face. It was fear.

"Shit, Dav," his dad said. "You okay?"

Davin nodded vaguely, his eyes not leaving me.

"Uh. Sorry…" I said, pointing in all sorts of directions like that made sense. "I was just… Uh…"

I pressed my lips together, thinking now was as good a time as any to start with that breathing before talking thing.

"Uh," Davin's dad started. "No, Avery. It's fine. Come on in and sit. I'll…uh…" He looked between me and Davin like he didn't know what to do.

"I'll get the broom," Davin said through clenched teeth before he picked his way carefully into the laundry.

"I'm so sorry, Mr Ambrose… Don," I amended quickly. "I didn't mean to…"

Don shook his head. "It's not you. It's just… Davin's very protective of his past. He doesn't like to talk–"

"Fuck's sake, Dad!" Davin snapped as he came back in, emanating more than fury.

"Dav, I was just–"

"Well, don't! No. We're not…" Davin huffed. "Fuck! No."

Don nodded slowly. "I'll, uh, give you some space."

Davin nodded back. "Okay. Thanks."

Don smiled at me and walked out. I just sort of hovered as Davin started picking up the broken bits of mug.

"Can I–"

"No, Avery," he snapped. "You can't do anything. There's nothing to talk about!"

I swallowed and nodded. "Okay. But I was going to ask if I can get the coffee going or something…"

He stopped what he was doing and looked at me, his expression seemed caught between exasperated and surprised. "What?"

I took a pointed deep breath. "Can I do the coffee or anything?"

He opened his mouth, then closed it again. "Uh. No. Thanks. It's fine."

I nodded again before walking further into the kitchen and pulling myself up onto the barstool. I was desperate to talk, to fill the silence. But quite aside from the fact I was supposed to be learning to let silence be, I knew how Davin in particular felt about inane chatter. So I said nothing.

Once he was done tidying up, he paused as he walked past me to kiss my hair, then got on with the drinks. I looked down to hide my smile, feeling like maybe I was getting the hang of this whole thing after all.

****

The next week, I was wandering around looking for Davin in my free lesson in a huff.

We hadn't talked about anything his dad had said and, while I was curious about what it had all been about, I also respected his privacy and the fact that Davin Ambrose wasn't known for sharing his feelings. If he even had them.

But I didn't want him to share his feelings with me now. I needed a lesson.

"There you are," I said as I walked into the meeting room.

He looked up at me and pulled his headphones off.

I blinked in surprise. "You heard me?"

"I felt my blood sugar spike. I assumed that meant you'd walked in the room."

I huffed a semi-sarcastic laugh at him. "Lesson. Stat."

He frowned. "Lesson? You've got a free now."

I rolled my eyes. "We won't mention that you're meant to be in class–"

"You just did."

"No. I need a lesson. Like a 'being not good' lesson."

"Now?"

I nodded.

"Why? What's happened?" he asked, leaning forward like he was half entertaining the notion of going to defend my honour or something.

"Ebony's had a…run in with a boy in PE."

"A run in with a boy in PE?" he clarified and I nodded.

230

"Yes."

"And how do you know this?"

I looked around a little guiltily. "Because she was having a rant at me by text."

"About a boy?"

I waved away his questions. "Yes. She talks to me about boys. Especially the ones she wants to mangle. She's very fond of…mangling. Now what do I do?"

"To what? Stand up to a boy for Ebs?"

I nodded. "Yeah. I guess."

He leant back in his chair and crossed his arms. "He's Year Nine?"

"Duh."

"Easy. You go up to him and you tell him to back off your little sister."

"That might work for you, gargantuan. But some of us are smaller than most of the Year Eights."

He looked me over and conceded that one. "True. What's the problem?"

"They're swimming and she's…not able to swim today due to…" I slowed to a stop.

"She's on her period?" he said simply.

I blinked in surprise. "Uh. Yes. You just…you just come right out and say that, do you?"

"Is that not what it's called?"

I nodded. "Um. Yeah. It is."

"So why would I call it anything else?"

231

That was a good question. "I don't know. Look, this boy is going to tease her mercilessly. Can you help or not?"

"I *can*."

"Ugh! Will you?"

He leant forward again, putting his elbows on the table and looking me over with a very thoughtful expression.

"What?" I asked him.

"Well, I do have one idea."

"Okay. Give it."

He shook his head slowly as he sat back again. "I don't know if you're ready for it."

"I'm so ready."

"I don't know if I want to impart it."

"Davin!"

He huffed that almost laugh and unfolded himself from the chair. "Look, what better way to get Ebony out of class than to get everyone out of class?"

"What?"

"I don't know how I feel using my powers for good instead of evil, but sometimes the ends justify the means."

"What are you on about?" I demanded and his eyebrow quirked.

"Keep your panties on." He pointed to his laptop. "Lesson. I'm going to teach you to set off the fire alarm."

"What? No! I can't..." I looked around in case anyone might have heard him.

"You can and you will."

"Davin, that's bad."

He nodded. "It's not good, that's for sure. But if you do something bad for a good reason, is it really so bad?"

"Yes!"

"Is it?"

"Davin–"

"I wouldn't impart this for just anyone, Avery. But since it's you… And Ebony… I feel moved to make an exception."

I bit my lip as I looked around. "I'm not sure…"

"If this guy teases Ebony, what's she going to do?"

I felt my eyes widen as I realised this was bigger than just Ebony being teased by a stupid boy. If he teased her, she was likely to hit him. And that would get her in more trouble.

I sagged a little. "Okay. Let's do it."

He sat back down and waved me over as he pulled his laptop closer with his other hand. When I got to him, he drew me into his lap and he opened his computer lid.

"All right. So it's a simple system to hack," he said, pulling up a screen I'd definitely never seen in IT. As he continued, his fingers played over the keyboard, his arms boxing me in. "Especially at school. Getting in the backdoor is simple as. And whenever we leave, we always leave it ajar just a little to make it easier to get back in."

I had no idea what he was doing, but he talked me through it with a bunch of words that seemed like they made sense, but when you combined them in that order they went straight over my head.

233

Finally he stopped. "Okay. All you have to do is hit enter."

I looked at the inoffensive little key. I'd used that button so many times for so many things. But never once to set the fire alarm off.

"Will we get into trouble for this?"

"We're setting it off in the science labs. They always get a pass when they find out it's a false alarm."

"So…no one's going to get in trouble for this?"

He shook his head. "Nope."

Including Ebony who would also not get in trouble for punching her classmate.

My finger hovered over the key.

I was still too good. I couldn't do this. Surely it was fairly innocent? And all for the greater good? Well it was definitely for that boy's greater good. I'd been on the receiving end of one of Ebony's punches, not that it had been entirely intentional, and I didn't wish that on anyone.

"Think of Ebs, baby," Davin whispered in my ear.

Well I was thinking about Ebony. But something in Davin's voice resolved me. I hit 'enter' and felt a little rush of adrenalin.

"Okay. Full disclosure," Davin said quickly as the fire alarm started blaring. "Someone's going to know it was me. They won't have proof, but they'll guess."

"What?" I rounded on him, adrenalin fading.

He shrugged apologetically. "I get out of most of it because I block the signal from going to the fire station. The worst the school gets out of it is another fire drill ticked off."

"Davin!" I snapped. "What happens when there's a real fire?"

"I only block that specific alarm," he said calmly like it was all fine.

"So they're going to know it was you."

He nodded. "But they won't know it was you. And I might not even get detention out of it."

"Mr Ambrose. Miss St John." I looked up to see the librarian frowning at us. "The fire alarm does not mean snuggle with your significant other. Get to the check point, please."

I nodded as I jumped off Davin's lap. "Yes. Sorry."

Davin was a little slower than me and I caught the mischievous glint in his eye as we passed her on our way out.

But that little flutter of pride and glee started up again in my chest as Davin and I fell into step with other kids and I realised that I'd done this. I hadn't done any of the programming stuff. But I'd hit the button.

I'd been decidedly not good and it felt good… As it were.

Sixteen: Davin

I'd all but told Avery if she wanted a date that weekend, it was going to be at one of our places because I was over people. Dad was away again, so I had to admit I wasn't upset when she chose mine.

"So, what have you got planned for me tonight?" Avery asked as we walked in the front door.

We'd stopped passed her place so she could change and pick up her overnight bag. I'd stopped to talk to her Mum for an unprecedentedly long time in which I think I'd had three coffees and Ebony had told me how much she'd loved Le Fanu and wanted to know what to read next. Avery had managed to pull me out of the house before Phil got home and, while I didn't hate talking to Phil, I *was* feeling incredibly deep in debt on my socialisation credits as it was.

"I didn't really have a plan. There is a plethora of movies you need to see before you die–"

"Now who's planning murder-suicide pacts?" she quipped and I very nearly let a smile slip.

"I was more thinking that there is really not enough time

for you to see them all."

"Okay." She grinned. "So what's on the agenda tonight?"

I don't know why or how she found everything so…stimulating. It didn't matter if I was showing her an old horror, a drama, something cult, or one of Gran's romantic comedies, she went into every single one of them enthusiastic to experience something new. And even if she didn't really understand the point of it or didn't like it that much, she never thought it was a wasted opportunity. She just put it in the experience basket and moved onto the next thing.

"I was thinking *The Godfather* tonight."

That pondering frown crossed her face and it was getting harder to deny I thought it was more than a little endearing. "I think I've heard of that. My granddad was obsessed with Dad reading the book when he was younger." She smiled fondly. "Dad's teen rebellion was *not* reading it."

Given the way Avery had turned out, I actually wasn't surprised by that in the slightest.

"Shall we order pizza in advance?" she continued as she helped herself to leading the way to my room.

I cleared my throat. "I've got dinner covered."

She looked back at me as she put her bag in the corner of my room that was apparently becoming hers. "Okay. What are we having?"

"Casserole."

"Naw," she teased. "Did you cook for me?"

"No. Gran sent it over."

237

Gran had not sent it over. Gran had told me in no uncertain terms that I couldn't feed my girlfriend pizza every time she came over so I had begrudgingly put together a casserole on the Thursday night that I could just throw in the oven when Avery was there. But I was not telling Avery that. Avery did not need to know that I had in fact cooked for her.

I got changed into a pair of jeans and a plain t-shirt and we went back out to the living room where I introduced her to *The Godfather*. While we were watching the second one, we had dinner and then I suggested we take the third one to the bedroom, if she was still amenable to watching it.

As I was working out where I'd dropped the remote for the TV, Avery cleared her throat for the second time as though she wanted me to look at her. So look at her I did. And I didn't quite understand what I was looking at.

Because Avery was holding up a pair of red Converses.

And they were far too big for her tiny little feet.

Which only meant one thing.

"What are they?" I asked, horrified.

"It's called colour."

"I don't like it."

Her smile made me feel a little less aggravated than usual. "Try them on."

"Ah. Hard pass."

"You can't just hard pass everything you don't like, Davin."

"Watch me."

238

"Would it kill you to add *one* colour to your wardrobe?"

I nodded. "It might. It's not a risk I'm willing to take."

She frowned at me and I swore she knew what that did to me. In case she didn't, I rearranged the growing bulge in my jeans.

"Need help with that?" she asked, that wry tilt back to her lips.

"Give me the shoes," I sighed, holding my hand out, knowing if I got my hands on her now then the shoes would be forgotten for hours.

She passed them to me and I dropped onto my bed to take my others off.

"How did you even remember what size I was?"

"My memory's good like that."

I nodded as I reached for the red ones. "When it comes to shopping, yes. When it comes to Math, not so much."

"Yeah, but my boyfriend's helping me with that."

I paused in tying up the laces to look at her. "Yeah. He is."

Because as well as helping her be not good and trashing her reputation, I had also for some unfathomable reason signed myself up for helping her pass Math.

She beamed at me again, hands clasped behind her back expectantly. Well I couldn't let that face down, could I? So I finished the laces, pulled my jeans down over the tops and stood up.

"Well?" I asked her.

She squealed, but it was tame compared to some of the

noises she elicited. "Oh, they look great!"

"I'll bet." I sat down again to pull them off.

"Don't you want to see?" she asked.

I sighed and got back up again. Pulling open my wardrobe door, I looked down at my feet. And it could have been worse.

"See?" she asked, coming up behind me and wrapping her arms around my waist while she peered around me.

"I do see. Can I stop seeing now?"

Our eyes met in the mirror and there really was no stopping that positivity, was there? Then I stopped to look at the two of us next to each other. Me in all black or near black and her in green and blue and orange and a bunch of colours I didn't care to know the name for. She was smiling and her eyes were bright. Meanwhile my eyes were almost always hiding behind my hair and my glasses, and I didn't remember the last time I smiled.

I knew we were different, but I'd never stopped to think about just how different. Or how other people might look at us. I didn't care what they thought of me. But I wasn't sure how I felt about what they might think of her.

"You okay?" she asked.

I cleared my throat and nodded, "Sure," as I slid out of her arms and sat on the side of my bed to take off the shoes.

"You sure?" she asked, dropping stomach-first onto my bed behind me, her head at the end.

"I didn't know I had the range of emotion for you to think

240

there was a time something was wrong."

She snorted and I looked back to find her on her back now. "I didn't either. Maybe you're growing as a person?"

"Please say it isn't true…" I muttered and she laughed.

I pulled the second shoe off and awkwardly spun around so I was lying over her.

"There was no deal about me getting emotions out of this."

She bit her lip as she tried not to laugh at me. But I shook my head before she could reply.

"Nope. None of that." And I kissed her.

She wrapped herself around me as our bodies pressed together. My hand made a beeline for the skin under skirt as usual. I couldn't help it. Her legs were soft and warm and she practically melted into me every time I gripped her thigh firmly, holding it against my hip.

As I slid my hand between her legs, she grabbed my wrist to stop me.

I pulled back to look at her. "You okay?"

She nodded and bit her lip uncertainly. "I just…don't want you to do that…"

My hand was anywhere *but* between her legs quick smart. "Okay. No worries."

"I want you to do something else instead…"

Well, hello. I was open to any and all suggestions. "What do you want me to do?"

"Have sex with me."

241

Except that, apparently. Why was I not open to that? "What?"

"Did you have *another* lesson planned for this date?" she teased.

What was happening here? "Sex isn't a lesson, Avery," I told her.

"Why not?"

I looked at her. "Why do you think it is?"

She wasn't shy about maintaining eye contact, that was for sure. "Because I want to know how to feel comfortable with a guy."

"You weren't comfortable with Miles?" I knew they'd had sex, but it's not like I'd cared what kind or how often. Now I suddenly cared. But only just a little.

"I don't know. I didn't think much of it at the time. And I wasn't...pressured into it or anything. I just felt..."

"What Avery?" I asked when she didn't elaborate.

"Like we were just going through the motions because we were meant to. I didn't *mind* having sex. It's just..." She shrugged. "I didn't feel particularly sexy. I wasn't as turned on. I rarely–"

"As turned on as what?" I heard myself interrupt.

Her cheeks went bright pink, but her eyes never left mine. "As turned on as I am with you."

Well, fuck me. The exuberant tyrant had actually rendered me speechless.

"Miles never made me feel the way you do. Looking back

on it, all I felt like was some shy, awkward, boring girl in bed."

I cupped her cheek uncharacteristically tenderly, really not liking the way he'd made her feel like that was even a possibility. "I keep telling you. There is nothing boring about you."

She smiled, but it didn't reach her eyes. "I just want to know if it's possible for me to not be that girl. If I can let go a little, really enjoy it, feel like I'm not doing it wrong."

"And having sex with me will teach you that?"

"I *want* to have sex with you, Davin. If it can count as a lesson as well, why not?"

Good Jesus. Why – how – did that feel so very wrong and so very right at the same time? I ran my hand over my chin as I thought about it. I was all for corrupting her. I was all for getting her off in the cinema, for getting us both hot and bothered at school to the point Mrs Mack threatened to hose us down, for showing her how to program the fire alarm and getting her to push the button, for getting her drunk for the first time and watching her enthusiasm rub off on my dour friends. But this...

There was something about this that made me pause. And I didn't know why.

"Are you not attracted to your girlfriend?" she asked, aiming for playful, but the doubt still snuck in. "Because you can tell me if you're not."

"Not attracted...?" I scoffed, my eyes sliding from her for

a second. "That is definitely not the problem here."

"Then what is?"

I huffed a deep breath as I rolled to sit up. "I get the lessons, Avery. I've accepted I'm all-in with helping you do this not good thing. But..." I sighed.

What the hell was it that was holding me back? Did I want her? Fuck, yes. So why was I hesitating? I'd never hesitated before. A girl says she wants me to have sex with her, I'm there. But Avery St John says she wants to me to have sex with her... And I stop to check with her if she's sure?

I got off the bed and stretched my neck, feeling weird and antsy. Well weirder and antsier than I usually was around her colour and...all that life.

"But what, Davin?" she asked.

I looked at her and saw she'd sat up and was watching me with the closest to unhappiness I'd ever seen on her face. I breathed out again, turning away from her as I tried to kick some fucking sense into myself.

"I'm not some virgin who doesn't know what she's asking, Davin. I'm not asking you to take my virginity or roleplay or introduce me to BDSM. I just want to have sex with you. If you want to, too. I guess I kinda thought that you wanted me the way I wanted you, and I wanted to see if it was different like that. If it was the lesson thing that turned you off or whatever–"

"Nothing about you turns me off," I said.

"What?" she asked.

244

I sighed and went over to crouch in front of her. "Nothing about you turns me off. Your obsession with neon and your unrealistic smile can blind me and annoy me, but I have no problem being turned on around you."

"So you don't not want to have sex with me?"

I huffed the closest I'd let myself come to a laugh. "I definitely want to have sex with you."

"I'm sensing a but…"

"I just want you to be sure about it."

She looked at me like I was testing her patience and that was a definite turn on. "Are *you* sure about it?"

I nodded. "Yeah. I'm sure about it. Why?"

"Then why don't you think I would be?"

That was a fair question. But she kept talking before I could answer.

"Just because you think you're more experienced, what? You think that means I don't know what I want?"

I shook my head, feeling like an absolute shit. "You know if I was intending to be condescending, you'd be perfectly aware of it."

"Then why don't you think I know what I want? I thought you didn't see me as that stupid little girl."

Ah fuck. I'd fucked right up now. I pulled myself to standing from my crouch so my legs didn't give out and sat next to her. "I don't, Avery." And I didn't. I thought she was a blight on my ocular nerves a lot of the time, but a stupid little girl? No. "I just didn't want you so wrapped up in this

245

being not good concept that you were just happy to sleep with me because I happened to be here and then you'd go and regret it later."

She crawled into my lap and took my face in those unbelievably small, soft hands. "I don't want to sleep with you because you just happen to be here. Why is it you never believe me when I say I like you?"

Because two people in my life liked me and they were obligated. Because how could anyone like me when I didn't even like myself? Because even if they could, I was not the sort of person that Avery St John would like.

I thought it best not to say any of that though. "Because you have a track record of having terrible taste."

She laughed. "Was that you actually implying something positive about yourself?"

"Take it to your grave, babe," I said as I pulled her to me and kissed her.

She slid her hand between us as best as she could without actually having to pull away from me more than absolutely necessary.

"Are you sure about this?" I asked her.

She did pull away from me then with the deepest, moderately adorable frown on her face. "Seriously?"

"I just…" I grunted. "I want to double check I'm not taking advantage. For my own piece of mind. No crossed wires."

There was no sign of unicorn farts and lollipops on her

face. She gave me this incredibly confidant, sexy half-smirk as those baby blues flashed. She reached behind her back to unzip her top, took it off tortuously slowly and dropped it on the floor before running her hand up my body.

"Yes," she said, leaning towards me.

And I was officially done for.

I'd thought the sultry goddess on our first date was near impossible to resist? I was completely powerless in the face of the woman in my lap just then. Avery could have asked me to go to school in a purple and neon green candy striped suit the next week and I would have agreed.

And the way she kissed me? I would have added a matching top hat. Complete with feather.

Her hands slid up under my t-shirt and I wasn't slow in helping her get it over my head. I found her lips again like I was going to forget how to breathe without them. But then she trailed them over my cheek and down my neck and my hands tightened against her hips.

Her body was so soft and warm against mine that it actually took me a moment to believe that it was in fact against mine because, for a moment, it felt like a dream. I held her close as we kissed, one hand always running over some part of her. I found the buttons on her skirt and slowly started undoing them. When she batted my hand away, I thought she'd changed her mind. But she just grinned at me and showed me there was a much easier to undo zip.

We pulled the skirt over her head, then she pushed her

shoes off and started climbing off my lap.

"Where are you going?" I asked her.

"Under the covers," she replied smugly as she clambered under and bit her lip. "You coming?"

"Hopefully not too quickly," I say as I stood up and wasted no time taking off my jeans.

She giggled and I was more affected by it than I used to be. "Good to know."

I pulled back the covers and she held her arms out for me. I can tell you I wasn't going to dawdle getting in beside her. I paused long enough to dump my glasses on my bedside table, then I was with her. I rolled half over her as she wrapped her arms and leg around me and beamed up at me.

"Can you see okay?" she asked, her finger tracing softly down my cheek under my eye.

I felt a smirk tugging on my lips. "Yeah. I can see okay."

She brought my face to hers and kissed me slowly, deeply. I felt my stomach drop and suddenly there wasn't a distance she could be from me that classified as close enough.

Her knee hugged my hip and I dragged my hand over hers and down her leg. She sighed as she arched into me, rubbing against me in a way that had me straining against my boxers. Her hands ran down my back until her fingers found my waistband and she made the very obvious move of pushing on it.

I pulled back enough to look at her and my witty quip died on my lips as I saw the look in her eyes.

"Are you–?"

"If you ask me again if I'm fine, I will…do something very out of character."

"Will you now?" I asked and she nodded. "You just look…"

"What?"

That hint of apprehension in her eyes turned into a failed attempted at hidden panic.

"You just look a little…nervous."

"Ah." She looked down at my chest. "It's not because I don't want to… I'm just… I don't want to be boring."

I could have smiled. But I didn't. "Lesson, then. Turn off the editor, baby. Whatever's going on in there, tune it out. Imagine you're having amazing, lazy sex in bed. What do you do?"

She licked her lip as she thought about it. "Okay. Okay. I can do that."

"Good. Now, is there something you want?" I asked her as I kissed down her neck.

There was a moment of hesitation then I watched the resolve send all those worries packing. "Yes," she answered, hooking her fingers in the waistband of my boxers. "Those off."

"Bossy," I commented, feeling an unbidden smile almost cross my face.

"Two can play at that game, Davin."

"Then tell me exactly what you want, baby," I said slowly

249

as I dragged my nose up her neck again and I loved the way she sucked in a breath as I did.

As she spoke, with only very little trepidation in her tone, she pushed against my chest and ended up lying over me. "I want your boxers off. I want my undies off. And I want it now."

I nearly fell for her right then. I'll be honest with you. She did something for me. Fuck, she did something *to* me. And there was a very lust-drunk part of me that was happy for her to keep doing it for as long as possible.

I did as she wanted and slid my boxers off, dropping them off the side of the bed as I reached for the bedside table and grabbed a condom. By the time I was facing her again, she'd taken off her undies and bra and, while her cheeks were flushed a gorgeous bright pink, there wasn't another sign of hesitation about her.

I thought it probably best not to check with her again that she wanted to do this.

Avery plucked the condom out of my fingers and ripped the packet open. She did the roll check and then she was sliding it over me. I gave my own hastily inhaled breath at the feeling of her hands on me.

"All good?" she asked cheekily.

Fuck it. I almost smiled again. "Super."

She laughed, hooked her leg around mine and I just followed as she pulled me onto her. I nestled between her legs and looked down at her while she brushed the hair off my face and looked up at me with… I didn't even know what that look was.

Something in me crumbled.

I pictured cliffs falling into the ocean.

Vast empires collapsing.

This implausibly small flare of life would have brought me to my knees had the physical action been possible.

She licked her bottom lip slowly as a smile lit her eyes, taking me in her hand and guiding me into her.

I thrust slowly and she lifted her knee higher around my hip to give me a better angle. She closed her eyes, a satisfied smile ghosting her lips, and rolled her hips to meet me.

I paused when I was all the way and she opened her eyes.

Seventeen: Avery

He was looking down at me like he'd never seen me before and it sent a thrill of excitement through me that had my heart fluttering like crazy.

"All good?" I asked again, more breathless this time.

He nodded almost stiltedly and I realised he wasn't looking at me like he'd never seen me before. He was looking at me like he'd seen me plenty of times before but just discovered he'd been missing something every single time. And that was a million times better.

I brought him down to kiss me, slowly again. I might have been more than aware that Davin wasn't a feelings sort of guy, but I was going to feel this.

As he kissed me back, seemingly in no rush to quicken the pace I'd set, his hand ran down my body and he started moving gently. Goose bumps flared across my body from where his hand touched like some tingly Mexican wave and it was one of the most pleasurable things I'd felt, ever.

I felt like I'd melted into a puddle of desire and passion and I just gave myself up to the moment.

There wasn't any worrying about whether I had my body in the right position against his or at the right tension (or lack thereof or the perfect combination of tense and relaxed at the right time) to try to get me off before he finished. There wasn't any worry about whether I was going too slow or too fast or if I was being sexy enough to make him feel good about it.

All I felt was Davin's hands and lips on my body, him inside me. I didn't think about how we moved together, it just happened like it was natural and it felt…different and amazing and, most importantly, right.

Sometimes Davin was kissing my neck, sometimes we just looked into each other's eyes like there was something deeper being communicated – although presumably that was just me – and sometimes we just kissed.

I didn't think about how long or short it took, I was just insanely comfortable. I definitely just let go. I definitely enjoyed myself. And I definitely didn't feel like I was doing it wrong.

The whole thing felt nice, but when I held him a little tighter he seemed to take that as a sign that something was working. He slid his hand between us and, just before he touched me, there was a smile in his eyes as he paused.

"Unless you want to do it?"

I giggled. "Not if you want to."

His lips brushed over my neck again as he said, "Oh I'd love to."

As he thrust, he ran his hand between my legs as lazily as he always started out, When I arched into him, it was like he knew he'd found the exact right spot and his touch became firmer as we started moving a little faster.

I could feel it deep in my stomach, a slow, strong flutter. As goose bumps flared across my skin from his lips on neck, the feeling of need and want in me rose. The tingling grew and tightened until I felt like there was this little ball of pressure in me that was going to burst. The flutter in my stomach was becoming a pull and my breathing was getting ragged.

As my orgasm hit, I held him tight and he slowed while I got my bearings and let the wave of extra sensitivity sweep through me. As it started abating, I bit his lip playfully, then opened my eyes quickly to see if he had actually smiled. But if he had, then I'd missed it.

He was just looking down at me with a heat in his eyes. "Okay?" he asked and I knew he wasn't actually asking if the orgasm was satisfactory.

I nodded. "Yeah."

He dipped to kiss me again. This time it was a little harder, a little deeper, and it matched his change in pace. Everything still tingled and every thrust just added to it.

I got completely lost to him, my hands threaded through his hair as my leg wrapped around his hip possessively, until he came hard and his thrusts slowed.

He kissed me slowly for a bit, ran his nose over mine, then

pulled out.

I held the sheets over me as he dealt with the condom, then thought I should probably go clean up a little. I saw one of his shirts on the floor next to the bed so I reached down and pulled it on before getting up.

"You okay?" he asked.

"Yep. Bathroom," I replied, feeling very okay indeed.

"Okay."

I headed for the bathroom, trying to keep the ridiculous smile off my face as I peed and cleaned up a little. I had a moment where I wished I'd brought my phone so I could tell Blair that Davin and I had had sex, but then realised as I headed back to Davin's room that it could totally wait and she wasn't losing out by me telling her tomorrow.

Oh. Okay, that was totally unnecessary.

I walked back into Davin's room to find him propped up against his pillows, the sheets only reaching his waist so his naked body was still on display, one arm behind his head, his dark hair still brushed off his face, and reading a book.

"Are you some sort of romance novel cover model?" I giggled.

He looked up at me, confusion obvious in his eyes. "What?"

I waved a hand to indicate him. "Is this normal?"

He looked around. "Is what normal?"

"Whatever it is you're doing right now?"

He blinked slowly. "Reading?"

"Sure."

"I read a lot, yes."

I mean, I knew that but… "Like that?"

He gave me a look that quite clearly told me he wasn't sorry about it. "I assume so. It feels normal. Am I supposed to read differently?"

"How do you turn the pages?"

He reached his arm down, flipped the page, then tucked his hand back behind his head. "I know it's old-fashioned, but…" He shrugged as if to say 'there we go'.

I had a very surreal moment where I realised just how much I was into the nerdy bad boy thing that Davin had going on. The unexplainably chiselled body, the dark hair, and the constant contempt on his face combined with the glasses, the intelligence, and the big hardback books to make one incredibly sexy package.

He might not have been the most stereotypical bad boy in history – I'd never seen him in a fight, he wasn't making his way through the entire female population of Mitchell College, and he had zero interest in motor bikes as far as I was aware – but the brooding, mysterious, dark parts of him sure gave him that bad boy vibe.

Which I had never been interested in before.

I'd never been into the bad boy thing or the nerd thing before, let alone the combination.

All my previous crushes had been charming, sweet, and popular. Some of them had been a little sporty. Others had been purely social creatures. They'd all been middle of the road, neither academically behind or inclined. Tom and Miles particularly had been the sort of guys who just exuded that something that you couldn't help swooning over. The cocky smile accompanied by the arrogant wink given by guys who knew they were hot and knew you knew they were hot.

Davin was decidedly not one of those guys.

He didn't make any effort to accentuate his looks, he didn't walk around like God's gift to anyone, and he certainly wasn't smiling winningly at anyone.

And yet I had actually never found any other guy sexier.

I wondered if that's what made everyone think being so good was a bad thing? The way I'd just described my previous crushes was the same way a lot of people could have described me. But this – Davin – was so much more interesting. He was so much more real.

"You coming back to bed?" he asked me, keeping his eyes on his book as he turned the page again.

"Aren't you getting dressed?" popped out of my mouth.

"I sleep naked," he said and I blinked. "Have for years."

"Oh… But…before…?"

He slid his eyes up to me. "I didn't want you thinking I was making assumptions."

I nodded quickly. "I see."

"Is that a problem?" he asked slowly like he was only just realising it might be.

We'd just had sex. Naked. So I guess it wasn't really that

big a deal. "No."

"You don't seem sure about that."

I shook my head. "No, it's fine. I'm keeping your shirt on, though."

He sighed and looked at me like he hadn't actually done that properly before. "What is it with girls doing that after sex?"

"What?"

"Putting on our clothes?"

I shrugged. "I don't know. I assumed it was sexy or something." Also it was the closest item of clothing to the bed and I'd felt weird about getting out of it naked.

He looked me over like he was trying to work it out. "I don't know. Is seeing a girl wearing my top a turn on?" He sat up, leaning his elbow on his knee, the book hanging by his leg. "Or is seeing Avery St John in my top a turn on? And is it a turn on because I know you've got nothing else on under it?" He cocked his head to the side. "Or is it a turn on because it's a blaring beacon that proclaims you're mine?"

My chest hitched and my breath caught. "Yours?"

He shrugged, like it actually didn't bother him at all. "In theory."

"In theory?" I squeaked.

He raked his hand through his hair slowly, his eyes on me intently. "You're wearing nothing but my shirt. That begs the assumption – or the reminder for those of us playing at home – that we've just been intimate." He rubbed his bottom lip like he was thinking. "Many might presume territory has been claimed. At least temporarily."

Holy shit.

I think I'd just set feminism back hundreds of years, but I felt okay with that. If Davin Ambrose wanted to claim me, I was going to let him. But I guess a part of my brain was expecting it went both ways. Still, one could never make assumptions with him.

He scooted to the end of the bed – keeping everything necessary under the blankets, even if I had just felt it all and more a few minutes ago – and held a hand out to me. I walked over to him like he was a magnet designed specifically for me and he pulled me down to straddle his lap.

"Yes, Avery," he said softly, with humour in those bright green eyes, and I looked at him in confusion.

"I didn't say anything."

"You didn't have to."

"Really? What's yes then?"

"Yes, it goes both ways," he said, slowly and deliberately. "I'm just less obvious about it."

Before I could say anything, he kissed me.

When he pulled away he said, "So… How did that live up to expectations?"

His eyes were serious as he looked at me and I knew what he was asking. I gave him a small smile and nudged his nose with mine.

"It exceeded expectations."

He looked mildly surprised. "Really?"

I nodded. "I didn't think our first time would be so…" I wasn't quite sure what the right word to use there was.

"So what?" he asked before I could decide.

"Different," I said before I'd properly thought it through.

A flicker of doubt passed through his eyes. "Good different I assume?"

I nodded again. "Of course. It was… I was…" Again at a loss for words.

"Amazing," he said softly and I looked up at him again. "Really?"

"Did you not think so?"

"How do I know if *I'm* amazing?" I asked.

"Do you think I enjoyed myself?"

"I don't know."

"How do you not know?"

"Well, just because you finished doesn't mean you enjoyed it."

"I could say the same about you."

I blinked. "Really?"

He looked me over like I worried him for a second, then his expression was just his usual brooding scrutiny. "Yes. It is entirely possible for a woman to orgasm without actually enjoying or wanting sex."

I looked down again. "Well…I enjoyed it. Very much."

He huffed that almost laugh. "I hoped so."

I shook my head, staring at his belly button. "No. Not

just…that. I mean…the whole thing. I was comfortable. I didn't feel like I was doing it wrong. It didn't feel wrong."

He tipped my chin to look at him. "It should never feel wrong, Avery…"

"I didn't mean with…him it did. I just meant… There's a difference between it feeling right and it feeling like just something you're doing. You know?"

He nodded slowly. "Yeah. I do…"

My heart skipped a beat in my chest because he'd spoken so quietly I wasn't sure if he'd ended that sentence with 'know' or 'now' and I didn't want to ask him to clarify. And when I say it skipped a beat, I mean it felt like it was about to thud out of my chest.

"Do you want to watch the movie? Or just go to bed?" he asked, that heat in his eyes making me feel very much like the latter was a wonderful choice.

But I didn't want him to think I was–

"Don't think. Just tell me," he said, his voice still soft.

"I thought I was supposed to think before I spoke?" I teased.

"Addendum. In bed, no thinking. Okay? I want to know what you want, unfiltered."

I looked down to hide my smile. "Okay. Let's go to bed."

Eighteen: Davin

The problem with Avery…

No. There were numerous problems with Avery.

But the problem with trying to give Avery lessons in being not good was that eighty percent of the time she was a confident, exuberant, happy person. Most of the things I could come up with to try to make her less good would do nothing to actually make her less good because she'd do it in a way that was painfully obvious it wasn't normal for her. And anything else she'd just do with her usual sense of wonder and awe.

So it made trying to teach her whatever it was she thought I was supposed to be teaching her fucking difficult.

I wasn't quite so desperate as to pull the streaking across the oval idea out of the rubbish pile, though.

I was pretty sure being not good had nothing to do with how she kissed me in the hallway or whether she got drunk at a party. It didn't have anything to do with getting off in the cinema and I was pretty sure she'd lost sleep over not telling Mrs Mack that she'd been the one to set the fire sprinklers off that day.

The way Avery talked about being not good had everything to do with whatever slip of confidence happened when she was faced with a potentially confronting situation. Not that she'd ever had any trouble being confrontational with me. I didn't do what she wanted? Fuck that, she'd push and prod and argue until I agreed. And for the guy who never did what anyone wanted, I gave in one hundred percent of the time, conveniently not feeling like she was bullying me or coming to dislike her at all.

I'll remind you, *"Plot furtherance lets you get away with a multitude of sins."*

But plot furtherance or otherwise, that wasn't going to help me try to teach Avery to be not good. I wasn't sure she had it in her to be not good. It was who she was. Not that she was going to like that assessment.

I pushed into the Common Room and wasn't surprised when the room went near-silent as everyone stared in shock that I was stepping foot into the hallowed hall. It's not like I wasn't allowed. I just couldn't remember a time I'd actually gone in there unless a whole year meeting had been called. But if I wanted Avery to keep rocking my world, I was going to have to, at some point, involve myself with her friends and this seemed like the least painful method I could come up with.

Slowly, people stopped staring at me and went back to their groups and their conversations.

Well most people.

Avery smiled at me and waved.

Blair grinned and nudged Avery.

And Molly and Krista – *"What? I know people's names. Just because I don't care doesn't mean I'm oblivious"* – giggled with Blair.

I nodded, took a breath and headed over to the corner of the room where they were standing. I plonked myself down on the counter masquerading as desk that ran around the edges of the room and nodded once more to the girls.

"Hi!" Blair, Molly and Krista all chorused and I grimaced, to which they all just giggled again.

"Hey," I replied.

Avery inserted herself between my legs and leant against me like it was second nature as they went back to their conversation while her fingers played absent-mindedly with the bottom of my blazer. I didn't bother listening to whatever it was they were talking about. Mainly because I didn't care about if that brand of eyeliner was better than another or whatever celebrity they were going on about. But also partly because Miles had caught my eye from the middle of the room.

His gaze raked over me and I knew I was being sized-up. I couldn't have told you if it was because he planned to come over and have it out with me. Or if he was just morbidly curious about his ex's new fling.

Body language will tell you a lot about a person. And

Miles' body language inherently told me that he was feeling threatened by something. It also gave me a sneaking suspicion that he and Cindy were not doing as well as me and Avery, or as well as they'd have you believe.

And 'well' here merely referred to how comfortable we were with each other. Physically comfortable in particular. It was perfectly tolerable to have Avery leaning against me while she talked to her friends and it was customary for her to have a hand on me somewhere. It had become my freakish new normal that, whenever we were together, at least some body part would be touching. Mostly this involved her leaning on me, but I had once or twice found myself taking her hand.

Miles and Cindy on the other hand looked like they weren't quite sure what to do with each other. Miles, for all his supposed charm and elegance, looked like he'd read about how to be casually intimate from one of the greatly repressed Victorians and the execution was a touch elusive. And Cindy looked rigid and uncomfortable under his arm like she'd really rather not be there.

The cynic in me assumed their relationship was not going quite according to plan. However another diminutive and less cynical part of me wondered if perhaps Cindy was feeling a little less cavalier about public displays of affection when the whole school now knew that she'd been fucking Miles behind Avery's back.

Deciding I'd probably maintained eye contact with my

girlfriend's ex for long enough, I threw a fleeting mordant grin at Miles, who gave me a weird sort of nod and finally looked away as though whatever Cindy was saying with Louise was suddenly the most interesting information in his existence.

"Don't you think, Davin?" I heard and looked at the four girls who were all staring avidly at me.

I blinked slowly. "About what?"

"Were you even listening?" Blair huffed.

"You know I wasn't."

Molly's smirk was humoured. "That we should probably book the limo now."

I might not have been listening, but that didn't mean I was ignorant of the topic on which they'd obviously landed. "I'm sure you can do whatever you'd like, ladies," I told them, subconsciously running my hand down Avery's leg.

Blair sighed. "Dates have to be in as well, Davin."

I assumed by the fact that they were all looking at me expectantly that even Avery expected we'd still be dating in…what was it? Thirteen weeks until the formal. That seemed like an awfully long commitment in which to be binding myself. But then Avery actually batted her eyelashes at me and I had that overwhelming urge to just cave again.

"Fine. Send me the bill or whatever." I shrugged.

All four of them squealed in excitement and I winced against the cacophony.

Unsurprisingly the whole room paused in what they were

doing to look at them. But Avery was, as usual, unfazed as she turned and flung her arms around me. I begrudgingly hugged her back as the other three made little 'aren't they cute' faces at me.

"All right. Enough of this," I said. I kissed Avery's cheek and gently pushed her off me.

"Oh! Are you too cool to hug your girlfriend?" Molly asked and I wasn't sure if I did or didn't like the wry glint in her brown eyes.

"Like liquid helium," I replied and they all looked at me in utter confusion. I rolled my eyes. "It's an incredibly cold substance that…"

They were all looking at me like I was suddenly speaking a different language.

I shook my head. "You know what? Never mind."

The bell rang and I had never been more pleased at the indicator of the tediously annoying structure of institutionalised education. I scooted Avery forwards a little so I could stand up. Not that she was terribly helpful as she didn't seem all that keen on moving any further away from me than necessary.

"All right. I'll see you later, babe." I didn't know why I insisted on making my movements known to her.

"Okay." She turned and gave me a huge smile.

I bent down to kiss her and she leant into me while the girls cheered. I pulled away with a scathing look in their direction.

"Ladies." I inclined my head. "I'm sure I'll see you all later as well."

They giggled their goodbyes at me as I grabbed my bag and swept out of the room. As I reached the doors, I almost ran into Miles.

He kicked his chin in greeting and I did him the service of tipping up an eyebrow in reply. Unlike most other people in this place, I didn't worship the ground he walked on and I could give zero fucks if I was in his way. Plus, the dude was at least a half-head shorter than me so I could sort of understand him feeling intimidated by me.

Miles shrugged out his shoulders and cleared his throat, heedless of the fact that he was really the only one in any position to actually make it through the door or that he was holding up the smooth flow of traffic. Which meant that half the Year 12 cohort were currently standing around watching Avery's ex and current boyfriends staring at each other.

Sizing each other up across a relatively crowded room was one thing. But I wasn't into whatever Miles thought we were doing here.

Miles cleared his throat again. "Davin. What's up?"

"Well it's certainly not the mass exodus of our classmates with the aim of getting to next lesson on time," I replied dryly.

Miles seemed to jump a little, then looked behind him. His eyes widened then narrowed before he looked back to me, gave a cursory nod and hurried out. I let his followers hurry

268

right on after him before inserting myself into the flow of students and headed for class.

I got through the next two lessons and actually arrived at Home Group before Avery. I was unbelievably relieved that she hadn't insisted on us sitting together in classes. I still got my seat at the back where neither teachers nor other students bothered me and she sat up the front with whatever friend she had in that class, usually Blair.

Avery did hang around to walk out to lunch with me though and I even found myself holding her hand without her needing to instigate such physical interaction.

"Are you coming to the Common Room again?" she asked me.

I huffed. "If it would please you, I'm seventy-three percent sure it won't kill me."

"Are you sure though?" she teased.

I picked her up and her legs went around my waist instantly as she giggled.

"Can you not do anything without sounding like some manic pixie?" I asked her, ignoring any correlation my brain made with the whole manic pixie dream girl trope.

"No." She was smiling warmly at me.

"Mr Ambrose!" the dulcet shriek of Mrs Mack floated down the corridor. "I *will* get the hose out if you keep this up in the hallways."

I looked back at her. "Is your office free, then?"

"Davin!" Avery giggled as she pressed her face into my

shoulder.

"Do you want another Friday, Mr Ambrose?" Mrs Mack asked.

I pretended to think about it. "I can't, sorry. I promised Avery I'd engage in some supposedly enjoyable activity."

"Put Miss St John down, Mr Ambrose, and get out of the corridor. I don't know how the hell you two are still together," I heard her mutter as she walked away.

I dropped the laughing Avery to the ground. "Yeah. You're laughing until you're joining me in detention."

"The couple that rebels together, stays together?" she asked.

I shook my head as I took her hand. "No."

She snorted as we walked away. "You sure?"

"Yes."

"No one will believe I'm too good if I get detention."

"To get detention, you'd have to do something worth getting detention. You might not be so good anymore, but you're no bad girl."

"What if I want to be?" she asked, swinging my hand in a very well-timed act of paradoxical behaviour.

Any idiot could see she didn't want to be a bad girl, but I wasn't going to pull her up on it just then. We had other things to address first.

"Then don't swing my hand like that and be less…chirpy."

"You always sound so disgusted with me."

I looked at her out the corner of my eye. "It's not disgust, Avery."

"What is it then?"

I hung my head back with a sigh as I stopped walking and she was pulled up short. "I just don't get how you're so happy all the time."

"I choose to be."

"For the love of all that's holy, why?"

"Why do you choose to be so unhappy?" she asked me.

Well I hadn't expected that. "I don't choose it. I'm just naturally talented in the finer arts of discontent."

She smiled, but there was an almost sadness in her eyes.

This was the time people usually told me to just pick myself up and be happy. Yeah, because thanks, I hadn't thought of that myself. Random stranger on the street tells me to just be happy and suddenly I'm magically fixed.

I think not.

But Avery once again surprised me.

"Can I do anything?"

I looked behind her because I couldn't look at her anymore. Somehow I felt like I was letting her down. "I'm fine."

"Are you? Because you don't seem it. You *can* talk to me."

She hadn't said anything after Dad's slip the morning after Vinny's party and I'd been more thankful that I cared to admit for that. I was grateful she was respecting my boundaries.

But I talked enough already, I didn't need more. Not about…that. "I am quite capable of talking to you, yes. And I will if I have some piece of communication I feel compelled to convey."

"Davin!" She did that thing where she stamped her foot, but I didn't impugn her for it this time. "You know I can do the whole woe is me thing too you know."

I blinked. "What?"

"I can bring myself down to your level or whatever."

I knew she was being sarcastic to try to get me to open up but I really didn't feel like analysing myself more than I was already forced to do.

So, "Have you ever stopped to think that maybe this obsessive desire to fit in is what lets people walk all over you?" tore out of my mouth.

"What?" she blinked and she actually pulled away from me a step, her hand jerking out of mine.

I groaned, absolutely furious with myself. I'd extra fucked up now. "Babe, that was not…" I sighed. "I didn't mean that."

She frowned at me and I felt no delight in seeing it on her face this time precisely because I had caused it. "Everything that comes out of your mouth is a carefully crafted string of words designed to show off how clever you are."

Usually that was true. When it felt like she was close to realising I was even worse than she thought I was, apparently not.

I reached for her again and I swear an eternity passed while she debated taking it or not. Finally she did and I felt my heart restart.

"Avery, I'm sorry. I…" I couldn't exactly lie to her could I? "While the question wasn't completely wrong, I didn't mean it the way it came out."

She frowned but I was gratified when she didn't pull away. "You think I have an obsessive desire to fit in?"

"I think it's a natural human quality and you're more concerned about being nice to others."

"So, yes?" she asked and I shrugged regretfully. "And you think that's why people treat me like I'm too good?"

I shrugged again. "The thought has crossed my mind."

She looked around and I was pleased people hadn't tarried in the hallway while we'd been talking. The lure of the freedom only granted by not being in the school building at break was obviously stronger than watching Avery have an argument with her boyfriend.

Finally, she drew herself up and nodded once. "Okay. So teach how to not care about fitting in and being nice to people."

For a guy who was an expert in the subject, I wasn't sure I was capable of teaching her that. Or that I wanted to.

But she wasn't as easily corruptible as she seemed to hope she'd be when we started this. So I could probably teach her that.

It was clear to me what her problem was now.

All I had to do was find ways to give her more exposure to and practise with confrontations. I needed to show her how to confront people when she had a right to and to stand her ground if someone confronted her. I also needed to do this without traumatising her, breaking the trust she had in me, or jeopardising our relationship.

And preferably avoid more confrontations between us.

Easy, right?

Nineteen: Avery

The two weeks of the holidays passed so quickly, I couldn't have said where they went.

Blair and I hung out either by ourselves or with Molly, Krista and a few of the others. I went for a few runs, finding the whole mindfulness thing a happy accident in my lessons. I watched movies with Ebony and listened to her whining when Davin didn't join us. And of course, I spent time with Davin as he tried to teach me how to be less nice to people. You'd have thought for the amount of time I'd spent with him, I'd have picked something up. But it seems I was a slow student. I did however manage to show my displeasure to the guy behind the counter at Hungry Jacks when he gave me a Coke instead of lemonade.

Davin's dad was home the first week of the holidays and I noticed that we spent more time at my place than his. I didn't dare bring it up because I wasn't sure how he'd take that. He and Dad talked books. He tried to convince Mum that the Gothic look was coming back in and she should include some darker shades in her designs – about which I was almost sure he cracked a joke. And he and Ebony bonded over books and the old movies he'd deign to let her join in on.

In his weird brooding way, Davin doted on my little sister, bringing her books to borrow and driving her to meet up with her friends and arguing the finer points of whether or not Edward Cullen was a respectable specimen of fiction. And I was almost convinced that Ebony was crushing hard on my boyfriend, but I had to say I didn't blame her if she was. Every time I tried to pinpoint the exact reasons why I liked Davin, it was like every one floated just out of reach and all I could come up with was a warm feeling in my chest and the truth I just did like him.

The second week Don was back at work and Davin and I spent more time at his than at mine – when he wasn't having dinner with his grandmother. Which, given that I'd suddenly turned into a proper hormones-raging teenager and thought about having sex with him constantly, was probably a good thing since I didn't have to feel self-conscious every time I wanted to – or did – do it.

Spending time with Davin, regardless of how physical we did or didn't get – because despite my new-found lust, we weren't actually constantly having sex – was actually enjoyable. He was nothing more than his usual moody, sarcastic self. He was grumpy and resistant to anything I suggested that might expose him to even the smallest bit of fun. But I still liked being around him. He showed me the movies he liked and talked to me about the books he liked. He asked me about things I liked and even listened to me while I told him, even if he looked like he regretted asking me, for example, why liquid eyeliner was better than wax pencil.

Despite his utter insistence that we do not buy into the total commercialism of gift-giving at Easter, I got him a Red Tulip bunny. He had no religious qualms about the concept, I was pretty sure it was just another thing he got to be grumpy about. But he did share half his bunny with me and I was pretty sure I almost caught a smile on his face while he was eating it.

There had been a time during the holidays when we were wandering around in town under the pretence of chaperoning Ebony and her friends. We found ourselves down by the river and I'd tried to convince Davin to get a paddle boat with me.

"No," had been his very definitive answer.

"Come on, Davin. It might be fun!"

"It won't be fun."

"You don't think anything's fun."

His eyes heated and my stomach fluttered. "You know that's not true."

"You don't think anything in public is fun."

"That's not *strictly* true…"

I snorted as I looked around and hoped no one was listening to him. "Davin!" I hissed.

"Avery!" he mimicked.

"We are not…" I flushed red and paused. "The cinema was public enough. We're not getting any more public than that."

He sighed dramatically. "Well, that *is* true." Then he'd almost smirked at me. "Today's lesson – jump in."

I looked at him. "What?"

He nodded. "Jump in."

I looked at the water and back at him. "No."

"Why not?"

"How about because that water is festy as, and you really don't want to be the instigator of my death by who knows what diseases?"

He stood behind me and wrapped his arms around me as we both looked at the Torrens. "Yeah. You're probably right about that," he'd said resignedly.

We'd also spent the holidays working on my terrible Maths skills. Davin called them abysmal and I didn't disagree. But, like with any other subject he put his mind to, Davin seemed to be the smartest person in Maths too, so I felt like I was in good hands.

As long as those hands stayed on the task *at* hand and didn't find themselves under my clothes. Which, to be fair, they usually didn't. Most of the time. When we were studying, Davin was strangely good at keeping his focus. He also usually kept me on the other side of the table. He was though very aware of his limitations and there were a couple of study session he cut short because I was apparently too tempting.

By the time we got back to school for Term 2, whatever Davin and I were seemed to be old news. There was nothing like a holiday break to make changes of the first term seem like old news. Much like this whole being in Year 12 business, dating Davin was just a fact of life.

On the Saturday of week one, Davin and I were at his house again and watching movies in his room. He seemed a little more cantankerous – he taught me that word and I quite liked it – than usual but I was trying to counteract as only I knew how.

"So what's today's lesson?" I asked.

"I don't fucking know, Avery," he sighed.

Even for him that was short and peeved off. "Hey." I put a hand on his chest. "You okay?"

"Yes. I'm…" He sighed. "Sorry. I'm fine."

"You sure?"

He grunted. "Yes. Fine. I just… I don't know how to make you be not good, okay? I don't know what lessons to give you to teach you how to be less…good! Have you ever thought about the fact that that's just who you are? You're just a good girl?"

I wasn't sure where this was coming from. I knew we hadn't been really sticking to the one lesson per date plan, but I felt like something about him was making me less good. Surely.

"I don't want to be a good girl, though."

Davin huffed and pulled his arm out from under me as he got off the bed. Although even obviously mad, he did it gently, just as quickly as possible. "Why not? What's so wrong with being who you are?"

Because who I was sucked. I didn't want to be called 'too good' like it was a bad thing. I wanted to be normal. It wasn't like Davin being himself was making him tonnes of friends. Although that did seem to be the point of his whole personality.

"So you're telling me you're quite happy being this closed off, grumpy guy?"

He shrugged. "It's who I am. I've accepted it."

"You don't have to."

"I'm *happy* to." The way he said the word, I was confident that was not the emotion he felt.

"Why?"

"It doesn't matter, Avery." He came close to snarling.

"I don't see why not. You want me to accept myself. Tell me what makes you so eager to accept who you are?"

"Because I have an ingrained sense of distrust and worthlessness after my mother killed herself and tried to take me with her!" he yelled. Then he turned around and spat, "Fuck!" with more emotion than I had ever heard from him.

I was shocked. Utterly and totally shocked. Everything stopped far worse than when Miles had dumped me in the school hallway.

My head was filled with something like buzzing

emptiness and I felt like I'd forgotten how to breathe. It was like what he'd said would be different if I just froze for long enough.

Of all the backstories in all the films and books and shows, that was not the one I was expecting for Davin Ambrose.

I didn't know what to say.

I didn't know what to feel.

He wouldn't want my sympathy, but I couldn't help but feel it. I tried to stop myself feeling sorry for him, but I couldn't. It was the moment you want to wrap someone up in bubble wrap and put them in your pocket to keep them safe for always. Like Tom Holland. That gorgeous man seemed like he needed to be snuggled. But Tom wasn't the one standing in front of me like every support he'd ever built for himself had just disintegrated out from under him.

Davin was.

I scooted to the end of the bed as he paced, muttering a string of no doubt hyperbolic ramble full of giant words I'd never heard of. But it was too quiet for me to hear.

"Davin…" I said softly and he jumped mid-pace like I'd struck him.

I watched him take a deep breath like that was the only thing stopping him from falling apart in front of me. There was a pain in my chest as I watched him and I wished I knew what to do.

I felt myself get up and I went to hug him. He pulled away from me with a look of complete contempt on his face. So I backed up and dropped onto the bed again.

"Dav, come sit back down…" I patted the bed next to me gently, hoping he'd stop his frantic pacing.

He looked at me, then the bed, me again, the bed again, and finally dropped onto it like he was on autopilot. My hands fluttered uselessly. The nosey parker in me was desperate to know more and I tried to ignore it, tried to remember I was respecting his boundaries.

"Davin, are you okay?" I asked because he sure as heck didn't look okay.

He gave a curt nod. "Sure."

"Davin–"

"We don't have to talk about it," he said quickly.

I wasn't so sure about that. I mean I wanted to be the mature person here and let it go, but… "You don't just drop a bomb on me like your mum killed herself, then say we don't have to talk about it."

He shrugged. "It's fine, Avery."

"It's not fine, Davin." I crawled into his lap and he glared at me. "It's just a little physical interaction. Suck it up."

"You can suck it if you want. I choose not."

I frowned at him. "Davin."

"What?"

I brushed his hair out of his face. He finally really look at me and sighed.

"I was about seven. Okay? Dad was at work. Mum had always been sick, but Gran was around to keep an eye on us

282

and they thought Mum was doing better. Well she was. Until the night she gave me a bunch of pills, then took us both to the bathroom. I woke up in her arms in the bath, freezing and vomiting and wondering why the water was red. Gran found me hiding under the vanity in the corner. She took me to the hospital, but it was too late for Mum."

I didn't need to ask what had happened to her.

God, I felt awful for him. And I felt awful for basically making him tell me.

"Davin, I'm so sorry."

He shrugged. "It is what it is."

"Are you okay?"

His whole expression was as cold as his tone as he replied, "I still get professional help, if that's what you're asking."

Well that I'd guessed from what his dad had said.

But, "It wasn't."

He nodded once and I wasn't sure he believed me.

Not sure what else to do, I pressed myself against him, wrapped my arms around his neck and hugged him tightly.

"What are you doing, Avery?" he asked.

"It's called comfort, Davin," I told him.

Eventually, slowly, he put his arms around me as well.

"This isn't so bad, is it?" I asked.

"I could think of a number of ways to make this better."

"I don't think sex is the answer."

"Actually, my first thought was to stop hugging."

I squeezed him a little and he buried his face in my

shoulder. I felt him take a deep breath and then his breath on my skin as he exhaled. There was nothing sexual about the situation, I just didn't know what else to do. I ran my hand over the back of his head in a way I hoped was comforting and he breathed deeply.

Neither of us said anything for what felt like a really long time.

But I didn't mind. I just wanted to be sure he was okay.

I was aware that the fact he'd just told me didn't necessarily make him any more or less okay than he had been carrying that around for the last eleven years. But I hadn't been there for the majority of the last eleven years, and I was just optimistic enough to hope that maybe there was something I could do that no one else could.

I felt him take a sharp breath in and exhale quickly, then he shook himself and sat up.

"That was…" he started, his eyes searching mine. They were clear and deep. "I'll drive you home."

I smiled in confusion. "Why would I want that?"

He looked down, then picked me up and put me back on the bed as he got up. "I just… I can't be around you right now. Okay?"

"What?"

He huffed and I could see he was angry. "You should go."

"Why?"

"Because–"

"Because you don't want me to see this broken you?"

His eyes narrowed dangerously. "I'm still the same person I've always been."

"If that's the case, why do I have to go?"

"Because I don't want you here."

I scoffed and crossed my arms. "So, you just get to push me away now? Is that it?"

"You don't get it–" he yelled but I interrupted.

"Oh no. I get it. Good little Avery couldn't possible see the cracks in your armour, Davin. Why? Are you going to take your feelings of worthlessness and throw them onto me? Am I not worth being here for you?"

"Excuse–"

"No." I stood up quickly. "I'll tell you something, Davin Ambrose! You're not worthless. You might feel like you're…you're unwanted or…or unlovable or something. But you are." I cleared my throat, realising that I didn't really know what I was going. "Wanted I mean. And worth…while? Anyway, I appreciate you. You seem to like to ignore that fact. But I appreciate you and I like you. I came to you because I saw you as a bad boy who could help me trash my reputation. But it's more than that now. I…" *have no idea what I'm trying to say and the look on his face tells me he's finding this no more comfortable than me.* "I… I could have gone to someone else. I could be in jail by now or on drugs or…pregnant! That would certainly make me less good…" I shook my head to concentrate. "My point is… I can't really do a lot about the whole mistrust thing I don't

285

think… But you're worth a lot to me and I really enjoy being with you…"

Okay. Now was definitely time to stop because he was looking at me like he didn't know if he was going to throw up, cry, or kiss me. And I don't think I'd ever been quite so terrible at trying to say what was on my mind. So I just took a deep breath and hoped he wasn't still trying to kick me out.

"You enjoy spending time with me…? Even after that?"

I smoothed my skirt like I felt any of the confidence I tried to inject into my words. "I've been the recipient of many of your outbursts and yet here I am."

"Here you are," he said, echoing his words from our first date. He sighed heavily and finally took a dang seat on the bed. "I'm sorry, Ave."

"What for?

"For…all that."

"You don't have to be."

"I do." He held his hands out to me and I took them as I sat in in his lap. "I shouldn't have…yelled at you."

"I think maybe if I had to carry that secret around with me for eleven years–"

"You'd dress in black and yell at people too?"

I giggled, but stemmed it pretty quickly. "Yeah. You don't just get to yell at me any old time though, mind you."

"And where was that attitude when Miles cheated on you?" he asked softly as he nudged my nose with his and wrapped his arms around my back.

"What attitude?"

"The 'I'll take no one's shit' attitude."

I wriggled self-consciously in his lap.

"You don't need lessons in how not to be good, Avery," he said tenderly.

"I do if I don't want–"

"You just need more confidence in yourself. You just need to stand up for yourself. You just need to refuse to let people walk all over you."

"And how do I do that?"

"You be the person you are with me. You show people you have a backbone. Fuck, I like you better now I know you have one."

"I don't know how to do that, Davin…"

"I've been thinking about that. It's one reason I snapped at you."

"What do you mean?"

"I mean that I've realised two lessons we need to teach you. I'm just not…sure how to teach them to you."

"Why not?"

"The first lesson involves you learning to stand up for yourself, to confront someone when they do something wrong. The second one is teaching you how to not cave when someone confronts you. Whether they're asking you for a favour you don't have to give them or they're dismissing you."

I didn't like the sound of it. But I could see the sense in it.

I could also see how and why he'd come to that conclusion.

"And we do those how?"

He sighed. "That's where I have a problem. We need to give you more exposure to confrontations. I just haven't worked out how to do that without you losing trust in me – in us – if things went wrong. And I was hoping to avoid more confrontations between us."

"So what do we do?"

He tightened his grip around my middle as he rearranged it. "Instead of lessons on dates, we'll do lessons at school."

"At school?"

It almost felt like he huffed a rough chuckle. "Don't worry. I'm not suggesting we stop dating if that's what you really want. I will deign to be seen in public with you if you insist. All I meant was that school seems to be the place where the big innocent doe eyes and the ditzy smile come out when you're faced with confrontation. So that seems to be the best place to help you out."

That seemed logical. Unfortunately. I didn't like that I had a confidence problem. I was supposed to be bubbly, confident Avery. But then again bubbly, confident Avery was also a goody-two-shoes. So I couldn't disagree that confrontation was what the bad boy ordered.

But it also a scary prospect. So I felt the need to change the subject a little.

"Will this involve more kissing in the hallway?" I asked playfully.

"I'm not sure how that would help," he said slowly. "But it can if you want it to."

"I wouldn't be opposed."

He nodded, making sure his nose bumped mine again. "Then it will."

"How about now?"

"What about now, Avery?" There was that almost humoured smile in his eyes.

"Can it involve kissing now?"

"Yes. It can involve kissing now."

I took his face in my hand and kissed him. I was still feeling a lot of conflicting feelings about his revelation and I'm certain a lot of that went into it. I wasn't sure if you could really communicate messages in kisses. But it felt like I was telling him I was there for him, if he wanted me to be. And I felt like he understood that. Until he'd had enough show of emotions for one night and flipped me over to shower me in a very different sort of kiss.

Twenty: Davin

It was the Tuesday after the unfortunate backstory reveal –
"Although Gran will be utterly thrilled." – and I'd stooped
to spending my time in the Common Room at breaks under
the guise of spending time with Avery. But I was perfectly
fine when she flitted about happily and left me to my
computer or my book.

I watched Avery laughing with a few people who, while I
assure you they've been floating around in the background
this whole time, have actually not been named, and I couldn't
stop my mind mulling everything over. I told myself it was
all research for helping her with confrontations, but it wasn't
that at all.

I'd been thinking about what she'd said over the weekend,
about how I was worth something to her. The fact she'd
delivered her… Calling it a speech seemed a gross insult to
speeches everywhere. But whatever she thought it was, she'd
delivered it so haltingly and awkwardly that I was sure she'd
meant every ill- conveyed word.

"I honestly can't tell you how I feel about that."

Because I wasn't sure what to do with it. I wasn't kidding myself that Avery could ever fall in love with me. And for that I was glad. I had no interest in being loved or being in love. Love was a fairy-tale after all. Something shoved down our throats to supposedly make life easier to get through.

But it didn't make life easier to get through.

Because by all accounts, my parents had been madly in love and it hadn't helped anything. She'd still taken her own life and clearly been so worried about sheltering me from the pain of life that she wanted to put me out of my misery before I realised I was miserable.

No. This 'love' business was simply meant to cause a distraction. But I didn't need the complications that came with that sort of distraction. Especially not with Avery, who quite clearly bought into the wide-eyed Disney version of love. And it suited her. If she wanted it, she deserved it.

"I'm a cantankerous bastard, but I couldn't bear it if I was the one who took that away from her."

I watched as Avery bounded up to Molly and Krista who were talking to three other girls about I didn't even know what because I had normal human hearing and was lucky to hear what someone said three feet away from me. The fact I had my headphones on as well had nothing to do with it.

Molly and Krista had endeared themselves to me the same way a vaguely amusing niece or nephew is thoroughly adorable while they're misbehaving for their parents for about the first hour, then you're over it and ready to take your whiskey to a quiet corner and wonder why you bother attending those dysfunctional family functions anyway.

They did treat Avery better than most people though. When they weren't being drawn into the overly excitable trap of high school cliques. Case in point, Avery had tried saying something to the girls after Krista asked her a question and it was all going well until one of those as yet unnamed people dismissed the idea with a disbelieving grimace and then everyone was jumping on the walk all over Avery bandwagon.

How do I know what happened?

"Plot furtherance," I remind you with a wink.

Meanwhile Avery laughed, nodded and waved it all off. As she started to move away, Molly caught up with her and followed her over to where Blair was. And like that, the slight cloud that had been almost invisibly hanging over Avery was dashed away in a puff of giggles and frivolous interest in whatever was on Blair's phone.

Now was usually the time of break when I caught Miles watching Avery.

And I say caught but, *"It's not like he's really trying to hide it."* Oddly.

And this fair Tuesday in Week Two was no different. I rubbed my chin, realising it was a little scratchy even for me, and passed a glance between Miles and Avery.

I didn't think she'd noticed. Honestly I think she was far too busy to notice. But I was the kind of person who'd sit and people-watch with no qualms about looking like I was judging the lot of them. Which meant I noticed quite a few of the things that went on at our school. One of them being that Miles had a propensity to eye off my girlfriend. I just didn't know if he was missing what he'd foolishly thrown away or if there was something else going through his mind.

I went back to my book for a while, then felt a kiss on either cheek and looked up hurriedly to find Avery taking a picture of me. Molly was standing on one side of me and Blair on the other. I raised an eyebrow at Avery as I dragged my headphones off.

"How quaint," I told her, being in no risk of deflating that smile.

She laughed and I didn't dislike it at all. "It's a keeper."

I kicked my chin at her. "I'll bet."

"Come on. Bell's rung."

I looked around and saw that people were indeed packing up their bags and heading out. I slid off the desk and slung my bag over my shoulder, getting ready for another two hours of tedium. I didn't even have Avery in my next double to ameliorate some of that tedium. So I spent that hour-forty wondering how in the hell to help Avery avoid yet another situation like the one at Recess.

When I got to Home Group, there she was as always, smiling and sitting eagerly in her seat. Mr Boyle did the roll, gave us the announcements and then we were free to go to lunch which is where we were when it happened.

"I put it to you that you let people walk all over yourself because you don't believe you deserve respect."

There. I just came out and said it.

It was a theory I'd been working on since the first night she came to my place and I'd asked her about why she let people take advantage of her and she'd responded 'what *about* me?' That had been all I'd needed to begin forming the hypothesis. My assessment of her problem with confrontations had strengthened it. I'd spent the last two hours perfecting it. And now it was fully formed and out in the world.

It was up to her to decide what to do with it.

What she did with it was blink at me in the way I knew a frown was coming. "What? In what way do I think I don't deserve respect?"

I'd poked the dragon, tiny and seemingly harmless as it was, and there was no going back. I was just going to have to hope I got out of it without anything catching fire. "In the way you put everyone else's needs before your own. If you think it will upset someone to stand up for yourself, you don't."

She crossed her arms. "Give several examples."

"We'll start with the biggest first." I knew by the look on her face as I paused that she knew what was coming. "Miles."

"No. That was…"

"That was what?" I pressed when she didn't continue.

"Who knew 'hooking up' could mean sex?" she huffed.

294

"Um…literally everyone else."

Her eyes widened. "Ohmigod, I *am* too good aren't I?"

I shrugged and was almost apologetic. "You said it, not me."

She pouted at me and gave a little huff. "Okay. Look, I know I shouldn't have let him get away with even just a kiss."

"Yes. But knowing you deserved to treat yourself better and using it as a lesson to actually treat yourself better are two very different things. You knew when he dumped you that you should have dealt with his cheating arse the moment you found out. But that doesn't change the fact that you're still wandering around like your feelings matter less than everyone else's."

She was surprised and I didn't blame her. I sounded utterly indignant and all on her behalf. For someone who professed to be proficient in not giving a fuck, I certainly wasn't walking the walk just then.

"So what's your brilliant lesson then, professor?" she sassed.

"You've just got to be…" I grunted in annoyance. *"It's not even less nice,"* I tell you. "You don't even need to be less nice, all right? I mean, you know there's a difference between being a total bitch and letting someone know their behaviour isn't okay, right?"

"Davin, I don't like…arguing with people."

"For someone who doesn't like arguing, you're sure not hesitant to go at it with me."

"You don't count."

Oh. Didn't I? "Really? Why not?"

"Because…" She stopped and looked at me uncertainly.

"No. Go on. I'm dying to hear this." I wasn't. Obviously. But I think we've long-since established that using words figuratively leant rather nicely to sarcasm.

She dropped her gaze to her hands that fiddled in front of her. "Because I'm not worried that you won't like me!" she snapped, then as though she'd just realised that she'd essentially made my point for me said quieter, "Okay?"

I scoffed. "Avery, it's not like I *don't* like you."

"No. I mean… Yes. To start with it was because I knew you didn't like me, so what did it matter? I wasn't losing anything. But…"

This was the conversation we'd barely started at Grill'd and I wanted to know how it ended. "But what?"

"Well it's not like you could hate me any more than you already did. So regardless of how much you do like me, I can tell myself I'm still not losing anything. Because however much you do like me now happened while I was being…this Avery."

"As opposed to *that* Avery," I said softly and she nodded. Any difference between this Avery and that Avery was subtle in my eyes to be honest, but she didn't want to hear that. So instead I pulled her to me and wrapped her up in my arms. "Baby…" I sighed. "Anyone who dislikes you for reminding them you deserve respect isn't worth the loss."

"It's easy for you to say that," she mumbled, the words nearly being lost in my shirt.

"Why? Because I don't have anyone to lose?" I asked, my tone hardening without my intention.

She pulled away, her face showing how utterly displeased she was with me. "Well because you won't accept you have people to lose. Without that it amounts to the same."

I didn't have to stand around and have her analyse me. This whole thing was about her character arc, not mine. I wasn't having a character arc. I wasn't doing character development. I refused.

I felt my nose scrunch in resentment, but I couldn't open my mouth for some reason. She needed more confrontation experience, but it wasn't supposed to be with me. And it wasn't going to be with me. Certainly not in the school hallway.

I huffed at her, turned and stormed off. I was too angry even for my mind to come up with retorts. My heart pounded and I wanted to hit something.

Just because Avery knew about my mum didn't mean she had the right to think she knew who I was. She was just…

Fuck.

She was just trying to show me she cared.

I'd fucked up again.

I was too proud to turn around and argue with her in the hallway but there was no reason for her to follow me when I was in a mood. So what else was I going to do except storm

297

angrily and dramatically through the few remaining students in the hallways until I got to my usual meeting room and threw my bag on the floor, heedless that I might have just broken my computer.

"Fuck!"

I whirled around to see Avery hovering in the doorway like she wasn't sure if she should come in or not. I'd been freaking out that she had no reason to follow me and yet there she was.

Seeing her, I was pissed off, I was surprised, I was grateful, I was relieved, I was wary. And I was sick of the havoc these conflicting emotional reactions were playing on my life.

"Davin–"

I felt my brows furrow. "What would you know about who I have to lose, anyway?" I spat because I couldn't deal with the rush of emotions flooding me.

She frowned, not intimidated by me in the slightest. "You've got your dad and your gran–"

I huffed humourlessly. "Two people obligated by familial bonds to feel affection for me."

"Well I'd include me, but you've made your disdain for anything resembling earnest emotions painfully obvious!" she yelled and I was glad we'd conveniently found ourselves in a meeting room.

As she stepped into the room, she slammed the door closed behind her and I could only blink at her in surprise for

298

a moment.

She'd actually yelled at me. Not once had she yelled at me. Ever. In all the time I'd spent being purposefully difficult, she'd never once yelled at me, never once been authentically angry with me. Exasperated plenty. Unwittingly amused definitely. But not proper angry.

"Avery…" I said slowly.

"Don't you 'Avery' me, Davin Ambrose!" she snapped, pointing her finger at me. Then she walked closer and hissed as though she hoped people weren't listening even though there was no one to listen now, "You want me to stand up for myself? Consider this me standing up for myself. You want to pretend people don't care about you? Go ahead. But pretending something's true doesn't make it so."

"I meant stand up for yourself with other people," I shot back.

Determination shone in her eyes. "No one else is currently disrespecting me."

"Technically I think this counts as me disrespecting myself," I commented dryly.

She huffed. "Well at least that's one lesson you don't need to impart! Apparently I do that plenty well on my own."

I sighed, her blatant criticism of herself enough to kick me out of my blinkered fury. "Fine. If I admit I have people to lose, will you admit your feelings are as valid as anyone else's?"

She opened her mouth, uncertainty marring her features

for a moment. I wasn't sure if she was hesitant to admit it or because I'd just done a total one-eighty and we all knew it.

"Avery you know this in theory." I hoped.

"Yes," she replied defensively. "The theory is easy to grasp. But even Communism works in theory," she muttered.

I shoved away the weird warmth that threatened to blossom in my chest. "Then it can't be all that difficult to believe."

"I'll admit it if you do."

I blinked. "Excuse me? I'm already admitting something."

"Two things." She nodded and crossed her arms again. "I'll admit – and put into practise – the theory that my feelings are as important as anyone else's if you do as well."

"I'm not following."

"For someone so smart, you sure can be dumb sometimes."

"Enlighten me." I frowned.

"You're constantly telling me to keep my feelings to myself. That's not exactly positive reinforcement that they're important now, is it?"

Well she had me there. That was a thing I did.

"How important is it that she admit it?" I ask, thinking it through.

Was it worth me risking a deluge of feelings and emotions? Was it worth me risking my own feelings and emotions? For that to happen, I'd have to acknowledge I had them. Except there was already something about Avery that made me contemplate considering the notion. How was I going to refrain if she was there with all her emotions on her sleeve, stirring up things in me I thought long dead?

"Well?" she asked impatiently.

"Fine!" I snapped. "Yes. I do think your feelings are important and the only reason I want you to keep them away from me is because I've spent years forgetting what they're like," I said to her quietly.

Her eyes widened and her mouth dropped into that perfect little 'o', but I ignored any and all thoughts inappropriate for the current circumstance.

"Davin..." she said, her hand reaching up to cup my cheek, but I grunted in annoyance.

"What is it about you that makes me even *think* these things?" I wondered.

I was just at that moment feeling a feeling. I was feeling fucking pissed off again. How dare Avery St John barge into my life and make me feel things. How dare she make me wonder if it was possible to keep a little light in my life even after she decided I'd been a mistake for long enough. How dare she have me considering I was even worth it. How dare she have me looking at her and questioning the way I'd shut myself off from the world.

And for the love of all that was holy, what was it about her that had me blurting out quite possibly the most vulnerable parts of me when we argued? I wasn't used to being vulnerable. But this was at least the third time that

Avery had me saying something I'd never intended to tell anyone.

"I'll make you a deal?" When I didn't look at her, she paused, then continued, "I'll still keep my feelings to myself *and* accept that they're just as important as anyone else's. Okay?"

Some of the muscles in my face twitched and I wasn't sure whether a part of me was trying to say something the rest of me didn't want to say or it wasn't used to making a third expression – "neutral and bored are both expressions, yes?"

"You don't have to do that," was all I could bring myself to say to her.

"No. I don't. But I don't want to make you any more uncomfortable than I do already."

I looked down at her, about to argue with her, but paused when I saw the rueful smile on her face.

"At least not yet."

I knew this time what the facial twitch meant. It was the definite, intentional suppression of a smile. "Look forward to it."

She put her arms around my shoulders. "Excellent."

I cleared my throat and heard myself say, "Speaking of things to look forward to…" What the fuck was I doing? "I wondered if you might want to meet Gran sometime?"

I hadn't looked at her. Mainly because I couldn't believe I'd just asked her that – why was I asking her if she wanted to meet my grandmother? I'd had this discussion with myself.

The two of them were going to be completely enamoured with each other. But then the mistake would be ended and Avery would move on and Gran would be left heartbroken.

Just Gran.

Not me.

But I also didn't want to look at her because there was this negligible piece of me that didn't want to see her reaction.

"Are you actually asking me to meet your gran? As in by choice? Not just convenience?" she asked and I heard the reluctance in her voice, which made my chest hitch objectionably.

She was presumably referring to the fact that she'd only met my dad because going to mine after Vinny's had been easier and Dad had happened to be home. Add to that the fact they'd spent less than about half an hour in the same room the next morning and most of that was me trying to get Dad to keep his well-meaning but giant mouth shut, this was definitely not the same as that.

Fuck. I wished she wouldn't look at me like that. She was obviously thinking quickly. There was this slight frown in her features and her eyes darted between mine agitatedly.

She was going to say no.

Of course she was going to say no.

I met her family because it made dating easier and that was an Avery thing. Meeting Gran was different. I was a closed off guy who was suddenly asking her to meet my closest relative. This was abnormal for me and she knew it.

This was nudging into serious territory and we were just meant to be a mistake.

Of course she was going to say no.

I looked away from her as I cleared my throat. "Forget I asked. I shouldn't have... Of course you don't... You don't have to–"

"I'd love to meet her, Davin," she said. Her face went from hesitant to warm.

I looked back down at her in surprise. "Really?"

She nodded enthusiastically. "Of course! Meet the infamous Gran? I would *never* pass that up."

"But you...?"

She cupped my cheek. "I was just surprised. I know how much she means to you. I'm flattered you want me to meet her."

I breathed out, feeling a sense of relief I reminded myself was preposterous. "Okay. Well I'll ask her when suits?"

Avery nodded, reached up to kiss me, then hugged me tight around the neck.

"Oh," she said without letting go. "Do you think this is the time for my peanut butter and chocolate brownies?"

"What is your obsession with the brownies," I didn't growl as I nuzzled her neck because, again, humans don't do that.

"Davin!" she giggled, making my cock twitch in learned anticipation.

"Avery?" I asked, my lips brushing her neck.

"This is serious!"

"Yes. Gran would utterly adore you if you brought brownies." I wrapped her up tighter and she squealed happily. "But she's not likely to share them."

"I'll make you your own batch then," she laughed before I kissed the hell out of her.

Twenty~One: Avery

"Mu-um!" I yelled as I ran around my room in nothing but my underwear at half past four the next Wednesday, furiously combing the tangles out of my wet hair.

Mum came skidding into my room with Ebs not far behind. "What?"

Ebony whistled as she saw me. "I *did* wonder why you didn't shower this morning," she said.

"Not now, Ebs," I pleaded.

"What's wrong, sweetie?" Mum asked.

"The curlers. Where are the curlers?" I asked, grabbing the bottle of detangler and giving that particular lock another spray. "Why is this happening now?" I muttered.

"Ave, you're just meeting Davin's gran," Ebony laughed. "It's not the end of the world if your hair's not perfect."

Mum and I both glared at her.

"You don't understand," I whined as I finally got the knot out. "Davin's gran means the world to him. I can tell. If she doesn't like me, I'm done for."

Mum gave me a weirdly knowing look – something

between pride, humour, and surprise – and I would have spent more time wondering what she was thinking had I not been in the middle of a crisis.

"I used your curler this morning. I'll grab it," Mum said gently as Ebony took another step into my room and frowned.

"Oh what, Ebs?" I huffed as I looked around for my volumising powder.

"He means a lot to you then?" she asked and I spared her a moment's glance to find her hanging over the back of my desk chair.

I tried to keep track of what she was saying and what I was supposed to be doing – I had two hours until Davin was going to pick me up. "Of course he does," I replied absently as I dusted my hair with the powder.

"No, Ave. I mean he *really* means a lot to you then?"

I turned to her for a moment as I picked up my hair dryer. "Um...well, yeah."

"Do you love him?" her voice was loud enough for me to hear but soft enough for me to look at her with slightly more concentration.

There was a look on her face I'd never seen before and I wasn't quite sure what it meant. She looked a little bit uncertain, but a little bit confused, and just a little bit like she needed me to be entirely honest with her. Sister to sister.

I breathed away the weird catch in my chest at the idea of Davin and love and smiled at her. "I'm not sure I can be trusted to know what love is, Ebs. I thought I loved Miles

and–"

"Yeah, but Miles was a shithead."

"Ebony," Mum half-heartedly chastised as she came back in. Then gave me an apologetic look. "Though to be fair, Ave, he sort of was."

I nodded. "Exactly. Maybe you *can* be too young to know what love is."

Mum passed me the curlers and gave me a smile like she knew Ebs and I were having some sister time and left again.

"I don't think you believe that," Ebony said, throwing herself stomach-first onto my bed.

"Why not?" I asked her as I ran the hair dryer over my hair.

"Because," she said, speaking louder to be heard, "I've never seen you like this before."

"Like what?"

"Well, no. I know you worry about what people think of you. But I've never seen you like actually worried. As in legitimately worried before."

I lowered the hair dryer as I tried not to compare my little sister and Davin too heavily. "What's that mean?"

Ebony shrugged. "You're not just worried that people will think your eyeliner's wonky or whatever. You want to make a good impression on Davin's gran because you care about him. It's new." She huffed a laugh. "You weren't even like this with Miles' grandparents."

I grimaced and we both laughed. The night I'd met Miles'

maternal grandparents was not one of my finest. And through no fault of my own. I went in there as my usual self and expected they'd like me because everyone did. But it did matter what I did because they were adamant that no one was going to be good enough for their little Miles.

Almost ironic really that he'd called me *too good* when I couldn't win them over.

I grinned at Ebony. "I wonder what they think of Cindy?"

Ebony returned my grin. "If he's smart, he won't have introduced them to her."

I nodded. "Probably wise."

I finished drying my hair and then turned the curlers on while I did my make-up.

"What are you wearing tonight?" Ebony asked after a while.

I pointed vaguely at my wardrobe with the lip-liner in my hand. "On the door."

I sort of noticed her head over to the wardrobe as I filled my lips in.

"Blue and black?" she asked.

"Yep. What do you think?" I turned in my chair to look at her. "Do you think Davin will like it?"

Ebony caught the skirt up in her hands and looked thoughtful for a moment. "Well, I like it."

I laughed. "And you and Davin like all the same things?"

She looked at me out of the side of her eyes. "Pretty much."

I gave her a warm smile and decided to agree instead of teasing her. "Good. Then I'm sure he will like it."

Ebony hung out in my room while I curled my hair, helping me hold the odd piece of hair and dousing me in hairspray as necessary. We didn't talk much – Ebony even sang along to the music a little with me – but it was a nice sisterly moment. She helped me into my dress and did up my necklace for me.

"What do you think?" I asked, giving her a twirl.

"You look really nice, Ave," she said with one of those rare smiles.

"You've got the disco coming up, yeah?" I asked her.

She nodded. "Yeah. Why?"

I ran my hand over my skirt. "You want to borrow it?"

Ebony and I were the same size even though I was a little (barely) taller.

Her eyes lit up and she nodded more vigorously. "Will you do my hair like that too?"

I put my arm around her. "Of course."

"Thanks, Ave."

I pressed my cheek to her head and blew her a kiss – knowing if I gave her an actual kiss she'd complain. "Anytime, Ebs."

I grabbed my clutch as we walked out and headed downstairs to wait for Davin.

When the doorbell rang at a little before six-thirty, I ran to get it.

"You're technically early," I laughed.

But he wasn't paying attention with his ears.

"*What* are you wearing?" he asked, looking me over.

I looked down. "You don't like it?"

"I didn't say that…"

"But?" I asked because his tone heavily implied a 'but'.

He scrubbed a hand over his chin. "I…"

I looked down again at the dress I'd bought the day I bought his red Converse – which he was wearing. I thought he'd like it, or at least have no reason to complain about it. It was one of those retro 50's swing dresses, pale blue with white polka dots, a thick black belt, with a black sweetheart neckline and halter strap. I'd paired it with red vintage-style shoes, I hadn't added any bows to my hair, and my clutch was black.

When I looked back to him, he looked thoroughly confused.

"You don't like it."

He shook his head. "I honestly don't know how to feel about it."

"What do you mean?"

"I mean…" He looked me over again and I was starting to worry about what he was about to say. "You've somehow pulled off completely sweet and innocent – perfect for meeting Gran – but somehow I still just want to throw you up against that wall and show you what you do to me."

I looked down so he wouldn't see the smile that elicited. I

mean, that had been the goal after all. "Take me to meet your gran, then maybe I'll let you do me dirty in the back seat on the way home," I told him coyly.

"Fucking Jesus, woman," he breathed. "Don't do that to me." He rearranged his pants to prove his point.

Then we both looked up sharply as Mum came into the hall. "Heya, Davin."

"Heather." Davin nodded, managing to look far less guilty than me at what Mum *could* have walked in on.

"What do you think, hun?" Mum asked him, taking my hand and making me twirl around.

I flushed as I looked up at Davin and didn't know why I felt so shy in front of him all of a sudden. Davin's eyes were pinned to me and his usual dour expression was somewhat softer than usual.

"She looks beautiful," he said.

"Ave. Brownies." Ebony came in with the two Tupperwares I'd put the brownies in the night before. "Hey, Davin."

He nodded. "Ebs. Good?"

She nodded. "Good." And passed me the Tupperwares.

I took them with a smile. "Thanks."

"Right." Mum smiled. "Do you two need to get going?" There was a look in Mum's eyes I wasn't sure I liked. Not if it meant what I thought it meant.

Davin nodded. "Uh. We probably should. Yes."

Mum looked at me like she was sorry for what she was

312

about to do and I groaned.

"What?" Davin asked and I hissed, "Mu-um!"

"Just one. Please?" she begged.

"It's not the formal," I grumbled.

Mum held up a finger. "Just the one. Then I'm done."

I looked to Davin, pretty sure I knew the answer was going to be a resounding heck no. But to my surprise he nodded.

"I can do a picture," he said simply.

Mum ushered him inside and put us against the cream wall of the hallway as she pulled her phone out of her pocket. "Okay. Okay. Just the one. I promise."

I gave Ebony the Tupperwares back, returning her wry smile. Davin sidled up close to me and put his arm around me and I instinctively put mine around him. I looked up at him as he flicked his hair out of his face. He looked at me with a humoured question in his eyes.

"What?" he asked.

I shook my head with a smile. "Nothing."

"Okay. Can I get one with you looking at *me* please?" Mum asked.

Davin flicked his hair again and we both turned to Mum.

"Great. Excellent. You both look *great*," she said earnestly.

I looked down to hide my smile as Davin and I pushed off from the wall. It wasn't like I didn't like what Davin was wearing. But it was still just his dark jeans and black top combination, no different to any other clothes Mum had ever

313

seen him in except his uniform.

"Thanks," Davin muttered as he cleared his throat. "Shouldn't be too late tonight."

Mum waved her hand and shook her head at him. "All good. Whenever."

I rolled my eyes at her as Ebony passed me back the containers and Mum shrugged.

"Okay. Home by curfew. Blah, blah, blah!" she said with a rueful grin.

"Bye," I called, my expression hopefully telling her to cool it.

"Bye," Mum and Ebony said as I took Davin's hand and led him out of the house.

"You do look beautiful, you know," he said, leaning towards me as we walked down the front path.

"I thought we didn't conform to traditional standards of physical beauty?" I teased and he did that huff that wasn't quite a laugh.

"I don't just think you're beautiful for your outsides. And you know that."

"So what makes me look particularly beautiful tonight, Davin?" I asked, swishing my skirt as I turned.

He opened the car passenger door for me. "You made an effort."

I looked up at him as I got into the car and smoothed my skirt over my lap. "I always make an effort. Thank you."

He leant down, leaning on the roof. "You made an effort

314

to win over Gran. Is it weird I find that sexy?"

He closed the door and went around to get into the driver's side. So I had a moment to myself to feel both thrilled that I'd at least impressed Davin and terrified about what his gran was going to think of me.

"It's sexy that I want to impress your gran? Or was it the idea of doing me dirty in the backseat?" I asked.

He took a deep breath. "You want to make it to meet Gran, then let's keep talk of backseat shenanigans to a minimum. Yeah?"

I laughed. "Okay. Deal."

He turned the car on and took me to his gran's house. He pulled into the driveway when we got there, then let out another breath.

"You seem nervous," I said, feeling a little concerned and nervous myself.

"Of course I'm fucking nervous," he grumbled. "I've never had a girlfriend, let alone brought her to dinner at Gran's."

I leant over and made him look at me. "It'll be okay. I promise I'll be totally lovable."

He dropped his forehead to mine for a moment, saying, "That's what concerns me." Then he pressed a quick kiss to my lips and got out.

I grabbed the Tupperware container for his gran, leaving his on the floor for later. I paused for a moment before I got out. I took a deep breath and reminded myself, "You can totally do this, Avery," then got out and followed him across the lawn.

Davin unlocked the front door, indicated I go in, and called, "Gran!" as he closed it again behind him.

"That you, Davin?" came a voice further in the house.

"No," he called back and I got the feeling it was an in-joke.

A gorgeous woman walked into the hallway and beamed with nothing but love at him behind me before her eyes fell to me. I watched them widen in surprised interest for a moment, then she just looked pleased to see me.

"Oh look at this gorgeous thing!" she cooed. "Oh, dear. You didn't have to dress up."

"This is Avery dressed down, Gran," Davin muttered as he went around me, his hand resting lightly for a moment on my back as he passed. He gave his gran a hug and let her kiss his cheek. "Gran, this is Avery. Avery, Ginny Wheeler."

I walked over to her. "It's really lovely to meet you." I held out the container, realising my hands were clenched rather tightly on it. I took a breath and tried to relax. "I, uh, made you some brownies."

She looked at Davin warmly as she took them from me. "That was lovely of you, dear. I'll get right to those." She passed the container to Davin. "But first let me look at you."

Ginny put her hand under my chin and looked me over like she was committing me to memory.

"Oh, Davin. Look at her. She's stunning. Posture, fashion,

316

those eyes… And that smile." Ginny leant towards me conspiratorially and I recognised the look of mischief in her eyes as the same I saw in her grandson's. "Dear, what are you doing with my Davin?"

I heard him mutter under his breath as he moved further into the house and I laughed. "I happen to quite like him, Ginny."

Her eyes fairly melted as she took my hand in hers. "You don't know how it warms my heart to hear that, Avery. Now come in. Come in." She started leading me into the house. "Davin *should* be making us drinks by now."

We walked into the kitchen and a big ball of grey fluff came trotting over to me with obvious curiosity. Davin turned and frowned at it.

"Flint! Come…" He petered off as the cat started rubbing against my legs.

I picked it up and held it close. I could feel it purring hard as it rubbed its head against my chin.

"Holy shit," Davin breathed and Ginny snapped his name. He looked at his gran and pointed at me. "He likes her," he said like he didn't believe it.

"Of course he does," Ginny said. "Unlike you, he recognises what a catch Avery is."

"What's that supposed to mean?"

"Just how long did the two of you go to school together before you started dating?"

"Gran!" Davin warned but, much like he was with most

people, she seemed determined to do her own thing.

"I'm only saying, dear, that I'd have liked to have met Avery earlier."

I hid a laugh as best I could as I put Flint down again, but Davin looked at me quickly and I knew he'd heard it.

"I see where Davin gets it from now," I said to Ginny.

"Gets what from?" she asked innocently.

"Most of what makes him…him."

She tutted, but it was somehow still elegant. "Davin wishes he were as witty and clever as me." Ginny threw me a wink as Davin exclaimed in protest.

"All right," he said slowly. "Have your drink, Gran. You can get to know Avery better from the living room, surely."

He passed Ginny a tumbler of drink and passed me a lemonade.

"Good idea. Avery, come and sit down. Make yourself at home, please." Ginny looped her arm with mine as we walked out and then called back to Davin, "Bring the brownies with you, Davin."

I laughed as she led me into the living room.

"All right, dear," Ginny said as she encouraged me onto the one couch and then sat on the other. "I want to know everything about you."

"Oh, God. I have no idea where to start."

She grinned at me conspiratorially. "Start at the beginning."

Twenty-Two: Davin

"This is already going far worse than I thought it would."

I'd expected Gran to love her. But even she'd surpassed my expectations. They'd both surpassed my expectations. Avery had won her over in record time. Damned Avery in that damned dress looking so damned...

"Fuck!"

Looking at Avery, I was completely torn. On one hand I was very interested in what doing her dirty in the backseat looked like – I was down to get my 50s roleplay on if that's what she wanted. But on the other... There was this foreign feeling swirling around my chest and stomach. It had everything to do with keeping Avery close, and nothing to do with even touching her.

I pulled on my collar, being so far from it choking me that the action was less than pointless. But I felt weird. I fucking *felt* for a start.

"Remind me I can do this. It's my gran and my girlfriend. How bad can it be?"

I picked up my water and the brownies, and followed them

into the living room. They were already laughing and Gran was looking at Avery like she could already picture the white dress and the great grandkids – who she would no doubt demand to send to Mitchell College also. Avery was warm and open and enthusiastic as always, throwing herself one hundred percent into the situation as she always did.

The one insignificant blemish in her perfect exterior was the way she looked into her lap as she brushed her hair off her face, the nervous tremor to her laugh, and the way she took a deep breath to accompany that questioning smile when she saw me walk in.

"And next year?" Gran asked her.

Avery sighed and looked back to Gran. "God. Next year. That's the question, isn't it?" She huffed a self-conscious laugh as she looked at me for a moment. "I don't know. Worst case, I thought I'd apply for Arts and hope I found something I was good at."

"Not the worst plan in the world." Gran looked at me. "He's going to do Arts, too."

"Majoring in English, of course," Avery said.

I nodded. "Although, I might only apply for Flinders now."

Gran frowned. "Oh no. Why?"

"Probably because Dad lectures at Adelaide," Avery offered, her nose wrinkling as though she felt guilty about it.

Gran looked between us. "Well I suppose that could make things difficult."

I shrugged as I sat down next to Avery. "I might. I thought…if the opportunity presented itself I could talk to him about it in a few months. See what he thought."

"Applications are due in October, Davin," Gran reminded me.

"And it's only May, Gran."

"Is it?" Gran asked me sardonically and I felt Avery suppress a giggle next to me. "And what does Dad teach, Avery? English I assume?"

"Yes. Medieval and Gothic literature."

Gran was already far too interested. That sent her interest sky high. "Medieval and Gothic? How about that." She looked at me pointedly and I rolled my eyes at her.

Avery nodded. "He and Davin already had a *huge* discussion about Gothic texts." She looked at me and I was sure the way she took my hand was totally subconscious. "What was it? Sexuality in…Victorian literature?"

"Well then." Gran barely contained a smirk and I was sure it wasn't just because she was interested by the fact I'd let Avery hold my hand in front of her. "Trust Davin to bring out the heavy topics at the dinner table."

"He convinced Dad to let Ebony read…" There went that pensive frown. "*Carmilla!*" she said in victory as she remembered it.

"Your sister?" Gran clarified and Avery nodded. "And how old's Ebony?"

"Fourteen," I answered for Avery.

Gran seemed to think about. "Could be too young. Could be old enough."

Avery smiled fondly, presumably thinking of her little sister. "When it comes to Ebony, it's pretty much always old enough. Emotionally anyway. She's an old soul."

I was pretty sure there were plenty of things that Ebony was still emotionally too young for, old soul or not. But Avery wouldn't have been thinking of them because she was far too respectable.

"And the two of you are close?" Gran asked.

Avery nodded. "Yes. Well we don't have a lot in common, but she keeps telling me she'd give anyone who hurts me a decent beating if she were bigger."

I watched Gran's eyes widen in surprise then she grinned. "I'm sure Davin is suitably prepared, then."

Avery laughed. "Oh no. He doesn't count. Ebony *loves* Davin."

Gran's eyebrow rose in my direction. "Really?"

"I assure you I've done nothing to earn it," I told her and Avery scoffed.

"He says that. But I'm starting to think that an actual thoughtful soul resides deep inside all that cynicism and sarcasm." Avery's hand squeezed mine and I couldn't stop myself returning it.

Gran leant towards Avery conspiratorially. "You know what, dear? I've been trying to convince him of that for years. I'm glad I'm not the only one who sees it."

"Brilliant. They're bonding."

In many ways, wasn't this exactly what I wanted? I wanted the two most important girls in my life – *"Do* not *read too much into that," –* to get along. Didn't I?

I'd almost convinced myself that I did. I'd almost convinced myself that this whole thing wasn't as bad as I was telling myself. Through dinner and dessert, I told myself it was fine.

Then the photo album came out and I was rethinking everything. I wasn't sure if I was more outraged or embarrassed. Not that I'd let either emotion show if I could help it.

"Oh, did he have no balloons at his party?" Avery asked as Gran showed her every piece of my tiny shame with absolutely zero fucks given.

Gran shook her head. "Oh no, dear. Davin was terrified of balloons–"

"Gran!" I snapped. "For all that's holy," was the closest I was coming to swearing in her house and getting away with it. Baby pictures were one thing. One terrible thing, but one thing. Stories accompanying those baby pictures were worse. "If you continue that sentence, I will–"

"What, dear?" Gran asked, looking at me over her glasses frames. "Berate me with your grandiose eloquence some more?"

Avery spluttered and I looked at her in annoyance.

"Having fun?" I asked Avery.

She nodded, still trying not to laugh, and I couldn't bring myself to be the cause of the smile falling from her face. I huffed and sat back in my seat. I waved my hand at Gran in a continuation motion.

"Fine. Proceed to embarrass me six ways from Sunday without the fear of *grandiose* retaliatory reprimand." I quirked my eyebrow at Gran and she did a terrible job at trying to hide her smile.

"Oh. Who's this?" Avery asked, running her hand over a picture.

Gran peered at the picture and looked up at me before answering. I knew who it was. "My daughter."

"My mother," I clarified, glaring at the woman who should know better than to tiptoe around the whole sordid past.

Avery put her hand on Gran's arm. "I am so sorry about what happened."

"Why? Did you run the bath?" I asked, more venom in my voice than I'd intended.

Gran shot me a look that was far too fast to decipher and just as well too. "Thank you, dear," she said to Avery, her tone nothing but sincerity. "It is what it is." She threw me a sideways glance before asking, "He told you the whole story then?"

Avery looked at me uncertainly and I gave her a single nod.

"I told her, Gran."

Gran looked between us and I saw her eyes soften immeasurably. I know she was telling me she was happy I'd finally opened up to someone we didn't pay exorbitant amounts of money. I hoped she knew I was telling her not to get too excited because it didn't mean anything.

I wasn't falling in love with Avery after all this. It wasn't a thing that was going to happen. This wasn't that gag-worthy romance story where I had no control over anything. It was my life. I was my own man and heaven forbid any writer who thought I was going to fall in love without my consent.

Avery was mildly entertaining and provided a temporary relief from my usual monotony. But when she was not good and one or both of us were bored, we'd just be that mistake and go our separate ways. That's all this was.

And I reminded myself of that fact as I watched Avery and Gran laugh and talk and fall irrevocably in love with each other, and I told myself that it wasn't heart-warming. I told myself they were the only ones falling.

Eventually, it came time that I should probably take Avery home. It was a school night after all and, after spending the night together more than a few times, I was pretty sure she didn't get up as early as she did, as happily optimistic as she did, because she went to bed as late as me.

So we said our good byes and Gran waved us off down the street.

"Your gran is something else," Avery said reverently.

I nodded. "She is…a special lady."

"I can see why you love her so much."

"What says I love her?"

She reached over and put her hand on my leg. The gesture was comforting, not sexual. "Actions speak louder than words, Davin."

I sighed as I shot her a sideways look. "The woman looked after me through the worst period of my life. Of her life. She found her youngest daughter dead and her grandson terrified, and the woman battled through it. Never once did she falter no matter how she might have been suffering on the inside. She stood stoic and tall for her family the way she felt someone had to while the rest of us all fell apart to varying degrees. That sort of thing earned…" I cleared my throat, "more than just my respect," I finished quietly.

She didn't say anything so when I stopped at the traffic lights I looked at her and found her looking at me thoughtfully.

"What now?" I asked her.

She smiled. "Nothing. I'm not at all completely convinced there's more to you than meets the eye."

I shifted awkwardly in my seat before driving on. "Good."

"You know…" she started, but didn't go on.

"I know a lot of things. Is there something particular to which you are referring?"

"It's not *that* late," she said and I heard the smile in her voice.

"Isn't it?" I asked, suddenly much more interested in

326

where the conversation was going.

"It's not. And I seem to recall there being something about doing me dirty in the backseat…"

I breathed out heavily as I told my cock to stand down while I concentrated on driving. "There has been some discussion of this, yes."

"There has."

"And did you have a specific location in mind as to where this could take place?" I asked, thinking through the actual logistics of having her in my backseat.

"I thought the backseat would be good."

I shot her a look and – yep – that had been intentionally sarcastic. I huffed and turned off towards my house instead of hers.

"Where are you going?"

"The closest place I can think of that we'd be guaranteed to get away with this," I told her.

She laughed and I took us to my house. Instead of just pulling into the driveway though, I opened the garage door which I never really bothered with and parked the car in before closing the door behind us. I turned the car off and turned to her.

"You want to do this?"

She nodded vigorously and I felt that smile tugging at my lips again.

"Okay, then."

She unbuckled her seat and clambered into the backseat

327

through the front ones because she was unrealistically short. Being slightly taller, I had to go around.

"Where are you going?" she asked from the backseat behind the front passenger as I got out.

I stuck my head back in and said, "Some of us don't fit through the front seats," before closing the driver's door and getting in the back.

She climbed into my lap and I awkwardly shuffled us over so her knee fit on the seat on my other side. Before I got my bearings, she unhesitatingly took my face in her hands and kissed me hard and I sort of just lost all ability to think clearly.

She ground against me as we kissed and hands slid over bodies.

"Condom?" she asked and I nodded.

"Pocket."

Between the two of us, we managed to get my wallet out of my pocket and the condom out of it with her only hitting her head on the roof twice. She just giggled and reached between us to undo my jeans. I was fucking glad when she released me from my boxers because I was more than ready for her.

She didn't delay in getting the condom on me, then she'd pushed her undies aside and was lowering herself onto me as she kissed me again. Her hands were in my hair and on my shoulders and mine were under her skirt on those soft, warm legs, holding her tightly and hopefully helping her with some of the work as she rode me.

And she didn't stop moving as she leant her forehead to mine and said breathlessly, "Maybe not as dirty as originally planned?"

I shook my head and replied, "I'm good with it," as I kissed her as though I couldn't get enough of her.

I felt her smile against my lips. "You sure?"

I nodded. "Besides, logistically, seriously dirty sex would be *really* uncomfortable back here."

She grinned. "I *did* promise you dirty…"

I almost laughed. "I can take you out of here and bend you over if you really want, but I'm good."

Her head fell back as she moved on top of me and that soft, satisfied smile crossed her lips. I met her thrust for thrust and she shook her head.

"Maybe next time," she said as though she was almost apologetic, but not quite.

I was perfectly fine with that. Whatever this was, it was incredible. I wrapped my arms tightly around her and held her as close as I could get her. "Yeah maybe," I mumbled against her lips as I kissed her again.

I'd never had anything against kissing before. It had always been vaguely pleasurable. But kissing Avery was addictive. Every time her lips touched me I felt something. It was like something shooting through my stomach and up into my chest. I didn't know what it was and I didn't want to know what it meant. I just needed more of it.

Her breathing started to come harder, she kissed me more fervently, and I felt her starting to tense in my arms, which I knew well by now meant that she was close. So despite the almost impossibly awkward angle, I slid my hand between us and ran it over her.

She sighed against my lips, "Don't stop, Davin," and I felt incredibly proud of her – it had taken a bit of time to get her to tell me what she wanted in the heat of the moment without her self-consciously losing her rhythm.

"Never, baby." My lips trailed over her cheek and down her neck and she sighed again happily.

I felt her thighs tensing firmer and then the rest of her body, including the arms that were around my head, and she let out that incredibly sexy whimper as she finished.

We moved more slowly and kissed more languidly as she got her breath back and her increased sensitivity dulled a little. I knew when she was ready for me to go harder again by the way she nipped my lip.

My hands gripped her hips as I thrust into her, her meeting every stroke in nigh perfect unison until I felt my orgasm building. I rested my head back on the seat and Avery seemed more than happy to take over the majority of the work until she tipped me over the edge.

She slowed again as I breathed hard.

I looked at her and felt that weird warming in my chest at whatever I saw in those bright blue eyes.

In order to not look at it too closely, I said, "I should

probably get you home."

She nodded almost regrettably but she was smiling. "I guess so."

I kissed her quickly. "Just let me get cleaned up, yeah?"

She slid off me. "Okay."

I looked back at her, unsure of what I'd heard in her tone. I took her chin in my hands and made her look into my eyes. "That was perfect, Avery."

She smiled shyly, biting her lips as her eyes hooded. "Right back at you."

I didn't know what had happened to me, but I was pretty sure that was enough of it for one night.

Twenty-Three: Avery

We'd been practising the whole me standing up for myself over the last couple of weeks with varying degrees of success. It was hard to overcome that feeling of hesitation I got that someone was going to not like me if I pushed back even a little.

It didn't even have to be a very big push.

I'd successfully stood up for myself when my Art teacher said to me, "I'm off to lunch. Can you finish cleaning up before you go, Avery?" the same way she often did.

I'd been very proud of my replied, "Oh, me too. My area's all clean. Looks like Faye and Rich left a bit of a mess though."

Miss Burnett had looked at me in some confusion for a second, then nodded and said, "Great. Thanks. I'll…uh…make sure they clean up next lesson."

I'd nodded and skipped my way out to see Davin and he'd done his darnedest to not look impressed with my minor victory.

Some things were easier than others though.

When Nina had said she didn't like Rose Byrne's dress in some article that was floating around, I hadn't disagreed with her even though I'd loved it. Davin had given me a very unimpressed look for that one since I'd been going on about it the night before.

When Kate was all about how long dresses for the formal were so early 2000s, even though about six people disagreed with her I couldn't do it. I didn't agree with her either, though. I'd just kept my mouth shut and shrugged when Molly asked me to back her up on the long dress team saying, "I don't know. They're both fine, I guess."

Strangely with Molly and Krista, as it had always been with Blair, it was a bit easier to say what I wanted without worrying I'd cause an argument or they wouldn't like me anymore. I wondered if that was because I hadn't really known them until after the whole thing happened. I still felt weird disagreeing with them. But it was getting easier because all either of them did was argue with me good-naturedly and once I even changed Krista's mind that peanut butter did totally belong with Vegemite.

I was trying to remember that I was allowed different opinions from my friends. I was allowed a voice and it mattered. And using that voice the right way wasn't going to (shouldn't) make people unhappy or dislike me.

At the formal committee meetings, I was still hesitant to push my own agenda when it seemed like no one (particularly Louise who was just mad that Mrs Mack had refused to let her have Forbidden Fairy-Tales as the theme) was interested in listening or someone told me – in any number of words – that whatever I said was a stupid idea.

Trina had asked my opinion on the colour scheme for the formal decorations after checking, "Your mum's an interior designer, right?"

I'd nodded and started saying that, "Lighter colours will open the space. But if you want to make it feel closer–"

"Exactly," she'd interrupted. "We need to go with the darker shades because we want intimacy. So I want that silver more gunmetal. I want the blues in the navies. I want the yellows to be deep golds. We want that red more maroon. And the green needs to be dark forest. The darkest forest you can get me."

I'd tried to clarify with an, "Actually, you still want some–"

But Trina was done with my opinion as she ran away with what she was convinced was right. "Dark. Intimate. Promoting togetherness." Then she'd glared at everyone like she was daring them to not promote togetherness.

I'd frowned and pretended to write the new orders down, but knew I was keeping some of the colours brighter. The committee had decided on mood lighting so we were at risk of people not even seeing half our hard work if we just dropped the brightness on everything. And I wasn't working so hard for almost half the year to walk into a formal that… Well actually Davin and Ebony would feel right at home in –

had Ebony been invited.

But I'd stuck to my guns and argued the benefits of having a bake sale at the school's Winter Fair to raise money for said decorations and even gone prepared for resistance based on possible allergies kids might have. So it was I found myself proudly in charge of my first bake sale and had half the committee volunteering to help, while Trina told the other half they were also helping.

Louise butted in on my bake sale sign when I was fixing it up in the Common Room at Lunch one day, telling me, "We needed something edgier and less cheesy."

And instead of reminding her that bake sales were supposed to have a certain sense of nostalgia and fun, I said nothing but, "I'll see what I can do."

Davin was in the Common Room with me and suggested, "She could steal the Metallica font and you could all paint your faces like Kiss."

It was obvious neither of us really knew what he was talking about, particularly when Louise gave one of those fake laughs and said, "We still want class, Davin."

Davin shrugged like it mattered little to him, levelled an apathetic stare at her and said, "Good luck with that."

As I tried not to laugh, I ended up just doing my own thing with the sign behind her back. I even added extra squiggly writing to up the cheese factor, explaining to Davin that, "We want cheese."

"I thought you were doing a sweet bake sale?"

I'd looked up and him in confusion.

"Not savoury," he'd added.

I'd smiled. "Just you concentrate on re-coding the school's screensaver–"

"Not a thing I do," he'd interrupted.

"–or whatever it is and leave me to my corniness."

He'd looked at me heatedly and nodded once. "You *are* the queen of corn, babe."

By Friday Week Four, even Davin agreed I'd made progress but that I still had work to do. And it was made all the more obvious when Louise came up to me with a stack of papers.

"I need you to take these to the Principal's PA for the formal budget," she said and I looked down at them.

The office of the Principal's PA – my good friend Mrs Hines – was literally on the way from the Common Room to practically any of the classes she might have after lunch.

"Louise, I–"

"I don't have time and she needs them this afternoon. So I need you to take them." She thrust them into my hand and I had no choice but to take them or let them fall on the floor. "Thanks, Avery. I knew I could count on you."

She started walking away, but I stopped her. "Actually, you can't. Not today."

Louise turned to me slowly and there was the sort of smile on her face like she was hoping for my sake she'd herd wrong. "Sorry?"

"I'm happy to help you when I can, but now is not one of those times." I faltered a little in the face of her astonishment, but I persevered. "It's just as easy for you. You take them."

I held the papers out to her again. She looked at them suspiciously, then turned that look on me for a moment.

"Okay…" she said slowly and I couldn't quite tell if that was murder or growing respect in her eyes. "No. You're right. Sure. Of course I can."

"Great. Thanks."

Louise took the papers back from me, looked down at them again and nodded. She cleared her throat. "By the way… You were right about the sign for the bake sale."

I blinked. "I was?"

She nodded. "You were. Cheesy and cutesy is definitely the right choice."

I smiled. "Oh. Well, thanks."

She shrugged and looked up at me. "No worries."

While I was on a roll, I thought I'd bring up the whole colour scheme thing. "I had a thought about the colours…" I started and she looked at me expectantly.

"What about them?"

"Well…I think Trina's last decision might be a little…too dark. When I said darker, I didn't quite mean–"

"You're getting the fabrics and stuff from your mum, right?"

I nodded. "Ye-es…"

"Cool. So what was this about darker?"

"The other day when we were talking about darker, I didn't mean like indistinguishable darker... Especially in the light you've chosen. I just meant maybe a little bit of contrast."

Louise nodded thoughtfully. "I trust your judgement. Go with your gut or whatever. I mean, stick to the colours. But shades and tones... Your call, Avery." Her smile was warmer now.

I nodded, smiling back. "Sure. I won't let you down."

Louise laughed. "I know you won't. You're Avery." But this time, the person saying that didn't leave it hanging like I was a pushover. "You always come through for people. I admire that." She waved the stack of papers at me. "I need to get these to Mrs Hines. I'll see you later."

"Bye, Louise."

"Bye, Avery."

As Louise left, I felt odd. I thought I'd feel happier, more victorious, more proud of myself. And I was proud of me for sanding my ground, but there was also something else in there as well. I started thinking something, but I hadn't quite got to the fully formed section of my thought process yet.

Davin walked over to me with slightly more bounce in his step than he usually had and tried to look me in the eye.

"Avery?" he said, some real emotion showing through. And that emotion was excitement. "Babe, you did it! You did it, without batting an eyelid. You totally put her in her–"

I put a hand on his chest and he paused in confusion.

"Now I know I can, that's the last time I do that," I mused.

"Hang on…" Davin stepped back from me. "What?"

"The last time I do that. Now I know I can." I felt my smile growing.

"I'm not following."

"Next time I'll probably just say yes." I shrugged.

"What?" he asked. "Why?"

I cocked my head to the side, feeling a sense of settled in myself that I didn't realise I'd been living without until I had it. "You know what, Davin?"

Panic hit his face for a split second, then he shook his head. "No. What?"

"I think I'm good."

He blinked. "You're good?"

I nodded.

"You're good?"

I nodded again.

"Good as in okay? Or good as in…?"

I grinned wider. "Good." I shrugged. "I'm a good girl."

His confusion was understandable. "I'm *really* not following."

"I could totally have taken the receipts to Mrs Nichol's office for Louise. It wouldn't have been a problem for me."

"But… You weren't required to. It's no more difficult for her to do her own job."

"Exactly. Which means it would have been no more difficult for me either."

339

"She's… She was trying to take advantage of you, Avery…" he said, but he sounded like he wasn't sure about something.

I shrugged. "Maybe."

"I'm going to need you to explain how that's okay."

"Well. I agree about the whole reminding myself that my feelings are important and standing up for myself more. But otherwise," I shrugged again, "why not do things for other people just because it's kind and helpful? I'm happy with who I am. And if that's too good, then consider me too good."

"Okay…?"

"I know I can stand up for myself when I need to now and I'm not so scared that people will stop liking me because of it. But I don't *mind* being helpful and kind, so I can do that when I want, too."

"So… So what have we been doing this whole time?"

I thought about that. "Well, we started out with a plan and…it changed, it evolved, it did its own thing."

"You don't say," Davin said not to me. Then he cleared his throat and looked me over. "So…are we…?" He coughed. "Are we done then?"

Oh. Um.

"I… Well, I still need a little help with the whole standing up for myself thing in…uh, in practice…" I said lamely, feeling my cheeks heating. "And you know… You're so good at lighting my indignation."

He nodded stiffly. "So… Not done?"

340

"Are you…bored?" I asked, wondering why it was so hot (and not in a good way) and awkward all of a sudden.

He shook his head and I noticed he wasn't looking at me. "I've told you, I could never be bored with you–"

"Uncomfortable, yes. But bored, no," I finished for him.

He breathed out heavily. "Exactly."

I tucked a piece of hair behind my ear. "Do you…still want to be dating?"

"Do you?" he asked.

I paused before I answered only because I realised that I really didn't want to be done with us. I really liked being with him and I was starting to think that it was more than just the benefits of him showing me how to be not good, which seems to have actually been him actually just showing me how to let myself acknowledge I was allowed to be respected.

Nothing about this experiment appeared to have gone to plan.

I'd wanted to be not good and ended up just realising that I actually quite like me, that I was okay with being good.

I'd thought Davin was just going to be my mistake. The bad boy I'd dated in my teens. A time I looked back on fondly, but moved on from quite happily and easily.

Only, now we were talking about the possibility of ending it, it felt like nothing about him had been a mistake. I didn't understand it and I didn't think it really mattered why. I just knew that I didn't want it to end.

But I wasn't sure what he wanted and he wasn't exactly

the touchy-feely, let's talk about – or even acknowledge – our emotions kind of guy. Although the fact he'd not actually definitively answered my question suggested that he wasn't thinking 'yes'.

Suddenly all the pride and happiness I'd felt on finally being okay with me vanished and I was left feeling weird and insecure.

"I mean… You could help me practise?" I said, sounding totally idiotic.

He ran his tongue over his teeth as he looked me over and I couldn't get a read on his expression. It was like he'd totally shut down, back to that completely stony-faced guy I'd pestered until he'd agreed to one date.

"Help you practise?" he repeated. He nodded once. "From what I saw, you don't need any more practise. Especially if you don't actually plan to use it."

"Oh… Uh. Okay. No worries. No, I get it. Sure."

"I think we can call that social experiment concluded then. Don't you?"

My heart beat feebly and I had to bite my lip to stop it trembling as I nodded. Once I had a little more control over my lip and my vocal chords, I said, "No. Sure. Of course. I mean, mission accomplished. Sort of."

"In the absolute loosest sense of the word, maybe."

I nodded, if only to pretend I was still that upbeat, positive girl whose heart wasn't currently crumbling to pieces. "Good. Well thanks, Davin. I appreciate everything you did for me."

He shrugged. "It provided a temporary alleviation of tedium."

The obvious disdain in his voice told me everything I needed to know. Nothing about this had ever been more than my experiment to him. He'd played his role and he'd played it well, he'd played it the way I'd asked him too.

"Of course. Well, I'll let you get back to your quiet existence, then. You can be as prickly as you like now."

He looked at me in condescension. "All I was waiting for was your permission," he said, his tone dripping that annoyed, sugary sarcasm I hadn't heard him use on me in a long time.

My throat threatened to close on me, but I plastered on a smile. "So I guess that's that. I'll talk to you later then, Davin."

His eyebrow rose slightly. "No. I'm actually all good on that. Thanks, though." He gave me a patronising bow of his head, picked up his bag and walked away.

I stood strong until he was gone, smiling at the other kids in the Common Room who looked at me in passing interest. Once he'd disappeared, I hurried as unsuspiciously as possible to the bathroom. I locked myself in one of the stalls and let the tears fall.

Maybe I wasn't going to look back on it and think of Davin as my mistake after all. But I was already realising that letting myself fall for him had been the biggest mistake of all.

I wasn't sure how far I'd fallen for him and I didn't want to work it out now it was over. All I knew was that I thought I was in love with Miles when he dumped me, but that hadn't hurt nearly as much as watching Davin walk away.

Twenty~Four: Davin

"So it's over."

The tortuous torment of that unflappable tyrant's social experiment was over and I was a free man again. No more dates. No more forced socialisation. No more being doused in annoying buoyancy constantly. No more early morning text messages. No more kisses I wish would never end.

"Wait no." I cleared my throat. *"She was sexy. So what? It's not like she was the only girl in the world who could inspire me to get hard."*

Nate had started turning up for dinner at Gran's with annoying frequency since Avery and I went our separate ways. He told me that his friends had missed me since Vinny's party, but I'd been busy with Avery and they'd served their narrative function. It seemed I had Gran to myself that night though, what with it being a night Dad was home.

"I can see my grandmother when my father's home without it meaning anything."

I pulled the bag with Flint's tuna off the passenger seat

and dragged myself inside.

"Davin?"

"Yeah?" I replied.

As had become the disturbing norm, Flint popped his head out of the kitchen, then looked at me with complete scorn at the lack of Avery with me, and flounced off.

"You met her once, you little shit," I muttered as I put his tuna cans away.

"And how will I be lulled into just letting anyone walk into my house if you assure me it's you?" Gran asked as she walked into the kitchen.

"Couldn't tell you," I replied as I turned to face her.

Her jovial façade fell as she looked me over. "Davin, dear. Are you–?"

"Fine." I stretched my neck and walked into the living room before dropping onto the couch.

Gran followed and I wished I'd had the energy to care more about the quizzical confusion on her face. She sat next to me and put the back of her hand on my forehead.

I pulled away. "What are you doing?"

"Checking you're all right. You look awful–"

"At least you're honest for once."

Gran tipped my chin to look at my eyes and she frowned. "Are you taking your meds?"

I ripped my chin from her light-as-a-feather touch and stood up quickly. "Excuse me?"

She propped her hands in her lap, exuding innocence. "In

346

difficult times, it's understandable to become…lax with these things."

I huffed an incredulous laugh. "Difficult times? No one offed themselves, Gran. My girlfriend and I broke up. There's a significant difference there."

Gran's eyebrow rose disapprovingly. "Is there?"

"Yes."

"Davin, your knowledge and skilful manipulation of the English language does not extend to an understanding of the emotions conveyed by that very same language."

I glared at her. "What exactly are you trying to say?"

"Only that it is perfectly reasonable to be upset that you and Avery broke up–"

"I'm fine, Gran!" I yelled. "I am in no way vexed that Avery and I broke up. I enjoyed her company and I care…" I coughed. "I cared about her. But I can do all of that without being so weak and foolish as to have fallen in love with her!"

"I see. So you weren't in love with her then?" she asked derisively.

"No. I wasn't in love with her." The idea was almost laughable.

"Well, that's something at least," she said as she picked up her knitting.

"If you must know, I was just supposed to be helping her trash her reputation."

"Were you now?"

"Yes. Her idiot of a boyfriend dumped her and said she

347

was too good so she wanted to prove she wasn't."

"Was he an idiot before or after he broke up with her?"

"Excuse me?"

Gran started on a new row. "Was he an idiot before he broke up with her or *because* he broke up with her?"

"He has always been an idiot."

"So, no more so because he failed to appreciate her the way she should be appreciated."

I huffed. "He certainly didn't appreciate her the way she deserved to be appreciated. He cheated on her, you know?"

She shook her head, her eyes on her knitting as I paced agitatedly. "I did not know. Go on."

"He cheated on her and then made her feel bad about herself."

"So you thought you'd help her?"

"She…persuaded me to help her."

"And how did that go?"

"It was fine. We dated. She…learned to stand up for herself. It was fine."

"And her reputation?"

"Is decidedly still firmly in place."

"So if you were *just* supposed to be helping her trash her reputation. What else happened?"

"What? Nothing."

"Nothing at all?"

"No. Why would you think something happened?"

"You just said you cared about her."

"Of course I cared about her. I'm not heartless."

"No. You're not."

"It was inevitable that two people who spent time together would grow to…some affection."

"But merely *some affection*? You didn't fall for her?"

"No!"

"Of course you didn't, dear."

"Love is nothing but a construct to lull us into moving through life with less resistance."

"Resistance to what, dear?"

I flapped my arms uselessly. "Resistance to… Pfft. Anything. It's a tool to placate us."

She nodded as she counted her stitches. "Naturally. It's not at all a real thing that has you is such a tizzy now."

"What?" I spluttered. "I'm not in a…tizzy!"

"No, dear. Silly me. This erratic pacing, lack of volume control and senseless rambling is definitely not a tizzy."

"I'm fine. Relationships end. Sometimes one of you kills themselves, and sometimes it's a matter of outlasting your usefulness."

"Of course. Because all relationships are only formed upon a person's usefulness to another."

"Exactly!"

"It has nothing to do with merely appreciating a person."

I scoffed. "No."

"And even though you obviously appreciated Avery, she is no longer useful to you."

"I'm just as useless to her now. Don't put this all on me."

Gran only nodded knowingly.

"And besides," I continued haltingly. "I wouldn't say I appreciated Avery…"

"No. Or you'd be far more agitated."

"I'm not agitated!"

"Sorry, dear. No. This is entirely normal behaviour for a man detached from matters of the heart." Gran of course managed to keep her voice at a normal, inside-approved volume while I downright lost my shit.

"I am fine!" I yelled.

"Yes. You always yell me."

"Only when you're being aggravating!"

"And why do you think I'm being aggravating, Davin?"

"Because you won't let go of this idea I'm not okay!"

"If you're so okay, why are you yelling?"

"Because I'm pissed off!"

Don't think that just because she was on the ball with the conversation that she'd stopped knitting. She hadn't. "Why are you pissed off?"

"Because I fucked up again!"

"How did you fuck up again?"

It was a testament to the sincere moment we were having that she didn't pull me up on my colourful language.

"Because I lost Avery!"

"And why does that matter?"

"Because I love her!" I snapped loudly, then froze.

350

Shit. I loved Avery. I'd actually fallen in love with the tiny gnat of positivity. She'd seen me as nothing but a means to an end and once that end was achieved – or abandoned – her relinquishment of my usefulness had obliterated the bottom out of my regular internal pit of despair. And that 'horrible sinking into a never-ending abyss' feeling I'd had for the last few weeks was in fact, apparently, heartbreak.

Nothing about this made any of it any better.

"So we've established that you're in love with her," Gran said serenely, still knitting.

"Yes!" I yelled.

"Okay. Good."

"Fat lot of good that will do me now we're over! So thanks for that!"

"You are most welcome, dear boy."

"I hope you're getting some satisfaction out of this!"

"Much."

"I want you to know I'm thinking *many* bad words!"

"I'm sure you are."

I grunted in annoyance.

"And you are or aren't taking your medication?" she asked evenly.

"Yes, I'm bloody taking my medication!" I snapped back.

Gran checked over the status of her knitting as she said, "That's all I wanted to know."

"That's all you…" I muttered angrily.

I loved the woman but I wanted to throttle her.

She might have had endless satisfaction out of me realising I was in love with Avery. But I had no such relief. Gran didn't have to go to school five out of seven days a week and see those shining golden locks sway as she laughed. Gran didn't feel that kick in the chest every time I bumped into Avery in the hallway or the classroom. She wasn't the one who wished she was still nauseated just by Avery's infinite inanity.

I was the one who had to deal with the way my stomach churned when Avery smiled up at me in passing like nothing had happened. I was the one who caught her scent during the day and felt it like a vice gripping my heart.

And a desperate desire to hang on to that in some form was the only reason I could come up with to explain why I found myself at the school's Winter Fair. Not that I was really participating fully in the day's events. I was just walking around and looking at everything, wondering if it hurt more or less to try to keep some part of Avery with me.

Which is when a rather out of breath Blair careened into me and stared up at me like she was simultaneously surprised and pleased to see me. And she failed to continue on her way.

"Can I help you?" I asked her as I pulled my headphones off.

She shook her head as she fought to get her breath back.

"No?" I checked. "All right then."

Just as I went to put my headphones back on and move on, she held a hand out to stop me and spluttered, "Avery and

Miles…"

I'm not quite sure what the feeling that spread through me was. But it was ugly.

"Avery and Miles what, Blair?" I asked slowly.

She swallowed hard, still trying to get her breath back. "At the bake sale."

I wasn't sure by that statement, nor by the look on her face, what was going on at the bake sale or why that had Blair charging around the fair. She was either trying to tell me the two had reconciled and she was sorry to be breaking the news. Or something bad was going down. Either way, I needed to know what it was.

"Where's the stall?"

"This way," she puffed and led the way.

And Blair, as only Blair and Avery could, babbled and waved her hands around the whole way. "I don't know what's happening… He just came up to her… Then it was…" She exhaled heavily. "And I was like…" She gasped. "And Avery! Then Miles…" She grunted in what I thought was disapproval. "But I wasn't sure. And I'd seen you around. So I thought I'd best get y–"

"Yeah. Thanks, Blair," I said absent-mindedly as I caught sight of them and a flood of relief hit me because they didn't look like two people reconciling. A flood of relief that was quickly dammed at the realisation that, if they weren't reconciling, then the something bad was happening.

"You think you're *so good* for dating that wannabe

badarse school loner?" Miles jeered. "You thought it would make me take you back?"

"Why would it have anything to do with you?" Avery asked him, glaring at him as though she couldn't care less that there were people crowding around them.

"You can't help that you're still in love with me, Avery."

Avery blinked. "I am not still in love with you. If I was in love with you in the first place. My dating Davin had nothing to do with you, idiot."

Miles scoffed, not believing her. "Really?"

"Yes. Really. Contrary to the fantasy land you've created in your head, I haven't been waiting around for you, using Davin as payback."

Miles squared himself, an ugly smirk crossing his face. "Is it true he dumped you because you were too boring? Even the bad boy couldn't stop you being too good!"

I was already walking over to them, not caring who was watching. I shoved Miles hard and he turned a glare on me.

Before Avery could respond to him, I'd pushed him into the stall behind him. One hand planted on the wall to one side of his head and my other balled into a fist I sent crashing towards him. But instead of punching him in his conceited face, I slammed it into the wood on the other side of him.

"Back off," I ground through gritted teeth. Not only because I was pissed at him, but also because apparently punching a wooden plank hurt like a bitch. Who knew?

There was a touch of fear in his eyes but he sneered,

"Coming to her defence even now?"

What did people see in this wanker? "Shut up, you twat."

"I can see why you were with him, Ave," Miles said, maintaining a very cool exterior. "Such passion."

"There was enough passion when she was moaning my–"

"Davin!" Avery said harshly. She put her hand on my arm and I looked at her. "Thanks. But I can handle this." There was a mixture of hatred and entreaty in her eyes.

Could she handle it, though? She was beautiful, gorgeous, sweet, kind Avery. She needed someone to protect her from fuck heads like her ex who thought they could walk all over her and treat her like shit…

But.

She also full well knew how to stand up for herself now. And she had no qualms about putting it in practice. This was her fight and I hadn't spent months trying to show her how to fight it to not let her now.

Against my better judgement and every fibre of my being screaming to do the opposite, I gave her a nod and stepped away. I told myself I could always step in again if she needed.

"Look here, Miles," she started, her voice only wavering a little as she looked around as though she only just realised there were people watching. "You don't get to speak to me like that. No one gets to speak to me like that actually. But you especially. You don't get to cheat on me and expect to get away with it – not only that but actually do get away with it – and then dump me only to turn around and behave all incensed that I went out with Davin. What have you got against him anyway? You don't even know him."

"Maybe I'm more surprised he decided to go out with *you* in the first place. Good girls aren't exactly his type."

Now, I know I didn't know Miles as well as Avery, but there seemed to be something else going on behind his contemptuous insults than his usual personality would normally allow. He seemed agitated, his mouth twitching constantly as though he was supressing a very specific emotion. I just didn't know what it was.

I opened my mouth to tell him Avery was exactly my type, but she beat me to it, emphasised with a finger to his chest. "Don't pretend to know what his type is. Just because I was obviously not yours doesn't mean I'm no one's."

"You like it boring then?" Miles looked at me with faux sympathy like I'd already proven his point for him.

I smirked but there was no humour in it. "I personally don't find three times a night boring. And that day we spent in bed…" My eyebrows shot up meaningfully as the crowd 'oohed' and 'ahhed' in humour and surprise. "But if that's what you consider boring, then I feel very sorry for Cindy. How *does* she keep up with you?" My tone heavily implied we were all aware of my actual insinuation.

Miles looked between Avery and me like he couldn't believe it.

"But you never…" he spluttered. "We never…"

Avery's grin was anything but saccharine and even if that

smile wasn't mine anymore I was devastatingly proud of her. "It's amazing what you get when you're willing to give, Miles," she said, merely adding credence to my previous insinuations.

Miles' face was total disbelief.

"You're not a very nice person really, are you?" she asked him, her head tipping to the side much more like a bird examining its prey than a confused ditzy teen pep queen. "Underneath all that charm and swagger, you're just like the rest of us. Desperate to be accepted, scared of being disliked. I'm not really sure why I thought you were any different."

There were some more exclamations from the people in the around us – some laughter and some muttering –and I found it dreadfully challenging to quell the rise of the left side of my mouth.

"Thank you, Miles, for saving me the trouble of still being with you when you didn't deserve me. You did me a huge favour."

Miles' face fell and there was a vulnerability in him as his shoulders slumped almost imperceptibly. Then he shook himself out and stormed off.

"Okay. Nothing to see here, folks!" Avery called, smiling at the gathered crowd. I noticed it didn't reach her eyes. "I hear the fairy floss station has free samples!"

The crowd started to disperse and Avery kept smiling at them until the flow of people was fairly standard for a school fair again. Then her eyes locked on me. Her smile was gone and I was pretty sure even Ebony would have felt the chill running down her spine.

Avery stalked over to me. "You!"

I took a step back. "Me what?"

"What the hell was that?"

"What was what?"

"You are too smart to be this dumb, Davin!" she hissed angrily. "Why did you get involved?"

"Blair found me. I thought I'd–"

"You'd what? Perpetuate that Goody-Two-Shoes Avery who needs a big strong boy to look after her?"

This. This is what you got for caring about someone. This is what emotions got you. They made you act without thinking and then you got yelled at.

"No. That's not what–"

"Then what? Felt sorry for me? You thought good little–"

"I'm sorry if I couldn't just sit back and watch you be yelled at by that arsehole."

"And what reason could you possibly have to–"

"Because I love you!"

Twenty-Five: Avery

I blinked as I tried to take that in. "I beg your pardon…" I breathed.

He looked around, his nose scrunching as he huffed. "I love you. Okay?" he snapped quietly. "So excuse me for not being able to stand aside while that shithead laid into you."

My heart was fluttering one second, then crashing another, only to thud heavily, then flutter again. My mind reeled and I was having trouble trying to work out what I needed to say.

"But you…" I breathed out heavily.

"I what?" he asked, his eyes narrowed.

"You didn't… You just asked me what I wanted…"

Why was it so hard to get enough oxygen into my lungs right now?

I'd spent the last month pretending that Davin didn't exist. At least not the Davin I knew. I'd spent the last month pretending that our relationship hadn't meant the world to me and that I hadn't felt completely raw and broken since it had ended.

I'd kept myself busy with my friends and the formal plans

and trying not to suck at the new material in Maths. I threw out basically every lesson Davin taught me in an effort to keep up the charade. All except one. I was suddenly very easily annoyed and had no trouble calling people out when they treated me or anyone else poorly. Otherwise, I was Avery.

In the school hallway, when all I got from him was a vague nod in passing, I'd made sure to plaster that warm smile to my face. Not that he'd ever seemed to look at me long enough to see it anyway. And I'd held onto that smile while my throat tightened and my eyes got hot. I kept it firmly in place until my cheeks stopped fighting it.

He'd stalked the school corridor with zero cares and his storm cloud of disdain for everyone around him. Mrs Mack could be heard yelling at him constantly from almost any corner of the school. He talked back to teachers with more contempt than usual. He skipped more lessons than usual. The real difference between Davin from before we were dating to after was the fact that he didn't prank anyone. No pictures were spread around the school, no fire alarms were pulled, there wasn't a single screaming goat to be seen anywhere.

For a moment, I'd wondered if maybe he missed me, too. But then I realised that I'd probably just ruined his little jokes for him.

Blair had given me the space I'd needed to try to get over it while also remaining stoically by my side, showering me in love and support. Even Ebony had been an unexpected force of support and cheer, although I knew she missed Davin too. Dad was awkward in his showing he cared about the break up, but at least he cared. And Mum surprised me totally by telling me she was never sure I should have rushed into anything so soon after Miles anyway. Once I'd explained to her what Davin and I had been doing and that I'd ended up falling for him, she'd changed her tune; she'd told me that she had actually warmed to him eventually and she was sorry it was over and I was hurting.

I'd spent a month hiding behind Little Miss Goody-Two-Shoes and her eternal optimism, pretending I was okay and I didn't feel sick every time I saw him and knew he didn't feel any more for me than a temporary alleviation of his boredom.

Only now it seemed like I wasn't just a temporary alleviation of his boredom and I'd spent a month squashing down the pain and the tears for nothing. Which gave me some very conflicting feelings, the strongest of which at the moment was indignant outrage.

"This is not the place to be doing this…" I muttered.

"What?" he asked.

I looked at him, annoyed and exasperated. "The school fair is not the place to be doing this. Okay. Let me just… Damn it."

I looked around to see what I could do with this blind-siding moment.

I was supposed to be manning the stall now with Blair,

Kate and Trina. But I really wanted to get Davin alone and find out what the hell he was playing at.

I held a hand out to the unrealistically tall boy with a horrible sense of timing. "Stay there. I need to make sure the stall is under control and then we are going to discuss why you think this something you just get to come out with. Okay?"

Davin nodded quickly, his lips pressed together like he knew exactly what I'd do to him if he opened them again.

I huffed at him and went over to the stall.

"Everything okay?" Blair asked, peering around me to look at Davin.

"I have you to thank for this?" I accused.

"What? For getting…" She petered to a stop and nodded. "When I saw Miles coming and I saw that look on his face, I might have gone to find Davin."

"Why?" I whispered sharply as Trina and Kate served people behind us.

Blair shrugged. "I don't know. I just know you've been miserable without him and he's been miserable, too–"

"Davin Ambrose has resting miserable face, Blair. That's just what he looks like!" I hissed.

"So he followed me?" Blair said, shrugging. "So what?"

"So he just told me he loves me!"

Blair squealed, but realised quite quickly that squealing was not the appropriate response and cleared her throat. "That's good isn't it?"

"It seems awfully convenient," I mumbled, then told her, "Whatever it is, I need to deal with it." I looked around. "Louise!" I yelled as I saw her walk past and she turned quickly.

"Yeah?" she asked and I waved her over. "What's up?"

"I need you to cover for my stall shift, please," I said.

Louise looked humorously surprised. "Um…why?"

I had no time for kind, nice or polite Avery. "Because Davin's just told me he loves me and I need to go and talk to him about it, okay? So can you please just do me this one favour? I will cover your emcee shift at the formal if it will make you do it."

Well if I'd wondered before, I knew now. That was respect in Louise's eyes. "You had me at love. Go. We'll work out if the favour needs repaying later."

I nodded as I picked up my bag and slung it over my body. "Thanks."

"No problem."

"Blair?"

"Yes?"

"If Mum and Dad come passed…?"

She nodded. "I will let them know you'll check in later."

"Thanks."

"Go get him!" Blair cheered quietly and I glared at her. "Don't go get him?"

I crossed through the meandering people to the huddled figure of Davin waiting for me.

I grabbed his hand and dragged him to the stairs that led from the school oval to the rest of the school.

"Where are we going?"

"Where's your car?"

"Usual spot. Why?"

"Your dad's at work?"

"Yes. Why?"

"We're going to your house."

"We are? Why?"

"Because that is going to give us the most privacy for whatever this is going to be. Okay?"

"Sure."

I dragged him to his car and got in. The car was silent on the way to his house. I wasn't quite so angry as to open my mouth and risk any ensuing argument turning into a crash. And the master of reticence was characteristically quiet.

Davin pulled into his driveway and I almost made it to his front door before him. I stormed down to his room, threw my bag on the floor and turned to him.

"Okay. What have you got for me?" I asked him, waving my hands.

"Wh-what?" he stammered.

"You said you loved me. And yet you didn't feel the need to say anything a month ago when we broke up. What's that about?"

"I thought you were done with me a month ago."

"So you say you love me but you didn't think to check?"

"I didn't know I loved you then!"

"Convenient."

"Sorry. But since when do you not just blither your stream of consciousness? I had assumed if you were amenable to our continued arrangement, you might have been more forthcoming."

"You weren't exactly telling me you wanted to be with me."

"I'm trying to tell you now!"

My confused and heightened emotions were ramping up my agitation, but I didn't know what his excuse was for yelling. All I knew what that it also fed my tension. "I'm not following."

He took a deep breath and seemed to come up with a speech pretty darned quickly. "I don't want to be your mistake anymore, Avery. I can't…" He huffed. "You might look back on this in ten years and realise it was a mistake. But I can't do it anymore."

"What does that mean, Davin?"

"I'm saying that I can't stand your incessant optimism ninety per cent of the time. It drives me crazy and I haven't been able to even look at sugar in months, but it's also one of the reasons I love you. I hate being around anyone, but when I'm not with you everything feels wrong. I'd rather be with you and unreasonably annoyed, than alone and uncomfortably relaxed. So, I can't be your mistake anymore, Avery."

I looked at him and it was the first time I'd really seen uncertainty in his eyes. I'd seen him ready to be rejected. I'd seen him uncomfortable in a social interaction. But I'd never seen him looking like he didn't know what was going to happen, like he didn't have control of the situation.

I'd never thought he could fall in love with me. I couldn't have said if I was in love with him – I hadn't looked too closely at how I felt for him because I hadn't wanted to know I loved him when I was convinced he could never feel the same. I hadn't wanted to wonder what the future was like when I we didn't have one. I'd just enjoyed living in the moment with him.

But, as I looked at him, I wondered if this – what I felt for him – was what love really was. Not the Disney version or the Netflix teen movie version; the kind you got swept up in and swooned over – which I'd had plenty of with Davin as well. But the real life kind, the long-term kind. Because Davin wasn't perfect. Anyone who met him would think I was crazy and I was wondering that myself. He was moody, he was rude, he was sarcastic and he was still a regular in detention. But despite that, I had this desire to be around him. Despite that, I'd missed him this last month.

Despite his terrible attitude and his hatred for everything I loved, I wanted to be with him. He made me smile – although, I don't think he was trying most of the time – and he made me feel safe and comfortable. My life had always been busy – I liked noise and colour and people – but Davin gave me some enforced quiet time and I was starting to appreciate the smaller things in life.

But I didn't get a chance to tell him all that because just as I opened my mouth he shook his head.

"I just… I don't want to just be your mistake, Avery…"

"I don't know what's going to happen in the future…" I started. I wished I could, but I couldn't.

"I know. And I don't expect you to. But if all I will ever be is just your mistake, I need to know. I feel like I'm helplessly falling more for you every day, and I just need to know if there's a chance you could ever feel the same. I don't expect you to love me, too. I don't even expect an answer now. I just… Can you think about it for me? If there's any chance I can be more than a mistake to you? And, if not, that's fine. But I need to know before I'm completely lost to you."

Right, well…

The heart flutters and ridiculous smile that elicited aside, I felt like if I just told him now that he was already more than a mistake to me that he'd feel like I was just placating him. But I had to say something.

I dropped onto his bed as I tried to work out what to say.

Davin walked over to me slowly and dropped into a crouch in front of me. He looked at me carefully, like he knew I needed a minute. I just wish it didn't feel like it was going to take far longer to piece together the jumble of words on the tip of my tongue.

Twenty~Six: Davin

I'd fallen victim to my own love story. I'd found myself the male lead in a romance novel with no control over what happened to him. And it was absolutely terrifying.

I tell you, *"Writers should not be allowed to do this to you."*

Anyone who tells you that falling in love is magic and rainbows and the most wonderful thing to ever happen to you is shitting themselves. It's horrible. Suddenly you can't imagine your life without this person and, while your chest gets all warm and tingly over that feeling, you're busy freaking the fuck out because you have no idea if they feel the same or if it will last.

Avery was looking at me like maybe she did feel the same, but she didn't say anything. She did lean towards me and kiss me, so I had to hold out hope she just knew me well enough by now that she knew how I'd react if she lay her heart out there.

If there was a heart to lay out there.

Because the chances that this tiny tornado of happiness

could ever fall in love with me were beyond low. They were non-existent. I'd done just what she'd said; I'd been my normal grumpy self, I hadn't tried to be charming, I wasn't sure I remembered how to be polite, and I hadn't stopped up breaking up. I couldn't think of a single thing to recommend me.

But all that was suddenly paling into insignificance as I realised I'd been crouching for-bloody-ever and my legs were suddenly not shy about whinging about it.

Not that that lasted long, because they just gave way under me, sending me sprawling and making Avery fall into my lap. She laughed and – all right, fine – I liked it. Okay? I liked it and while it was still my life's purpose to make her frown as often as possible – she needed someone to moderate her – I also wanted to hear her laugh as often as possible.

"So I fell for you," she giggled.

I rolled my eyes. "God, really?" I muttered, but that smile was tugging at my lips.

Her laughter faded and she was looking at me intently. It was like I was supposed to have understood something, and obviously didn't.

"No?" she asked and I felt thoroughly confused.

"What am I missing?" Do you know?

She took my face in both her stupidly small hands and the only description I had for what happened in my chest was that my heart skipped a beat. I had half a mind just to leave and be done with it. No girl was worth all these aggravating emotions, surely? But it was my house, so leaving would be a little weird.

"Oh, screw it," she muttered and that was the second time that day she'd sworn. Colour me impressed. "There's no way I can do this anymore without you overthinking and overanalysing. So now's as good a time as any."

She paused and I didn't care for it. Then she licked her lip and took a deep breath.

"Davin, you are nothing a girl looks for in a boyfriend. But you're everything I need. I don't think we have anything in common, but I want to be around you. If I'm not already in love with you, then I'm definitely halfway there. You haven't been just my mistake for a while now, I just didn't think you could ever actually like the annoying gnat of positivity."

She was smiling, but I knew enough about this shit to feel a little guilty. I wrapped my arms around her and shook my head. "Me, either. But I started falling the moment you kissed me as though I wasn't just that guy and I don't think I'll ever stop."

"I don't think I want you to."

"No?"

She shook her head. "No. Because what if you stopped and I didn't?"

I related to that. "That's the worst part about this."

"As well as the best?"

"Fuck, no."

"What's the best part, then?" she asked softly.

"You."

She smiled so warmly that I felt it in my heart. I don't want to be quite so wanky as to say I felt that cold exterior of my heart cracking. But the slight cracking sound – similar to ice caps melting – perhaps did a better job of suggesting that.

"Is now when I offer you my watch or my ring or my Year 12 jumper or something?" I asked her.

She giggled. "If you want."

I grabbed my jumper and pulled it over her head. And she got completely lost in it past the point of adorable.

"Fuck it," I said, pulling the chunky silver ring off the middle finger of my right hand – *"Which I had conveniently actually been wearing this whole time, don't you know."* – and took her hand. "Where do you think it will fit?" I asked her.

She grinned and held up her pointer finger. I slipped the ring on. There was a little wiggle room but, when she held her hand upside down and shook it, it didn't fall off.

"Perfect," she said, smiling up at me.

"That you are, baby," I said and kissed her again.

A thought suddenly occurred to me.

"So we are dating again, yes?" I asked and she nodded. "This means I still have to go to the formal, I suppose."

She laughed. "Yeah. I'm afraid so."

I just took a breath in. "Yay."

****

"So, I can't pretend I'm doing this entirely under protest and against my better judgement," I tell you two weeks later as I pulled on my tux jacket and dragged my hair a little off my face.

Avery still drove me insane more often than not. She exasperated me with her constant carpe diem and joie de vivre and I needed a nap after spending any time with her as much from the mental exhaustion as the physical exhaustion.

"If you get my drift." I wink.

But it was undeniably true – I would prefer to be annoyed by her every second of every day than go through another one without her. It was sheer and utter madness and I still didn't know what the hell I saw in her, but I was completely in love with everything she was. Especially the parts I hated.

Dating Avery with no impending finish hanging above my head was daunting. Identifying neither of us were waiting for one of us to get bored anymore, but comprehending that either of us still could, was terrifying. It was one thing to fall in love with her and know that we were just doing this until it could be over. It was another to know she loved me but that could change.

I'd lost people – person – before and I'd spent most of the wake of that too scarred by the experience to feel anything more than a guilty hatred for what happened. By the time my feelings had numbed to it, I'd had nothing left with which to

372

grieve and I kept myself in a position to never go through anything remotely similar. So the idea of losing Avery was filled with more foreboding unknowns than I had ever let myself experience. A single month of losing her had given me enough of a taste to be suitably petrified of what forever could look like.

"Still, a boy likes to be jilted in love now and then. Right?"

I straightened my tie in the mirror and looked myself over one last time.

"That's right, we're doing the mirror bit."

I was in a full and proper tuxedo. It was as per Avery's request as much as for if I was doing this thing then I was going to do it properly – I'm a recluse not a vagrant, and I'm perfectly aware that there is a time and place to be proud of one's appearance.

The jacket and trousers were black, my shirt was white, and my tie was – of all the colours she could have picked – hot pink. I hadn't seen Avery's dress, but she'd acquired the infernal tie for me, telling me it would match perfectly. With that in mind, the red Converse she'd bought me would have been a touch on the nose. But I was still me for all my talk of 'right place and right time' so I'd gone with my usual black ones. I had also thought that Avery might appreciate it if I didn't have my hair hanging in my face all night. Not that it seemed to like this being swept to the side bollocks.

"You ready?" Dad asked, popping his head into my room

after knocking and not waiting for an answer.

I nodded. "Yeah. I think so."

He leant in my door way and nodded approvingly. "You scrub up well."

I flapped my arms rather uselessly. "Not half bad."

"Come on, Gran wants to see before we go."

I rolled my eyes. "Fine." I put my phone and wallet in my pocket, picked up Avery's corsage, and followed him out to the living room.

It was the first time in a long time that Gran and Dad had been in the same house without it being some big occasion. I always thought that Dad felt a bit guilty for leaving Mum and me in the house alone and that he wasn't here for us when we needed him. And I was pretty sure Gran felt much the same but also, because it had been her daughter, that she was partially responsible somehow.

"Oh, look at you!" Gran said, smiling at me affectionately as she looked me over. Until she got to my shoes, then she frowned. "Davin!"

"What?" I shrugged. "Avery knows me."

"It's her last formal."

I shrugged again. "And she'll find this fitting." Gran looked somewhat sceptical. "I promise."

She sighed. "All right then. Are you sure you don't want me to drop you off with your dad?"

"God. You'd think we were getting married," I tell you. But I could see by the look on her face what it meant to her.

374

To see Avery that is. I don't think she really cared about seeing me off on my first formal. I nodded. "Sure. Why not."

Gran did a pretty decent job of hiding her enthusiasm as she picked up her purse. "Come on, Don," she said perfunctorily as she led the way out of the house.

Dad looked at me with a knowing smile. "Yes, Ginny," he called before we followed after her.

Dad and Gran got into the front and I folded myself into the backseat of Gran's tiny Barina. But I didn't complain because Gran was far too excited.

We drove over to Avery's place and they flanked me as we walked up the front path and I rang the bell.

"Davin, look at you!" Heather cried warmly when she opened the door.

It suddenly occurred to me that having Dad and Gran drop me off (and come in) meant that my parents – for lack of a better word – were meeting Avery's. That made it seem terribly real. But too late now. Besides, I had wanted it to be real, so I could hardly complain when it was.

"Heather, this is my dad Don and my grandmother Ginny."

Heather turned her welcoming smile onto them. "Oh, so nice to meet you. Come in. Come in. Ave and the girls are still upstairs–"

Yep. We're doing that, too.

"–but she assures me she's almost ready. The others are in the living room."

375

I nodded and walked in, followed by Dad and Gran. Heather took us through and there was indeed a gathering of people in their front living room. There were a few parents milling around, as well as the other three girls' dates who kept to themselves in one corner.

"Now, you all get one drink before you go so choose wisely," Heather chuckled. "They're over there on the table when you're ready. Don, Ginny, come and meet my husband and the others."

I watched as Dad and Gran went with Heather and then just sort of stood at the archway wondering what I was meant to do now.

"Hey, Davin."

I turned at my name and saw Shaun, who I thought was going with Blair?

I nodded to him and headed over. "Hey," I said.

"That Avery's corsage?" Zac asked.

Different Zac, because there is in fact more than one person with the same name.

I nodded. "Yeah. I thought it was…her."

Adam smiled. "Definitely her. Did you make it?"

"My grandmother helped. By which I mean I sort of wondered if something similar was a good idea and she hijacked the idea and now we have this."

This being a creation of such hideous vibrancy that I felt almost dirty holding it. Gran had spearheaded the operation in which we took two giant bows from K-mart, one rainbow and one white with little shiny rainbow unicorns, pulled them apart and rearranged them on a bracelet with other bits of shiny stuff and diamantes. It was definitely more than I'd originally envisioned, but I had a feeling – a few too many of those lately – that Avery wasn't going to hate it.

The guys all laughed and nodded.

"Yeah, my mum got super excited when I went to the florist. Totally insisted she help. She ended up doing most of the work," Shaun said and the other two nodded like they knew exactly what he meant. Shaun indicated Avery's corsage with the beer in his hand. "That though is brilliant."

"I wish I'd thought of that," Adam agreed.

"Mu-um!" I heard Avery's voice from the top of the stairs. "We're ready!"

Heather pushed through the people. "Okay everyone. Let's do this." She pointed at us. "Boys, you ready?"

We all looked at each other. I didn't know about them, but I wasn't feeling particularly ready. But we all nodded, looking a bit like stunned mullets as we did.

"Excellent," Heather said, then walked into the hallway and called up the stairs, "Who's first?"

"Molly!" came the answer.

"Adam, you're up." Heather waved him over.

Adam gave us all a look, to which the others gave him a sympathetic 'we're behind you' sort of expression in response. As he passed, Zac patted him companionably on the arm.

And then Molly did her entrance down the stairs and met Adam at the bottom.

We went through the same thing with Blair, then Krista.

By that time, I'd worked out the drill. Stand in the archway at the bottom of the stairs so everyone's parents could watch my reaction to seeing Avery coming down the stairs in her formal dress. Then I give her the corsage and we pause to have our photo taken before we come into the room.

I shook myself out and psyched myself up to be the unwanted centre of attention.

"You'll love it," Molly whispered as I walked past her and I nodded in…well I wasn't sure what.

I took my place and then promptly forgot the drill as she appeared.

She was wearing a cropped black top with cap sleeves and a simple neckline that looked more made from glittered lace than material. And sitting low enough that her waist was on display was an A-line skirt in a hot pink that exactly matched the tie she'd bought me. Her hair was probably the simplest I'd ever seen it; side part, soft at the front where it went over her forehead, wide bun and a single braid through the top. Likewise, her makeup was minimal – no winged eyeliner for once – and her lips matched her skirt.

It wasn't like she was actually any more beautiful than I thought her on a daily basis, but for some reason she completely took my breath away as though I'd never seen her looking so perfect.

By the time I'd taken it all in, she'd done her elegant descent down the stairs and she was standing in front of me.

"Hey," she said, her eyes shining with warmth and a crooked smirk on her face.

"Uh. Hi," I said and held up the corsage for her.

She looked down and one of those bright smiles lit her face and I felt it in my chest. "Oh, Dav. It's gorgeous. Thank you."

She held her hand out and I slipped it onto her wrist before I collected myself and we turned to the room.

We did the photos. Avery had a glass of bubbles and I had a beer and we all hung around chatting – or in my case listening – for a bit until the limo arrived to take us to the Hyatt for the formal.

As we walked in, it could have been worse. I'd heard about Louise's push for Forbidden Fairy-Tales, but even I had to admit what they went with was a much better choice.

'Once more with feeling' hung from the ceiling in giant letters and I wasn't going to ask how they got there. There were pictures all over the Hyatt's ballroom of our year level from way back when most of them were in the junior school. There were whole class photos starting in 2006 with the tiny little five-year-olds up to the most recent whole Year 12 shot from a few weeks previously. There were pictures from the Year 5 production, the Year 10 production, school camps, sports days, and every talent show, fair and fundraiser the school had ever held in the last twelve and a half years.

"This isn't cheesy at all," I tell you over the music blasting from the DJ's speakers.

Avery gripped my arm tightly with hers as she looked around in excitement. I knew what this meant to her. It was really our last big hoorah as a year level and she'd been part of the huge effort into getting it all ready. She was one of the ones who'd been at the school since reception so she had a lot of history with all these people and there was something scary about the fact that was coming to an end.

Watching the way her face lit up as she and the girls looked over the photos and reminisced about this and that, I got this strange sensation. It started in my chest and spread its way up to my face. It was a legitimate smile trying to worm its way out. I didn't really think it appropriate, so I shoved my hands into my pocket and nudged it away.

The formal passed in somewhat of a montage-like blur of having pictures taken, talking with people, eating, and dancing. Although I sat and watched Avery enjoy the dance floor unless it was an opportunity to hold her close. Which is not to say I was the slow dancing kind. But I could partake of a groove if it meant she was rubbing her body against mine.

And it was just one of those times that she was looking up at me with such tenderness in her eyes that I was sure I'd done nothing to earn and in no way deserved.

"I assume now is not the time to tell you I love you?"

I scoffed. "Since when have I ever been able to tell you what not to do?"

"Isn't that kind of corny though?" she asked, her nose wrinkling sexily.

I felt a full blown smile tip up both sides of my mouth. It felt like the first time in eleven years that I'd smiled. In fact, it wasn't just a smile. It was a laugh as well. I looked down at the tiny erratic creature who'd been the one to bring it out of me.

I sure as hell didn't appreciate life any more than I had at the start of the year. But I appreciated Avery and her place in my life. I truly preferred every moment of discomfort I spent in her presence and I'd long given up hope I was ever going accrue any socialisation credits back in the black. I'd accepted that she was going to be the ray of blinding positivity to cut through my swathes of dark clouds. I loved her and I fucking didn't care who knew it anymore.

"Everything about you is corny, baby," I reminded her. "Don't stop now."

She sighed happily. "In that case... I love you, Davin."

"That's my good girl."

I kissed her, not hiding the smile on my lips as I did.

Epilogue

Avery

I'm still a morning person. Even Davin's absolute refusal to wake up before midday whenever possible couldn't change that. I was always going to want to live life to the fullest and he was just going to have to live with that.

For all our talk of lessons, it wasn't like Davin had changed me. I was always going to be that tiny tornado of positivity, living life loud and proud. But my new appreciation for the quieter things in life had given me good balance; my concentration was better, I felt like I'd become a better listener, I could take a breath and relax for a minute. I also had a better understanding of Ebony and it felt like our bond had only grown deeper.

Every day before school, I still woke up with the sun. I still sung as I showered and dressed. I still sung as I called good morning to Ebony who was dragging herself out of bed, grumbling about the annoyance of it all. And I was still singing as I twirled into the kitchen a little before my parents.

Some people still treated me like I was that stupid little

girl who didn't deserve their respect. But I didn't let them get away with it anymore. I wasn't the girl who'd told herself that letting Miles get away with cheating on me was the nice thing to do.

Teachers still treated me like I didn't know anything sometimes. And I was the first – okay second after Davin...third after Ebony – to admit that academic intelligence wasn't my strength. But with Davin's help, I clawed my way up to a B average and I knew that, even if I wasn't one of the 'smart kids' at school, I had plenty of other strengths to be proud of.

Even now I don't think I could tell you why Davin and I work. We're two complete opposites, but I can't imagine being with anyone but him. For all his extreme grumpiness, he makes me happy. He's that one adorable cloud on a sunny day.

Davin

I'm still not even a people-person. Even Avery's goddamned exuberance and love of...everything couldn't change that. And I didn't care if she nipped my ear lobe, I wasn't waking up for anything before midday unless it was a school day.

Now was the time I was supposed to be glad we lived in Australia. Were this any other teen romance bullshit, we'd have to worry about what we'd do when we moved to opposite sides of the country now that we'd nauseatingly fallen in love. Well I'm pleased to report that we didn't have to worry. Nine times out of ten, we endured our tertiary education in the state in which we were born and bred. Or maybe that was a South Australian thing?

My school morning routine did change slightly because Avery thought it a brilliant idea to wake me at eight-twenty-five. But she made up for it by having a travel mug of coffee ready for me when I arrived at her place to drive her and Ebony to school.

People didn't avoid me quite as much as I would have liked them to anymore. And while that was a constant font of wretchedness, I did get Avery out of it. Blair, Molly and Krista were about the only ones who didn't back off after the death glare and I'd started to find them more a source of morbid entertainment. I still wasn't enlightened as to the infinite mysteries and adventures of life and for that I was glad.

So the only obstacles Avery and I were going to face in the near future was if she kept insisting on sneaking colour into my wardrobe – which wasn't exactly easy to do since even navy blue tends to stand out among all-black, but she kept trying – or if she didn't stop wriggling so much in the bed in the morning.

Because there was no way in hell I was going to be waking up. Even if she kept rub– Hello.

You know what? I'm going to have to get back to you on that one…

Being Not Good

Thank you so much for reading this story! Word of mouth is super valuable to authors. So, if you have a few moments to rate/review Avery and Davin's story – or, even just pass it on to a friend – I would be really appreciative.

Have you looked for my books in your local or school library and can't find them? Just let your friendly librarian know that they can order copies directly from LightningSource/Ingram.

If you want to keep up to date with my new releases, rambles and writing progress, sign up to my newsletter at http://eepurl.com/doBRaX.

You can find the playlist for *Being Not Good* on Spotify by following this QR code:

Thanks

Well if you made it this far, an extra thank you to you!

This book is particularly close to my heart and a lot of time and effort have gone into it by a lot of friends, family members, and readers.

Attempting to write a satire novel for the first time is never easy when you spend most of it worrying that people will forget you're writing satire and just assume you're a terrible writer who confused the list of don'ts with a list of dos.

So thank you to everyone who helped me with this one, who made sure my goals were being conveyed in the manner in which I intended, and those who cheered me along every time I freaked out and wanted to throw it into the nearest volcano (FYI I just Googled this and apparently it's only 433.8km away which is a lot closer than I expected).

And a special thank you to the people who dealt with me as I turned into Davin for about three months.

Thank you to the Convocation for reading the random, out of context bits I sent you and encouraging Davin on from the beginning. I know you're a little biased, but it helps anyway.

Thank you to Emily for going through it and asking the hard questions about what the heck I thought I was doing. We work wonders together and I'm really happy to have had you on board for this one.

Thanks to my beta readers who answered my weird questions about how to make sure Davin didn't just sound like a weirdo, who told me what was and wasn't working, and reassured me I hadn't totally messed it all up.

My books

You can find where to buy all my books in print and eBook at my website;
www.elizabethstevens.com.au/YoungAdultBooks.

About the Author

Born in New Zealand to a Brit and an Australian, I am a writer with a passion for all things storytelling. I love reading, writing, TV and movies, gaming, and spending time with family and friends. I am an avid fan of British comedy, superheroes, and SuperWhoLock. I have too many favourite books, but I fell in love with reading after Isobelle Carmody's *Obernewtyn*. I am obsessed with all things mythological – my current focus being old-style Irish faeries. I live in Adelaide (South Australia) with my long-suffering husband, delirious dog, mad cat, one guinea pig, two chickens, and a lazy turtle.

Where to find me:
Website: www.elizabethstevens.com.au
Facebook: https://www.facebook.com/elizabethstevens88/
Twitter: www.twitter.com/writer_iz
Instagram: https://instagram.com/writeriz
Email: elizabeth.stevens@live.com

Made in the USA
Middletown, DE
11 December 2019